A Time to Heal

A Novel

By

Cassandra J. Sperry

ISBN 978-0615880891

Second Edition

A TIME TO HEAL

For Dawn,

My editor and own real life Allie;

Fate made us sisters,

God made us friends.

CHAPTER ONE

Susannah woke up from the recurring nightmare she'd had for what seemed like a lifetime. It had actually only been four years. It felt so real, but when she woke up she knew it was not.

In her bedroom, things that were dear to her surrounded her. Pictures of her mother, stuffed animals, collected since childhood, a jewelry box filled with all sorts of things, some even jewelry; including the diamond ring from her engagement.

Susannah could see some of the objects in the dark. She knew every square inch of her apartment so well that she could walk through it in the dark.

The nightmares came less frequently now. When they had first begun they had been an almost nightly occurrence. Now she only had them when she was too stressed.

Unbidden, the nightmare seeped into her mind. She was sitting at the kitchen table drinking coffee when Wayne came in.

"Honey, we hit the jackpot. I won the lawsuit." He said.

"That's wonderful." Susannah told him, putting her coffee cup down on the table.

"I thought you'd be pleased." Wayne said.

"I am pleased. It's just that we've been going through this for a while, it's overwhelming." She answered.

"Well, it's over now. We're going to be on easy street from here on in."

He helped Susannah up out of her chair then hugged her.

Susannah bid her mind not to remember Wayne's lies and emotional abuse. She lay back down trying to sleep. She had trained herself to think happy thoughts to go back to sleep.

First, she thought of him. He was thirty-two, six foot two, two hundred pounds, well built and muscular, but not grossly so. He had silky jet black hair. The kind you'd run your fingers through in moments of passion. His eyes were diamond-ice blue and sparkled mischievously. He was ruggedly handsome with a finely chiseled nose on a perfectly ovular face. His lips were full and strong. He was tan from working outdoors.

Second, she thought of how they would meet. He'd walk into the office demanding to see her boss. She would politely inquire as to whom he was and ask him to state his business. She would be shaking inside, but outside showed her to be as cool as a crisp winter morning. He'd practically bellow his name and tell her it was none of her business what his business was. She'd call her boss on the phone relaying he had a visitor and who that visitor was. She'd hang up and escort Mr. Bad Attitude in to see her boss.

Third, she'd go back to her desk, sit down and try to control her raging hormones. She'd never met a man who ignited her fire the way Mr. Bad Attitude did.

That's as far as she went. She couldn't imagine going further with her story.

Warm milk usually helped her get back to sleep. She sat up, swung her legs over the side of the bed, stood up and went to the kitchen. Susannah warmed up milk, drank it and went back to bed.

Closing her eyes she saw Mr. Bad Attitude. He stood before her all in black so handsome she wanted to cry. She drifted into a sensual slumber that helped her sleep better for the rest of the night.

The alarms startled her. It took a moment for her to realize it was real and not a dream. Sitting up, she swung her legs over the side of the bed and stood up, heading to the shower.

After showering, Susannah followed her morning routine. She dried off, dried her hair, got dressed, put her make-up on then braided her hair.

Going to the kitchen, she made a nutritious breakfast eating in the breakfast nook. Rinsing off her dishes, Susannah set them in the dishwasher then did her daily cleaning.

Before leaving for work she checked to make sure all of the appliances were off.

Climbing into her car, Susannah started it. While it idled down she put on her seatbelt and turned the radio on.

Driving to work she sang along with the radio; her only stop was to pick up a Diet Coke to drink after she had coffee.

Arriving at work, she parked in her usual spot in front of the door to her office. Unlocking the door, she heard the familiar click that told her it would stay unlocked until her boss locked up that evening.

Walking to her desk, Susannah put her purse in the bottom right hand drawer then went into the kitchenette to start a pot of coffee brewing.

Going to her desk, she pulled a pad and pen to her to take down the messages from the answering service Mr. Latham used.

Several times she'd suggested picking the messages up instead of calling to get them, but Mr. Latham had said he didn't want to burden her with the task.

Susannah called, wrote down the messages, chatted with the operator for a few minutes and then hung up.

Setting aside the messages for Mr. Latham, she tackled the work on her desk. It seemed there wasn't enough time in her workday to complete her work. She was efficient, well organized and energetic, but it seemed there was more work than she could handle.

Mr. Latham walked into the office.

"Good morning, Miss Roberts." He greeted her.

"Good morning, Mr. Latham. How are you this morning?" She answered.

"I'm fit as a fiddle and you my dear?" He said.

"I'm fine, thank you." She told him.

Nathan Latham was in his early sixties. He'd been in business for more than thirty years and showed no signs of slowing down or closing his law practice.

He walked into his office. Sitting down at his desk he called, "Oh, Susannah."

Susannah smiled. He'd called her name that way from the day he'd hired her as his Legal Secretary.

"Yes Mr. Latham." She called back.

"Would you bring an old man a cup of coffee?"

"You're not old, coming right up."

Susannah went to get Mr. Latham a cup of coffee. Taking it to him, she sat it off to the side of the papers he was working on then turned to go back to her desk.

"Susannah?" Nathan said.

She turned back to him. "Yes?" She answered.

"I've been thinking, there seems to be a lot more work for you to do now that we're in this technological age. Would you be offended if I hired someone to assist you part-time?"

"No, I was thinking the same thing before you came into the office."

"It's settled, I'll write up a job posting and we'll get it in the paper within the week."

Susannah nodded and went back to her desk. She worked steadily until lunchtime, glad that she'd soon have an assistant to help with her workload.

At noon she took her purse out of the drawer she'd put it in and walked to Nathan's door.

"I'm going to lunch, Mr. Latham. Would you like me to pick something up for you?" She said.

"Are you going to Tilly's café?" He asked.

Susannah nodded.

"My usual, number twenty-two, no onions or lettuce, strawberry cheesecake and iced tea."

"I'll be back in an hour."

Susannah went into the bathroom to refresh her make-up and check that no hairs had come loose from her braid.

Leaving for the café minutes later, she was hit by the warmth of the day. It took her almost no time to reach Tilly's.

Susannah ordered her usual, the sandwich special, traditional cheesecake and iced tea. She'd eat in today as she usually did.

When Susannah turned to go to a table Alexander took the moment to observe her.

He watched her walk to a nearby table to wait for her lunch. Her red hair was pulled neatly into a braid. Her green eyes sparkled when she'd looked at him. She had a Cupid's bow mouth and her nose turned up slightly at the end. Her figure was shapely; her walk was flirty, but held tightly in control.

She sat gracefully arranging her skirt around shapely legs.

Susannah waited patiently with her hands folded in her lap for her lunch, which she knew would be brought to her soon. When it arrived, she dug in heartily, well mannered and gracefully.

Eating her sandwich, she felt someone watching her. Subtly looking around she found Alexander watching her. He politely nodded his head.

Blushing she looked away.

Ah, so she's not used to being watched. Alexander thought.

The fact that she blushed, like a maiden, pleased him. He had heard her name when the server said it when he'd brought her lunch.

He watched her until she finished eating her cheesecake and drank the last of her iced tea.

Alexander thought it was a good thing he'd eaten alone today; otherwise his brother would have razzed him for being curious about the young woman.

Susannah stood up, still aware of being watched by him. She walked to the counter to order Mr. Latham's lunch. While she waited she chatted with the cashier.

"How's work going?" Olivia asked.

"I'm busy; Mr. Latham is going to put an ad in the paper for a part-time assistant for me." Susannah answered.

"When is the ad going out?" Olivia asked.

"At the end of this week." Susannah told her.

"Friday is my last day here I graduate from the university this weekend. Do you think I'd have a chance?"

"I can only advise you to apply."

Susannah's order came up.

"Tell Nathan Tilly says 'hi.'" Tilly said.

"Talk to you later, Olivia. I have to take Mr. Latham his lunch before he thinks he's going to starve to death."

Susannah walked back to the office and gave Mr. Latham his lunch.

"Number twenty-two, no onions or lettuce, strawberry cheesecake and iced tea." She announced placing his lunch before him.

"I was beginning to think I'd waste away to nothing." Nathan repeated her words to Olivia.

He handed her the money for his lunch.

"You knew I'd have your lunch her promptly at one o'clock as I do everyday. Tilly says "hi." She told him.

Nathan opened the bag, waving away her mention of Tilly. He'd been a widower for six years she could tell he was lonely.

"You should ask her out. She's in her late fifties; she'd make a great companion." Susannah told him.

"What do I want with a woman nagging and bossing me around?" Nathan asked.

"You've known Tilly for nearly forty years. She's neither nagging nor bossy."

"I don't need a wet behind the ears girl giving me advice."

"I'm not a girl. I'm twenty-six and I'm certainly not wet behind the ears. Speaking of girls, one of Tilly's cashiers' last day is Friday; she'll be graduating from the university this weekend. She wants to apply to be my part-time assistant."

"Tell her to apply. I can't make promises, but I will be fair. Now get back to work before I fire you missy."

Susannah knew darn good and well Mr. Latham wouldn't fire her. She'd worked for him since she'd graduated from the university five years ago. They made a great team. She knew what he needed almost before he told her.

She turned to leave, then turned back, "Make sure you eat that sandwich before you eat your cheesecake." She walked out without waiting for a response.

The afternoon flew by as it always did when she was busy. The sooner she got an assistant the less overworked she'd be.

Driving home from work Susannah thought about the man in the café. He was similar to the man she fantasized about to erase the nightmares when they occurred.

She remembered she was out of coffee so stopped at the store a few blocks from her apartment. Walking through the store she remembered a few other things she needed. She went to the checkout.

The man from the café was in front of her. He didn't notice her; she made certain not to draw attention to herself. He was in profile to her. At six foot two he was well built and muscular, but not grossly so; he had silky jet black, a finely chiseled nose with full, strong lips.

After making her purchases Susannah went to her car, put them in the backseat and drove home. She stopped at her mailbox, withdrew her mail then took her packages to her apartment, unlocked the door and went in.

After putting her packages away she played the messages on her answering machine.

Her mother had called, Allie Cole, her best friend since kindergarten left a message, and there was another message that left her in shock.

Wayne! What could he want after all these years? Why was he calling? She had let him know she never wanted to hear from or see him again. The message he left begged her to call him. He missed her and wanted to try again.

Susannah forced herself to move, she was shaking uncontrollably.

Going to her room, she changed into jeans and a t-shirt. Afterward she went into the bathroom to wash off her make-up, apply moisturizer to her face, then unbraided and brushed her hair.

No matter how much she bid them to go away, the feelings overwhelmed her. She was young and vulnerable again. Wayne had been a partner in a construction company that had gone bankrupt. Instead of telling her he was broke he made up an elaborate story about a big construction project he was bidding on.

A week later he told her he'd won the bid. The story went on for several months. The company was waiting for business to pick up; they had to liquidate some assets. The senior partner was felled by a heart attack. One of the associates had run off with some cash.

Next he told her he'd have to sue the company because they had backed out of the deal. Susannah was so stressed out and tense she couldn't think about anything else. Wayne always assured her that everything would be okay, he asked her to just be patient, believe and trust in him.

For the next several months Wayne told her he was visiting his attorney, talking to his partner and generally made up excuses about why the money wasn't being given to him. He had bought her a diamond engagement ring two months before everything had blown up in his face.

The money for the ring had come from her savings account; he'd talked her into putting his name on her account.

Susannah finished her daily after work rituals, then went into the kitchen to cook dinner. Putting on a pot of coffee she took out ingredients for bacon, lettuce and tomato sandwiches. She set the bread, Miracle Whip and sandwich ingredients on the counter.

After getting paper plates and paper towels from the cupboard, she put bacon on a plate, covering it with paper towel. Putting it into the microwave, she set the timer to cook it. While she waited for the bacon to cook, Susannah sliced tomatoes and shredded lettuce.

The microwave dinged. She took the plate out, put the bacon on another plate covering it with paper towel. After dumping the grease into an empty coffee can, Susannah repeated the process with the bacon.

She toasted bread, putting Miracle Whip on it. She set the table in the dining room. When the bacon was cooked she put her meal on the table.

Just as she was sitting down to eat the phone rang.

"Damn." She muttered.

She went to answer it. "Hello."

"Don't hang up, Susannah, it's Wayne." He said.

"It hasn't been that long that I don't recognize your voice. What do you want?" She answered.

"I want us to reconcile." He told her.

"I was just sitting down to dinner; I don't have time to talk." She said.

"I won't keep you long; can I come over in an hour?" He asked.

"No, we have nothing to talk about." She said and hung up.

Going back to the table, she went to sit down again. The phone rang again. Swearing under her breath, Susannah chose to let the answering machine pick it up in case it was Wayne again. She waited for the answering machine to pick up.

When her mother's voice came on Susannah went to answer it.

"Hi Mom, what's up?" She asked.

"Are you screening your calls again?" Laura Roberts asked.

"Yes, Wayne called while I was at work today and he just called again." Susannah told her.

"What does he want?" Laura asked.

"He wants us to reconcile. He wanted to come over in an hour." Susannah said.

"Of course you said no." Laura said.

"Yes Mom. I'm not going through that again. I've listened to enough lies and gone through enough emotional and psychological abuse to last me a lifetime. Unless he's done a one-eighty, which I doubt, I want nothing to do him."

"I remember everything he put you through; I wouldn't trust him any further than I could throw him."

"Don't worry, Mom, I'm not reconciling with him." Tired of talking about Wayne, Susannah asked, "Why did you call Mom?"

"Grandma and Grandpa Nelson are coming to spend two weeks with us. They'll be here Saturday."

Susannah loved her mother's parents. "It will good to see them again. It seems like forever since we saw them."

"It's only been three months Susannah."

"I know, but I've been so busy at work lately everything seems like it happened a long time ago."

"You need a vacation."

"I have too much work to do. Mr. Latham is going to hire a part-time assistant for me. I hate to cut you off, Mom, but I was just about to eat dinner."

"You should have told me, we could have talked later. I love you and I'll talk to you later."

"Okay, I love you too."

Susannah hung up the phone. She went back to the table to eat her dinner. The bacon and toast were cold. She was so hungry she didn't mind.

After dinner she rinsed and scrubbed off the dishes she'd used and loaded them into the dishwasher.

She went through her apartment and did the work she'd been putting off because she hadn't felt like doing it.

Unbidden, memories of the man she'd seen watching her during lunch came to mind.

He was handsome with his diamond-ice blue eyes, a finely chiseled nose on a perfectly ovular face. His lips were full and strong that looked made for kissing.

Susannah damned the memory that remembered such vivid details.

It would take more than one night to get the things done she'd put off doing, so she did the worst first. Climbing into bed after midnight, Susannah was exhausted. Setting her alarms she dozed off.

First her dreams were ordinary, plain and boring. Suddenly her dream man was there dressed all in black, smiling a devilish smile that invited her to join him. She did join him.

He kissed her so sweetly and gently she wanted to cry. The dream was so sensual she squirmed in bed not noticing when she kicked the blankets off. Her body was warmed by the sensuality of her dream.

Just as he was taking her clothes off her alarms rang. She cursed their timing. Susannah lay in bed as her body temperature adjusted back to normal. Her breathing shallow and panting became normal. Getting out of bed she went to take a shower.

While showering she remembered the dream. Her dream man had been gentle and kind during their lovemaking; she'd felt loved and cared for.

It had been nothing like Wayne's fumbling attempts at lovemaking. She'd never gone further than kissing him or any of her other boyfriends.

Her friends had given into their boyfriends and had found themselves pregnant or had been dumped. Her mother had taught her that giving into a man just because he pressured her wouldn't make her feel loved and cared for.

She'd lost many boyfriends because she wasn't willing to sleep with them. She hadn't minded; her mother had always been there to console her when she'd been dumped.

After she was dressed, Susannah went to make a light breakfast.

When she finished eating, she rinsed her dishes loading them into the dishwasher. Closing it, she washed off the counters. Susannah tackled more of the work she'd put off. Before leaving for work she checked that the appliances were off.

Driving to work she stopped to pick up a Diet Coke.

Unlocking the door to her office, she listened to the familiar click that told her it would stay unlocked until Mr. Latham locked up that evening.

Susannah followed her morning ritual of making coffee and calling the answering service.

Sitting at her desk, she sighed. All the work she had to do almost overwhelmed her. She'd be glad when Mr. Latham hired her assistant.

He walked in.

"Good morning, Susannah." He said.

"Good morning, Mr. Latham." She answered.

"We need to talk Susannah. Please come into my office." Nathan said.

"Yes sir." She replied, following him into his office.

"Please sit down." He said, gesturing to a chair in front of his desk. "How long have you been working for me, Susannah?"

"Five years sir."

"Would you say that in the time you've been here you have helped bring this office into the technological age?"

"Yes sir."

"Would you say you've helped organize and keep this office running smoothly?"

"Yes sir, what's with the interrogation?"

"I realize how valuable you have been to the firm so I have talked to my partner and attorney. We've set you up as an associate to the firm."

"I didn't know you had a partner. What does that mean?"

"He's been a silent partner out of choice. You'll receive five percent of the profits."

Susannah was speechless, her mouth dropped open.

"I've surprised you."

"Yes sir."

"At the end of every quarter you'll receive your share of the profits. Will that suit you?"

"Yes sir."

"Susannah, we've been together for five years; Now that you are an associate I think it's time you stopped calling me sir or Mr. Latham. My name is Nathan, please use it from now on."

"Yes sir, I mean Nathan."

"I've drafted a job posting for the paper. Please look it over and edit it. Make any changes necessary and return it to me for approval." He said, handing the posting to her.

Susannah took the paper from him and went to her desk. She had so much work to do; Nathan wanted to get the posting in the paper within the week. She carefully looked it over, moving some of the words and rewording others.

After typing it up, she printed it out, saving it to her hard drive. She took it in for Nathan's approval.

He looked it over as carefully as she had. "This looks good. Take it to the newspaper. I'd like it to be in this Sunday's edition."

"How long do you want it to run?"

"Two weeks daily, three Sundays."

"I'll go now. Don't worry about the phones; I'll have the answering service take messages."

"Very well, take your time. Enjoy the beautiful weather we're having."

"I'll be back in a bit."

Susannah called the answering service asking the operator to answer the phones while she was gone.

She walked to the local newspaper office to place the job posting in the classified section. Talking to the director of classifieds, she told him Nathan wanted the ad to run two weeks daily, three Sundays starting the upcoming Sunday.

The director looked over the posting Susannah had handed him and told her the rates. She chose the most cost effective one. The whole process had taken approximately fifteen minutes.

Susannah was proud of herself; it wasn't often that she was. After all Wayne had put her through she'd doubted she would ever have confidence in herself, or just plain be happy again.

It had been her best friend Allie who had stumbled onto the truth about Wayne's business deal with the construction company. She had told Susannah that Wayne was lying and had been for a while. Susannah had gotten angry with Allie for making up such a story.

Two days later she'd received a call from her bank. Wayne had withdrawn a large sum of money from her account. That's when everything he'd been telling her was revealed to be lies. There had never been a deal with a construction company.

Susannah confronted Wayne with the lies he'd told. He couldn't handle the pressure anymore so packed his belongings and took off. She hadn't seen or heard from him since, until he'd started calling recently.

She hadn't pressed charges against him for the money he'd taken. She'd wanted the whole nightmare to be over and didn't want anything more to do with him.

When Wayne left Susannah called Allie. They had made up and Allie stayed up all hours of the night with her talking and crying until Susannah could no longer cry and so she wouldn't be alone. She convinced Susannah to talk to a counselor and help her work out her issues.

Susannah agreed and had been going to see a therapist for the last four years. She had other issues, her father's abandonment, having faith and trust in anyone or anything, other than the ones with Wayne.

Back at the office she went to talk to Nathan.

"Nathan?" She said.

"Yes?" Nathan said looking up from the papers he was working on.

"The ad will run for two weeks, three Sundays, beginning this Sunday." She said handing him the bill.

Looking at it he said, "This is reasonable, I thought it would be more."

"I chose the best size ad for our needs."

"Do we have any applications from when I hired you?"

"Yes, I'll bring one in so you can make the necessary changes."

Susannah went to get an application and took it into Nathan.

"I'll look this over now so we can make the changes."

She went back to her desk to tackle the work that was piled there.

Half an hour later Nathan called, "Oh, Susannah," as he giggled like a little boy.

Susannah smiled, she knew he thought it was cute to call her by the song name.

"Yes, Nathan." She answered.

"I've made the changes to the application. Will you type it up?" He said.

Susannah walked around her desk into Nathan's office. He handed her the copy she'd given him with the corrections he wanted made. She looked it over. The application was going to take time to revise, a lot of time.

She'd have to put aside her regular job duties to type it up. Getting right to work, she typed up the application with the changes Nathan had indicated.

The work was tedious and frustrating, but she enjoyed it because it gave her less time to think. She needed to concentrate on something other than the recent phone calls from Wayne.

Susannah painstakingly typed the application. She wanted it to be just right so she wouldn't have to redo it.

Half an hour before quitting time the application was complete. She took it into Nathan's office laying it on his desk next to the pile of papers he was working on.

She hadn't taken a lunch hour that afternoon. As she turned to leave, Nathan stopped her.

"Take the rest of the day off. You didn't take a lunch break today. I'll see you in the morning." He said.

"Have a nice night.   See you in the morning." Susannah replied.

She went back to her desk. Closing the file she saved it to her hard drive.

Going to the kitchenette, she dumped the coffee, making sure everything was in order before she left. Gathering her things from her office, she shut down her computer and called the answering service.

Taking one more look around, she left.

CHAPTER TWO

On her way home she decided to treat herself to dinner at her favorite restaurant. Going in she was seated by the hostess; when her server came she ordered her usual meal.

She'd been there often enough the staff knew her by name. Her server stayed a few minutes to chat, then went to give her order to the cook.

While Susannah waited for her food she watched the traffic outside. She watched as a familiar black Ford Mustang pulled into the parking lot.

Wayne.

She started to get up, but changed her mind staying where she was. Maybe he wouldn't notice her when he came in. As luck would have it he saw her and asked the hostess to seat him at her table.

"You're not welcome here." Susannah snapped after the hostess left.

"I wanted to talk to you about reconciling. You haven't returned my calls." Wayne said.

"I didn't return your calls because I want nothing to do with you." She told him.

"I have the money I borrowed from you." He said, reaching into his pocket.

"You mean stole, don't you? I don't want dirty money, Wayne. Heaven only knows where the money came from."

"I worked for it and saved a little from each paycheck to give back to you. I'm glad I bumped into you tonight."

"Hello, Darling, sorry I'm late." Alexander said sliding in next to Susannah.

She looked at him in surprise. Fortunately Wayne's gaze was focused on the stranger who'd just sat down next to her.

"Hello, I'm Alexander Arthur." He said extending his hand to Wayne.

Wayne weakly shook hands with him.

"Wayne Loomis." He answered.

Susannah took pen and paper out of her purse, writing her name on it. Slyly she showed it to Alexander so he'd call her by name. Putting his arm around her, he gently kissed her on the side of the head.

"How do you know my Susannah?" Alexander asked.

"We were engaged once." Wayne answered.

"What a coincidence, we're engaged now." Alexander told him.

Wayne looked at the naked ring finger on Susannah's left hand.

After seeing Wayne look at Susannah's hand Alexander said, "We've only just become engaged. Susannah hasn't picked out her engagement ring yet. She can't decide if she wants one already available or if she wants one custom designed."

"Congratulations, when is the big day?" Wayne asked.

"As Alexander told you I haven't decided on a ring yet so we haven't picked a date." Susannah said.

Wayne looked from one to the other trying to determine if they were telling the truth. They looked to him like a couple in love, but were they?

Disgusted by Wayne's scrutiny, Alexander said, "Have you ordered yet, love, I'm famished."

"Yes, darling. I'm having Rib eye steak, baked potato, the buffet, and Diet Coke." She answered.

"Your usual. I'll have the same with the exception of coffee." Alexander stated.

"Michael is our server tonight." Susannah informed him.

Alexander subtly motioned for him to come over.

"Yes, sir what can I get you?" Michael asked.

"I'll have the same as the lady with the exception of coffee."

"Yes sir." Michael answered.

He took Alexander's order to the kitchen.

"I wanted to stop by to give you the money I owe you, Susannah." Wayne said standing.

He took her hand, pressed the money into it, closed her fist and walked away.

Susannah sat staring after him.

Alexander looked at her saying her name. When she didn't respond he waved his hand in front of her face.

She blinked a few times then turned to him.

"Did you say something?" She asked.

"No, you're still in love with him aren't you?" Alexander said.

"Of course not. I'm not sure what my feelings for him are. I still feel so vulnerable around him after four years and I can't figure out why." Susannah blurted out.

"Do you want to talk about it?" Alexander asked.

"I can't tell a total stranger my problems." Susannah answered.

"Sometimes it's easier to talk to a stranger."

The conversation was interrupted when Michael brought Susannah's and Alexander's dinner.

"Thank you." Susannah said when he placed the food in front of her.

"May I have A-1 steak sauce, please?" Alexander asked.

"Sure thing." Michael said.

"Are you going to tell me about it?" Alexander coaxed.

"I don't want to burden you."

Noticing she was still holding the money Wayne had given her, Susannah shoved it into her open purse and began eating.

Alexander watched her eat slowly, chewing her food well.

They sat in silence while she ate.

"You have to be the most exasperating female I've ever met." Alexander grumbled.

"How so?" Susannah asked.

"You're sitting with a good looking man, no conceit intended, who's willing to listen to your problems, even pot shots at males and you're ignoring me." Alexander said.

"You are good looking I admit, but I once thought Wayne was good looking then he revealed his dark side." Susannah answered.

Michael brought the steak sauce, sat it on the table and left.

"Everyone has a dark side."

"Yes, but not everyone's dark side makes them do things to hurt others."

"You can't forgive him?"

"Not unless my memories can be erased."

"He hurt you that bad?"

"Enough to make me want to give up on men entirely and live in a cave like a hermit."

"So he made one mistake and you're not willing to forgive him."

"It's not so much forgiving him as forgetting. His mistake dragged out for a while. Why are you interested?"

"Just curious I guess."

"Curiosity killed the cat."

Susannah began eating again. She wanted to get away from Alexander as quickly as she could. His probing questions brought back painful memories of the period in her life which she wanted to forget.

Her therapist told her she was managing her life and must confront her past. How could she when it hurt? The things that hurt worst were mistakes she'd made in her life which she couldn't forgive herself for. It hurt too much to remember because she couldn't forget or forgive herself.

Sometimes she wished she'd get amnesia so the memories would be gone and she could start a new life.

"Penny for your thoughts." Alexander said.

"They may not be worth that much." Susannah answered.

"Are you always this pessimistic?" He asked.

"Not usually, I'm just too stressed out. I have to leave." She answered.

Susannah tried to stand to leave, but Alexander was in her way.

"Excuse me, I'd like to leave."

"We were having such a stimulating conversation."

She scowled at him.

Alexander leaned into her whispering, "Your friend is watching us. What will he think if you leave?"

"Damn, I didn't notice."

"Obviously, don't you like my company?"

"It's not your company, it's your questions I don't like. Excuse me, I'd like to go to the restroom."

Alexander stood so Susannah could leave.

Susannah went to the restroom, coming back several minutes later.

"If I promise to behave myself will you stay and have dessert with me?" Alexander asked.

"All right, but will you move to the other side of the booth? I have a space problem." Susannah said.

"Meaning?" He said.

"I can't have anyone, not even my fiancée, too close in my personal space." Susannah told him.

Although his closeness made her flush and uncomfortable, she didn't mind it with him.

Alexander moved to the seat across from Susannah.

"Better?"

"Much, thank you."

"What would you like to talk about?"

"Anything except my personal life, past or present."

"Where do you work?"

"I'm Nathan Latham's Legal Secretary."

"Nathan Latham, he and my father went to law school together. How is he?"

"Fine, not ready for retirement. He just made me an associate in the firm."

Alexander remembered the name Susannah had written on the piece of paper.

"Susannah Roberts? You're Susannah Roberts."

"Yes, how do you know my name, is something wrong?"

"No, Nathan has mentioned you several times when he's come to the house for dinner. You wrote your name on a piece of paper when I sat down, remember. We were supposed to go on a blind date a couple of years ago."

"We were?"

Alexander put his hand to his heart in pretense of anguish. "I'm hurt you don't remember."

"I vaguely remember Nathan wanted to set me up with the son of a friend he went to law school with. If I recall correctly I came down with a nasty case of the flu."

"You do remember." Alexander exclaimed with mock enthusiasm. "What happened to rescheduling our date?"

"I asked Nathan not to set me up anymore, I was still vulnerable. I still am, but not as much as I was then."

"How long has it been since you've been out on a date?"

"Four years, we weren't supposed to be talking about my personal life, remember."

"You brought it up."

Susannah thought back over the conversation and came to the conclusion she had brought it up after Alexander asked where she worked.

"What do you do when you're not pretending to be engaged to women you don't know?"

"I work in construction. I'm buying Arthur and Sons Construction from my mother."

Susannah went pale.

Alexander watched her face go from a healthy pink to a sickly white. He motioned for Michael.

"Bring my fiancée some water please." He ordered.

"Yes sir." Michael said.

Alexander moved over next to Susannah.

She was in shock. Her ears were ringing, her vision was blurred and her heart pounded so that she thought it would leap out of her chest.

Michael brought a pitcher full of iced water and a glass.

Alexander motioned him away. Pouring water into the glass, he put it to Susannah's lips.

"Drink this."

Susannah obediently drank the water he offered. His voice came from deep within a tunnel.

The manager came over. "Is everything all right?" He asked.

"My fiancée isn't feeling well. She'll be fine in a moment."

The manager stood hovering over the table.

"Don't hover, she needs space to breathe."

The manager left.

Alexander got Susannah to drink more water. Her color was coming back.

"Are you all right?"

"No, I'd like to leave. Please excuse, me. I'm afraid I won't be able to have dessert with you after all."

Alexander stood up to let her out. "Would you like me to drive you home?"

"No, I'll just pay my bill and go home. I'm really sorry about dessert."

Susannah went to get her bill, paid it and went out to her car. Once inside she let the tears flow. Why hadn't she made the connection when Alexander had introduced himself?

There weren't that many Arthurs in town that she could have missed his connection to Arthur and Sons Construction. She felt like a fool. She'd had dinner with the one man in town she should have avoided.

Alexander hadn't recognized Wayne's name because he didn't know what he'd done four years earlier.

Someone was tapping on her window. She looked, Alexander stood there.

She turned on the car and rolled down the window.

"Yes." She said.

"Is it safe for you to drive home?" He asked.

"Yes, please move away from the car so I can leave." She said crisply.

Alexander's look of concern became a scowl as Susannah backed up and drove off.

As soon as she got home Susannah unlocked her door, went inside, locked the door and turned on every light in her apartment.

Knowing the nightmare would occur, she went over her bills, and otherwise tried to occupy her thoughts. By midnight she was exhausted physically and emotionally. She'd taken a warm bath and had blow-dried her hair.

When she climbed into bed the sheets were cool. Lying down, she closed her eyes. Alexander stood before her all in black. He was the most handsome and sexiest man she had ever met.

She couldn't believe she'd told him so much about her relationship with Wayne. People were right when they said it was easier to talk to a stranger.

Before she fell asleep, Susannah's last thoughts were of Alexander.

The nightmare started again. She sat at the table drinking coffee. Wayne was telling her he'd hit the jackpot. He was lying. Her heart beat wildly, she was anxious and her breathing was labored.

The nightmare suddenly changed. It wasn't Wayne talking to her anymore it was Alexander. His face was full of concern.

"It's going to be okay, Susannah. Wayne won't bother you anymore. He's gone away for good." Alexander said pulling her close. His voice was calm and soothing.

Susannah felt loved and cared for, like when she'd been sick as a child and her mother had taken care of her. She snuggled closer to Alexander.

He stroked her hair back from her face. All night in the dream Alexander was there. Her heart pounded. She was sweaty. She kicked off the blankets. She shot up suddenly wide awake.

Going to the bathroom, she turned on the light and took a washcloth out of the linen cupboard. Running it under cold water, she looked at herself in the mirror.

She didn't look different, but she felt different. Taking off her nightgown, she rubbed the washcloth over her sweaty body. She ran it under cold water again and rubbed it over her face and neck.

Putting her nightgown back on she hung the washcloth on the towel rod to dry.

Going to the kitchen, she turned on the light.

Warming milk in the microwave, she thought about the nightmare and dream. Why had the nightmare suddenly turned into a dream starring Alexander? Did she subconsciously think of Alexander as her knight in shining armor? The last thing she needed right now was to get tangled up with a man.

She didn't trust men, period. No matter how decent they seemed to be you just never knew. Wayne had fooled her and she wasn't going through that again.

After drinking her warm milk, Susannah shut off the lights going back to bed. It was a long time before she went back to sleep. Finally her alarms went off. Susannah gratefully climbed out of bed.

Her dreams had been a collage of things that had happened in her life, some good and some bad.

Intermittently Alexander had popped into the dreams taunting her with his sexy smile and flirty ways.

She followed her morning routine.

Talking to herself, she said, "I'm in a rut. I have to find a way to break the monotony in my life."

Alexander popped into her mind.

"I don't need a man to make me happy." She stated automatically.

Driving to work, she stopped to fill her gas tank and get a Diet Coke.

When she arrived at work she followed her usual morning routine, then started on her work. When Nathan arrived she was hard at work.

"Good morning, Susannah." He greeted.

"Good morning, Nathan." She answered.

She followed him into his office to give him his messages and the paperwork she'd finished.

The day went quickly. Just as she was getting ready to leave for lunch Alexander walked in.

At the familiar tinkling of the bell above the door, she looked up.

There was a smile on her face to greet the visitor. Her smile turned to surprise when she saw Alexander.

"May I help you?" She asked surprised to see him.

"Yes, you can join Nathan and me for lunch." He said.

"Thanks, but I'll be eating alone." She told him.

Going to Nathan's door, Alexander said, "Nathan, can you persuade your secretary to have lunch with us?"

"Susannah, we'd be honored if you'd join us for lunch." Nathan said.

Alexander looked back at Susannah with a grin.

She was scowling at him. "All right." She accepted.

Susannah led the way out the door after asking the answering service to take messages.

"How does Tilly's sound?" Alexander asked.

"Fine, Alexander, fine." Nathan said.

"Susannah?" Alexander questioned.

"Tilly's is good." was all Susannah could manage to say.

As they walked to Tilly's Nathan and Alexander kept up a steady stream of conversation. Susannah was quiet as she always was when she was uncomfortable.

When they arrived at Tilly's there was a line waiting to order.

"Maybe we should go somewhere else." Alexander suggested.

"No, we'll just have a long lunch." Nathan answered.

When it was their turn to order Tilly stepped up to take it.

"How are you Nathan?" She asked.

"Fine Tilly and yourself." Nathan said.

"I'm well, what can I get you?"

"Susannah what would you like?" Nathan asked.

"The sandwich special, traditional cheesecake and iced tea." Susannah answered.

Tilly didn't need to write down the order since Susannah ordered the same thing every time. Alexander and Nathan ordered.

"I'll bring your order out when it's ready." Tilly said.

Susannah reached into her purse to pay for her lunch.

Alexander pulled out his wallet, "I invited you to lunch, I can claim it as a business expense." He said to Susannah.

"Mother is having a dinner party this Saturday and would like you to be there Nathan." Alexander said as they sat down.

"How is your mother?" Nathan asked.

"Lonely since father passed away last year." Alexander answered.

"Lovely woman, your mother." Nathan said.

Susannah listened to the conversation between the two men. She was unusually quiet.

"You're not saying much, Susannah. Is something wrong?" Alexander said.

"No, I have nothing to contribute to the conversation." She answered.

"How's your mother?" Nathan asked.

"She's fine, glad to finally have warm weather. She hates the cold winters and keeps threatening to move to Florida." Susannah told him.

"What does your father think about that?" Alexander asked.

Nathan scowled at Alexander.

"My father left us when I was born." Susannah stated blankly.

"I'm sorry." Alexander apologized.

He thought to himself, her father left when she was born, her former fiancée hurt her. No wonder she's distrustful of men.

"How are things in the construction business, Alexander?" Nathan asked.

"They've started picking up. If all goes well I should be getting a new contract this week." Alexander told him.

He physically felt Susannah tense.

Nathan knew the story of Susannah's broken engagement. He'd pried it out of her shortly after she'd broken it. Susannah had told him about the situation Wayne had caused four years earlier.

"The two times we've met you've become upset when I mentioned my construction company, Susannah. Why?" Alexander asked.

"It's none of your business." Susannah snapped. "I'll go see what's holding up our order."

She stood to go to the counter. Alexander put his hand on her arm.

"Take your hand off me." She hissed.

"I will when you sit down." He snarled.

Susannah sat down.

Alexander removed his hand from her arm.

"My mention of the construction company triggers an unusual reaction in you. What's the problem?"

"I told you it's none of your business."

"You may as well tell him, Susannah. He'll just investigate on his own and learn the truth." Nathan suggested.

Tilly picked just that time to deliver their orders.

"If I can get you anything else just holler." She said and walked away.

Susannah glared at Alexander, then at Nathan and back to Alexander.

"I'm waiting." Alexander said.

"You can wait until hell freezes over." Susannah stated.

Ignoring both Alexander and Nathan, she began eating her sandwich. They had no alternative but to eat their own lunches. A tense silence filled the table as they ate.

When she was finished eating, Susannah went to refill her glass with iced tea. Arriving back at the table, she sat down quietly sipping her tea.

It was obvious that everyone was finished eating. Susannah stood and the men followed her out the door.

Alexander and Nathan followed at a leisurely pace. When they arrived at the office Susannah was getting messages from the answering service. Afterwards she busied herself with the paperwork on her desk.

Nathan and Alexander went into Nathan's office and closed the door.

Growing up Susannah had learned to control her outward emotions, but hadn't learned how to let the gaping wounds inside heal.

She believed her mother didn't trust men because her husband left so had never married again. Laura Roberts had not let Susannah know how much her husband's abandonment had hurt her. She'd certainly never encouraged Susannah to distrust men, only to be wary of them.

Susannah was hard at work when Alexander came out of Nathan's office an hour later.

"Good-bye, Susannah, see you later." He said.

"Not if I can help it." She said under her breath.

"Oh, we'll be seeing each other again, count on it." He told her.

"Do you have super hearing?" She asked.

"No, but I do have good hearing."

"Don't let me keep you from your work."

Alexander chuckled, "You can't get rid of me that easily. You have a good day." He said blowing her a kiss.

Susannah blushed, watching him as he went to his car. She went back to work after he left unaware that Nathan witnessed her watching him. She worked steadily for what seemed like hours.

Normally she didn't take breaks, today she made an exception. Walking to Nathan's office door, she lightly knocked.

Nathan looked up from the papers he was working on.

"Oh, Susannah what do you need?" He asked tiredly.

"I'm going to take a break and walk to Tilly's for iced lemonade." She said.

"Pick one up for me too, please." Taking money out of his wallet he handed it to her. "My treat."

Susannah took the money. While she was turning to leave Nathan said, "I'll cover the phones while you're gone."

"Okay."

She took her time walking to Tilly's. It was good to get out of the office for a while.

Tilly was surprised to see her. "What are you doing here, Susannah?" She asked.

"Taking a break, may I have two iced lemonades please?" Susannah answered.

"Sure thing coming right up." Tilly said handing the order to Olivia.

"How are things at the office?" She questioned.

"Busy, there never seems to be enough time to get everything done." Susannah told her.

"Olivia told me Nathan is going to hire a part-time assistant for you."

"Yes, the advertisement will start running in the classifieds next week."

Olivia handed Susannah the iced lemonades. Susannah handed her the money, took the change putting it in her pocket.

She spent a pleasant few minutes talking to Tilly and Olivia, then left. On her way back to the office she ran into Wayne.

"Isn't this a nice surprise, seeing you twice in two days?" He said.

"Get out of my way. I have to get back to work." Susannah snapped.

"Surely Nathan can spare you for a few minutes." Wayne said.

"He may be able to spare me, but I don't want to talk to you." She told him.

"It's been four years, Susannah. Can't we let bygones be bygones?"

"You embarrassed and humiliated me, then left me to explain everything to our friends."

"I'm truly sorry for having put you through that, Susannah. I'm back for good and I'd like you to give me another chance."

"You don't deserve another chance. Good-bye Wayne."

Susannah walked around him quickly going back to her office.

She took Nathan his iced lemonade, handed him the change and then went back to her desk.

Taking a small drink of her iced lemonade, she let it run down her throat as she held her head back and closed her eyes.

"You look like you're in heaven." Alexander said.

"I was until you walked in. What do you want?" Susannah snapped.

"I came to see Nathan on business. We have an appointment." He stated.

"I'll tell him you're here." She said.

Susannah picked up the phone and put in the number to get Nathan.

"Yes." Nathan answered.

"Mr. Arthur is here to see you." She said.

"Send him in." Nathan said.

"Go right in." Susannah said hanging up the phone.

She ignored Alexander as he walked past her desk.

Turning back to her work, she found it difficult to concentrate. In her mind those diamond-ice blue eyes seemed to penetrate right through her.

She tried to recall the last time any man had affected her as Alexander Arthur did. No man ever had. Not even Wayne and she'd fancied herself in love with him.

When Alexander came out an hour and a half later Susannah hadn't made much of a dent in her paperwork. Her mind kept wandering to Alexander.

"Susannah?" Alexander interrupted her reverie.

"Yes, Alexander." She said softly.

"Are you busy Saturday night?" He asked.

"No, why?" She asked, still half in her thoughts.

"I'd like you to be my date at my mother's party."

"All right."

Alexander raised an eyebrow at her. She'd agreed too easily. He looked into her eyes; they were in a dreamy state. He knew he shouldn't take advantage of her vulnerability, but he couldn't help himself.

"I'll pick you up at seven. Drinks at seven thirty, dinner at eight."

"I'll write down my address."

Now she sounded more like herself.

Susannah wrote down her address, handing the slip of paper to Alexander.

"I'll see you Saturday at seven."

"I'll be ready."

Alexander gave her a salute and walked out.

"Have you decided to start dating again?" Nathan asked from his doorway.

"It would seem so, wouldn't it?" Susannah answered.

"Alexander is kind, caring, decent and compassionate. You could do worse." Nathan stated.

"If you recall I did." Susannah reminded him snapping out of her euphoric state.

"Young Loomis is a fool and egocentric. How did you meet him?"

"I met him on a blind date. He was a friend of Allie's fiancée John. Not even he knew Wayne was so egocentric. If he had known he wouldn't have introduced us."

"We both have work to do. I know you don't like discussing Loomis."

"Thank you."

Susannah turned to the pile of papers on her desk, then looked at her watch.

It was four thirty. She sorted through the papers dividing them into groups. Those that weren't urgent she put in one pile. Those that weren't urgent but needed attention soon were put in another pile. She continued this until she was satisfied she had order.

She tackled the worst of the piles first. Her watch alarm went off telling her it was five o'clock. Marking her place in her paperwork, she went about closing the office for the night.

"Good night, Nathan. See you in the morning."

"Good night, Susannah. Have a good night."

CHAPTER THREE

Susannah went home. Taking her mail out of her mailbox she went to her apartment. Unlocking the door, she felt the familiar melancholy. She'd had it occasionally since her break up with Wayne.

The melancholy usually triggered violent and vindictive thoughts. She never acted on the thoughts and always told her therapist about them. The medication she took that helped her better manage the things in her life seemed to be useless sometimes.

During her melancholy moods Susannah believed nothing would ever get better in her life and she'd always be alone. Shrugging off her mood wasn't easy, but she tried her best.

Putting the mail and her purse on her desk, she went to change clothes and wash off her make-up.

Susannah was more aware of her loneliness at dinner that evening. She was glad she had Saturday to look forward to. She didn't understand why she had accepted Alexander's invitation. Maybe subconsciously she wanted to rid herself of the loneliness she'd been experiencing recently.

For the rest of the evening she mindlessly watched television, not being aware of or caring what she was watching.

Going to bed, she checked her alarms, turning them on for the next morning. Lying in bed, Susannah thought about Alexander. Nathan had said he was kind, caring, decent and compassionate.

That made him a good candidate for a companion, but what parts of himself did he keep hidden? She'd learned the hard way that outward appearances were deceiving.

Drifting off to sleep, she dreamt her father came for her.

He stood at the door. "May I come in Susannah?" Thomas Roberts asked.

"You walk into my life after twenty-six years and expect me to let you in?" She asked.

"I made a mistake. I want you to forgive me and get the chance to know my little girl." Thomas said.

"You gave up that chance when you walked out on my mother when I was born." She told him slamming the door.

He pounded on the door. Ignoring him she went to bed.

The pounding was replaced by a ringing phone.

She got up, going to answer it.

"Thank Heaven you're home." John said.

"John, it's eleven o'clock, a little late to be calling." Susannah told him.

"Allie and I were in an accident. We're at the hospital and Allie needs you." John explained.

"I'll be dressed and on my way within fifteen minutes." She said.

Susannah went into her room quickly dressing. Going back to the living room she put on her sneakers.

After grabbing her purse, she rushed out the door down to her car.

"How bad is Allie?" Susannah asked when she arrived at the hospital.

"I don't know. She has you listed to be notified in case of an emergency. No one is telling me anything." John told her.

"Did you tell anyone you're her fiancée?" Susannah inquired.

"No, they didn't give me the chance. They wanted me to contact you." He said.

"How did you find out?"

"As I told you on the phone I was with her. She was driving and was hit broadside by some damn fool who didn't think it necessary to come to a complete stop at a stop sign."

"Are you all right? You're not hurt are you?"

"I'm fine, just shaken up. I rode in the ambulance with Allie when they brought her to the hospital."

Susannah went to the reception desk waiting for the reception clerk to help them.

"May I help you?" She asked.

"I'd like to see Allison Cole." Susannah said.

"Your name." Cathy asked.

"Susannah Roberts."

The receptionist called back to the emergency area.

After several minutes Nurse Nancy came out.

"Susannah Roberts?" She said.

Susannah stepped forward acknowledging her identity.

"This way please." Nurse Nancy said.

Susannah and John followed Nancy.

"I'm sorry sir, but you'll have to wait here."

"This is Allison's fiancée, he will see her." Susannah insisted.

Nancy looked from one to the other, seeing the stubborn set to Susannah's jaw she shrugged continuing to walk toward the room Allie was in.

Allie was hooked up to some machines and had an I.V. in her arm. She had bruises and scratches, her head was bandaged where she'd hit it on the window.

"Miss Cole has been given medication for the pain." Nancy said then walked out.

"Allie." Susannah said.

She waited for what seemed like hours instead of the mere minutes it took Allie to open her eyes.

"Susannah, is that you?" Allie asked.

"Yes, and look who's with me." Susannah said, putting her hand on John's arm.

"John, what happened?" Allie asked.

"We were in an accident. Do you remember?" John said.

"Yes, how are you? Are you hurt? How are the people in the other car?"

"I'm fine, I wasn't hurt. The people in the other car had a few scrapes and bruises, but otherwise they're fine."

"I'm glad. John I'd like to say something. Promise you'll be quiet until I'm finished."

"I promise."

"I've been thinking the last few weeks. We've been engaged for over two years we should get married."

John's mouth dropped open. He'd been trying to get Allison to set a wedding date since the night he'd proposed.

"Aren't you going to say anything?" Allie asked.

"I'm speechless." John admitted.

"You two have a lot to talk about. I'll leave you alone." Susannah said turning to leave.

"No, don't leave Susannah. This concerns you too." Allie said.

~ 44 ~

"How?" Susannah asked suspiciously.

"You will be my maid of honor, won't you?" Allie asked.

"Of course, you know I will." Susannah said.

"Good, I have something to tell you both." Allie said.

"You have our attention, darling." John said.

"I'm pregnant." Allie stated.

"What!" John said happily.

"I'm pregnant." Allied repeated.

"I heard you the first time. How did this happen? We took all the precautions." John answered.

"Nothing is one hundred percent preventative, except abstinence of course." Allie reminded him.

Susannah was uncomfortable. She stood shifting from one foot to the other.

A doctor came in. "How are you feeling, Miss Cole?" He asked.

"Like I've been run over by a Mack truck." Allie told him.

"We're going to admit you for a few days for observation. You may have a concussion."

"Why am I hooked up to these machines?"

"After you told us you're pregnant we thought it best to monitor the baby. We want to make sure the accident didn't cause harm to the fetus."

"The baby is going to be all right isn't it?" John asked anxiously.

"Yes, we just want to monitor it for a few days. They'll take you to your room soon."

The doctor left.

Pulling Allie into his arms John asked, "How do you feel, darling?"

"I'm a little sore, otherwise fine."

Susannah excused herself to use the restroom. When she went back Allie was being taken to her room.

"You may as well go home, Susannah. There's nothing more you can do here tonight." Allie told her.

"Are you sure? I can stay if you want me to." Susannah said.

"No, you have to work in the morning. John will call if we need anything." Allie said.

"If you're sure, Nathan won't mind." Susannah said.

"I'm sure, now go get some rest."

"Okay." Susannah kissed both Allie and John on the cheek. "I'll call you tomorrow." She said and left.

"I'll be back, Darling. I'm going to walk Susannah to her car." John told Allie.

"All right, don't be gone long." Allie said.

"Why won't Allie let me stay?" Susannah asked.

"You know Allie, she can give all the love and support you need but has a difficult time accepting them." John told her.

"I know, but after being with you for so long I thought she might have given herself a break." Susannah responded.

"No matter how long we're together she'll never forget how Gregg treated her." John said.

Susannah sighed as they reached her car.

"Let me know if you need anything." She said.

John reached over to pull Susannah into a hug.

"We will, take care of yourself." John said opening her door.

Susannah stepped into the car to drive home. As she drove she thought how fortunate Allie was to have John to love and care for her.

Arriving at her apartment building she went to her apartment, unlocking the door. The blinking light on her answering machine was like a beacon in the dark room. Turning on the light, she pushed the play button.

It was Alexander. He'd wanted to talk and was sorry he'd called so late, but couldn't sleep. He wished her good night and said he'd talk to her later.

Susannah went to her room, undressed, put her nightgown on and climbed into bed. Her dreams were vivid and imaginative. Alexander was in all of them.

She would remember the last one the most. He was a knight in shining armor dressed all in white. He rescued her from an evil villain who was trying to force her to marry him.

Susannah thrashed around in bed unable to wake up. The dream wouldn't let go. Finally she was free, riding in front of Alexander off into the sunset.

The alarms woke her. She was exhausted. Sitting up, she climbed out of bed hoping a warm shower would wake her up.

After showering, Susannah dried off, got dressed, braided her hair, brushed her teeth and put make-up on.

She'd pick up breakfast on the way to work this morning. She had to get out of the monotonous habits she'd been in since her break up.

Looking around her apartment she saw it as drab and lifeless. She could afford to spruce it up. She thought about redecorating after Nathan hired her assistant.

Her apartment was clean, just dull. On her way to pick up breakfast she thought about what she could do to change things.

Arriving at work Susannah sat her fast food breakfast on her desk, then went about her morning routine.

She was tired of her dull, boring life. She wished something exciting would happen. Her mother's words came back to her, "be careful what you wish for, you just might get it."

Susannah leisurely ate her breakfast. The paperwork on her desk wasn't going anywhere. It would still be there when she finished eating.

Nathan came in just as she was throwing away her trash.

"Good morning, Susannah." He said.

"Good morning, Nathan." She replied.

"I need you to take a letter." He told her.

Susannah picked up pen and paper from her desk following him into his office. She sat down in a chair opposite Nathan.

While he dictated she wrote down what he said in shorthand. It took Nathan several minutes to dictate the letter.

"I need that typed up right away. I want it to go out in today's mail." He said.

"I'll get right on it." Susannah answered.

She went out to her computer to type the letter. After typing it, she printed it, then typed the envelope to put it in. Going to Nathan's office, she placed the letter in front of him to read and sign.

Nathan read the letter, made a few changes and handed it back to her.

Susannah took the letter to her desk making the changes Nathan had indicated. Printing it on the office letterhead again she took it to Nathan for his approval.

He checked it over, signed it and handed it to Susannah.

She made a copy for her files. Taking it to her desk, she folded it into thirds, put it in the envelope, readied it for mailing and placed it in the outgoing mail.

Picking up the phone she dialed the hospital.

"Ruby Memorial Hospital." The receptionist answered.

"Allison Cole's room please." Susannah said.

"One moment."

"Thank you."

There was a click then the phone in Allie's room was ringing.

On the third ring Allie answered.

"Hello." She said.

"Hi Allie how are you." Susannah said.

"Hi, Susannah I'm feeling better today." Allie told her.

"I'm calling to check on you of course. I also wanted to discuss the wedding. Do you have any ideas about what you want?" Susannah asked.

"I only decided a few days ago to set a date so I haven't thought about all the details." Allie said.

"You aren't going to change your mind, claim you were under the influence of drugs." Susannah said.

"I'm not going to change my mind and I wasn't under the influence of drugs." Allie told her.

Susannah laughed, "Okay, do you want to wait until you're home to discuss the wedding?"

Allie caught Susannah's humor. "Yes, my mind will be clearer then."

"I have to get back to work. Call me if you need anything."

"I will, love you."

"Love you too."

Susannah hung up.

The morning went by quickly as it always did when she was busy. Going to lunch she nearly walked into Alexander.

"Good afternoon, Susannah." He said.

"Hello, Alexander." She replied.

"Do you mind if I join you for lunch?" He asked.

"No, I'd like the company." She told him honestly.

While they walked to Tilly's Alexander took Susannah's hand, holding it as they walked. It felt natural to hold hands with Alexander.

"What can I get you?" Tilly asked when it was their turn to order.

"I'll have the chicken dumpling soup, traditional cheesecake and iced tea." Susannah said.

"I'll have number eighty-two, a chocolate chip cookie and coffee." Alexander said.

"Will this be together or separate?" Tilly asked.

"Separate." "Together." Susannah and Alexander said simultaneously.

"Together." Alexander said before Susannah could argue, handing Tilly the money for the order.

She took the money saying, "It will just be a few minutes."

"You don't have to buy me lunch." Susannah said automatically.

"I know I don't have to, I want to." Alexander said.

"Thank you." She said.

"My pleasure, Miss Roberts." He said.

They made polite conversation while they waited for their lunch.

When Tilly brought it they took it to an empty table sitting down to eat.

"How has your day been?" Alexander asked.

"Busy, I'll be grateful to have an assistant." Susannah answered.

"Nathan told me about your workload." Alexander told her.

"It's getting worse everyday." She said.

"Can I ask you a personal question?"

"Sure, but I reserve the right not to answer."

"Last week when I told you what I do for a living you turned white, why?"

"It's a long, boring story. I don't know you well enough to tell you."

Susannah began slowly eating, careful not to burn her mouth.

Alexander gave her a quizzical look.

"What better way to get to know someone than to tell them about yourself?" He asked.

"Your question is too personal. Besides, I hardly know anything about you except what Nathan has told me." She answered.

"What did Nathan tell you?"

"That you're caring, compassionate and I could do worse."

"Remind me to send him a bottle of his favorite Brandy."

"I'll do no such thing. I don't encourage drinking."

"You don't drink."

"No, I don't like the way I feel the next morning. Besides, I like to be in control and alcohol doesn't allow me to do that."

"You don't dance around with a lamp shade on your head do you?"

"No, I talk too much and have no restraint."

"Very interesting."

Susannah finished her soup and started on her cheesecake."

Alexander finished his sandwich and ate his cookie.

When they finished eating they left. Alexander lightly put his hand on the small of Susannah's back, escorting her out sending chills down her spine.

They walked silently back to her office. Alexander followed her in.

"Thank you again for lunch, Alexander."

"My pleasure, ma'am. I want to check to see if Nathan has a few minutes to talk."

Susannah went to work. The rest of the day went by quickly. She had plenty of work to keep her busy.

Saturday morning she slept late. Upon waking she took her time getting out of bed.

On the weekends Susannah did the cleaning she hadn't been able to do during the week, which included laundry. She was grateful for the laundry facilities in her building. She didn't like the idea of going to the Laundromat.

After doing her chores Susannah thought about what she'd wear to Mrs. Arthur's dinner party.

This would be her first date since she'd broken her engagement.

Pulling open her closet doors she peered inside. There was the purple floral sleeveless dress, or maybe the pink cotton dress that went down to the floor covering her shapely legs. There was also the short black-strapped dress.

Susannah couldn't make up her mind. It was just past two o'clock. She had plenty of time, Alexander wouldn't be there until seven.

She went to her spare bedroom to get the cross stitch project she was working on.

She still couldn't decide on a dress.

Going to the phone she dialed Allie's number, she'd know what was appropriate to wear to a dinner party.

Allie picked up on the third ring.

"Hello." Allie said.

"Hi, Allie, it's Susannah." She said.

"How are you, we haven't talked in a few days." Allie said.

"I'm well, how are you feeling?" Susannah asked.

"Good, John won't let me do anything around the house. He wants me to stay in bed all the time." Allie told her.

"I'd do the same. I would liked to have been able to take time off work for you." Susannah said.

"Susannah, you know I don't like being coddled."

"Would you rather that John ignore you? Gregg would have, in the past we've both made bad decisions when it came to men."

"Don't remind me. Don't get me wrong, I am grateful to have John. I'm still having a hard time believing he's real."

"Speaking of being real that's why I called. I'm going to a dinner party tonight and don't know what to wear."

"How about your black-strapped dress that's always tasteful."

"I'm afraid it may be a little too short."

"No, it's just right. Who's your date?"

"How do you know I have a date?"

"You've turned down almost every invitation John and I have extended since you broke your engagement. You wouldn't be going to a dinner party without a date."

"Alexander Arthur."

"Arthur. Doesn't he own Arthur and Sons Construction?"

"He's buying it from his mother."

"How did you meet him?"

"I'll tell you some other time. I need to get ready for the party."

"Wear the black dress, it will knock his socks off."

"Who says I want to knock anybody's socks off?"

"We've been friends since kindergarten. I know you almost better than you know yourself."

"All right, I'll wear the black dress, but if I get into trouble I'm blaming you."

"Naturally, you always have blamed me when we got into trouble."

"That's because it was you who talked me into doing things we probably shouldn't have."

"I'll let you go and get ready for your date now. If you're smart you'll wear the two inch heels I gave you for your birthday."

Susannah heard a click and had no one to argue with.

Going to her closet, she pulled out her black dress and the heels Allie mentioned. Gathering the rest of her ensemble, she laid them on her bed.

Taking a leisurely bubble bath, Susannah tried not to let Allie's suggestion of knocking Alexander's socks off bother her.

After her bath she put on her robe. She'd wait until it was almost time for Alexander to arrive to get dressed.

While waiting for the time to pass she gave herself a manicure and pedicure.

Susannah couldn't imagine why she was taking such pains with her appearance for this dinner party.

She suspected she was more aware and interested in making a good impression than she'd admit to herself.

After her nails dried Susannah went to get dressed. She slipped on clean panties, the matching bra, silky nylons, a slip and finally the black dress; the shoes Allie suggested completed the look.

She sparingly put on her make-up. What should she do with her hair? She put it in a braid for work so it didn't get in her way.

Wanting to look sophisticated, yet demure, she tried several different styles, finally choosing to sweep it all to one side to frame her face.

When her bell rang at seven sharp butterflies danced in her stomach. Taking deep breaths and putting a smile on her face, she went to answer the door.

When she saw Alexander her breath caught in her throat. He wore a black suit, white shirt and black tie. He looked good enough to eat. She absently reached out to hug him then pulled back, embarrassed and apologetic.

He was so attractive her eyes welled with tears.

"You look lovely this evening, Susannah." Alexander stated.

It took Susannah a moment to compose herself.

"You look very nice yourself. Please come in." Susannah said.

Alexander held out a single red rose.

Susannah took it. "Thank you. She found a vase to put the flower in. "Should we be going?"

"Yes, Mother doesn't like late entrances."

"I'll get my wrap and purse."

They were soon on their way. Susannah put her hands on her stomach to calm the butterflies that were still dancing there.

"Are you all right?" Alexander asked.

"Yes, just a few butterflies." She answered.

"Relax, we're just common folks." Alexander said.

"You may be but I should tell you something." Susannah told him.

"What?"

"Now is neither the time or place."

"You will tell me soon."

"It's something that may jeopardize our relationship."

"How?"

"Could we please just get through this dinner party first? I'll tell you another time."

When I get up the nerve to tell you what my former fiancée did to your family. She thought to herself.

After a short drive they arrived at the Arthur family home. Alexander pulled up in front of an ordinary home in an ordinary neighborhood.

"This is where your mother lives?" Susannah asked.

"Yes, what did you expect?" Alexander answered.

"I don't know; not this." She said.

"I told you we're common folks."

Alexander opened his door, stepped out of the car and closed the door. He went around to Susannah's side, opening the door he extended his hand to help her out.

Keeping hold of her hand he escorted her to the door. Opening it, he ushered her inside.

"Look who finally made an appearance." A small gray-haired woman said.

"Hello, Mother, this is Susannah Roberts." Alexander said.

"Hello, Susannah. Welcome to our home. Make yourself at home. Alexander put her wrap in the closet." Tina Arthur said.

"Yes, Mother." Alexander obeyed.

Tina ushered Susannah into the living room, introducing her to the rest of the Arthur clan.

Everyone welcomed her like a long lost friend. Nathan was there too.

Alexander came into the living room. Standing next to Susannah he lightly rested his hand on her waist.

"Tell me big brother, how did you meet such a beautiful woman." A young man, who resembled Alexander said.

"I rescued her from a fate worse than death."

The young man, Charles, raised an eyebrow at him.

"Her former fiancée was bothering her at Matilda's. I sat down next to her pretending to be her new fiancée."

"Leave it to Alexander to have such luck." Charles said.

There was more chit chat and Susannah was well aware of Alexander's leg touching hers as she sat beside him. She was thankful when dinner was ready so she could regain her composure.

Everyone sat down at the table, joined hands and Tina offered the blessing.

Susannah had never been religious so saying the blessing was foreign to her.

As the food was being passed, Susannah took a little of everything passed her way.

"Nathan tells us you're his secretary." Patricia Arthur-Warren said.

"Yes, he hired me when I graduated from the university and I've been with him since." Susannah replied.

"I can't imagine sitting in an office all day doing paperwork. I'd rather be outdoors, one with nature." Kristin Arthur said.

"Kristin, eat your dinner." Tina admonished.

"Yes, Mother." Kristin answered.

"Do you like your work"? Patricia asked.

"Yes, it's interesting, never boring and keeps me busy." Susannah replied.

"I've put an advertisement in the paper to hire a part-time assistant for Susannah." Nathan said.

"This technological age seems to complicate things more than need be if you ask me." Charles said.

"You have to keep up with the times, little brother; otherwise you'll get left behind." Alexander stated.

The rest of the meal was eaten in genial and comfortable conversation and companionship.

Susannah offered to help clean up after dinner, but Tina shooed her out of the dining room.

Alexander ushered her into the living room.

"How long have you been with Nathan?" Charles asked.

"Five years." Susannah answered.

"I've been with Arthur and Sons Construction since I was sixteen. At first I only worked weekends and summers. Now I work full time. I love watching the buildings rise up from the dust so to speak." Charles said.

"That's how I feel about my job. I start out with a small project and when it's done it seems to have developed a life all its own." Susannah said.

"Would anyone like coffee?" Patricia asked carrying in a tray laden with coffee, cream, sugar and mugs.

"That will hit the spot after the delicious dinner your mother made." Nathan stated.

As the evening wore on Alexander saw that Susannah wasn't as comfortable as she pretended. She shifted in her chair every few minutes, not being able to stay still.

"It's time I took Susannah home. She's had a long week." Alexander stated standing and reaching for Susannah's hand to help her up.

She was relieved that he had made excuses to leave. As he went to get her wrap, She said to Tina, "Thank you for a lovely evening and the invitation to dinner."

"It was a pleasure to meet you. Now that you know where we live you're welcome to visit anytime." Tina said."

"Thank you, I will when I have time." Susannah accepted.

"Good night, Mother. Good night all." Alexander said escorting Susannah out.

CHAPTER FOUR

The trip to Susannah's apartment was tense. Alexander parked in front of her building.

She put her hand on the door handle. He put his hand on her arm.

Susannah turned to him a question in her eyes.

"It's time we talked." He said.

"What about?" She asked.

"Why you're uncomfortable around me." He stated.

"Who says I'm uncomfortable around you?" She queried.

"Ever since I told you who I am you've kept your distance, both physically and emotionally. I want to know why."

"You're imaging things."

"Am I? May I come up to your apartment with you so we can talk?"

"I'm tired and as you said, I've had a long week."

"You told me you need to tell me something."

"We barely know each other."

"We could get to know each other if you'd let us."

"This isn't the best time. Now if you'll excuse me, I'd like to go inside."

This time when Susannah went to open the door Alexander didn't stop her. He watched her get safely into the building and drove off.

The message light on her answering machine was blinking when Susannah walked in the door.

She turned on the lights, put her purse and wrap away, and went to play her messages.

The first one was one from her mother. It was very important that she call back. The next one was from Wayne.

Not really wanting to talk to anyone, she chose the lesser of two evils and called her mother.

The phone rang three times before her mother picked up.

"Hello." Laura said.

"Hi, Mom it's me." Susannah greeted.

"Are you sitting down?" Laura asked.

"No, why?" Susannah asked.

"First your grandparents aren't coming this weekend, Grandpa is sick. Second, brace yourself, darling. I have shocking news."

"What is it Mother?"

"Your father is here."

"He's here in town or he's here at your house?"

"At the house, he wants to see and speak to you."

"No. He hasn't given a damn about me in twenty-six years why should I give a damn about him?"

"Watch your language, young lady. I did not raise you to curse."

"I apologize for my language, but I absolutely refuse to talk to the man who left us when I was born. He can just go back to wherever it is he came from. I want nothing to do with him."

"Susannah you at least owe it to him to let him explain."

"I owe him nothing. He left you when I was born."

"There were extenuating circumstances. Won't you at least hear what he has to say?"

"All men have excuses for their actions, he's no exception. He hasn't thought about me in twenty-six years. I don't think that just because he shows up in town at his convenience I should let twenty-six years of neglect just be forgotten.

"Susannah! He's not Wayne, not all men lie."

"No, they just walk out without explanation and reappear years later."

"You're very cynical for a woman your age."

"I have reason to be. I'm very tired Mother. I just came back from having dinner with the Arthurs."

"The Arthurs? As in the ones Wayne had a deal with."

"The very same."

"What in Heaven's name possessed you to have dinner with them?

"Alexander Arthur invited me."

"He's the oldest Arthur child."

"Yes, I met him earlier this week when Wayne accosted me at Matilda's."

"I'd like to hear more about this acquaintance."

"How about tomorrow at brunch. I'll pick you up in the morning."

"It's a date. I love you Please think about talking to your father."

"I love you too, Mom. See you in the morning."

Susannah hung up. Her father was at her mother's. What could he want after all of these years?

She wouldn't think about it tonight. She'd think about it after she'd had a good night's sleep.

Going to her room, Susannah undressed and put on her pajamas. She set her alarms to get up in the morning.

Going to the bathroom she washed off her make-up, took down her hair and brushed her teeth.

Back in the bedroom, Susannah shut off the light, walked to the fan, turned it on and climbed into bed.

The nightmare began again it was more real than usual. In the nightmare her father, along with Wayne betrayed her trust.

They told wild stories about the people in Susannah's life. Alexander Arthur was their main target. They told her she couldn't trust him. He only wanted to get her into bed and then he'd dump her like so much garbage.

She woke up covered in sweat and anxious.

It was three o'clock in the morning. Susannah burst into tears.

She cried for several minutes. Climbing out of bed she headed to the kitchen. She warmed up milk and drank it.

Going back to bed, she turned on the television to have subtle noise so she could fall asleep.

Soon Susannah was asleep again. She dreamt she was in a beautiful field of wild flowers in assorted colors. Alexander stood at one end and she stood at the other.

He called her name. She was afraid to go to him. Almost every man in her life had betrayed her or brought her pain.

When her alarms went off Susannah was thankful. She dressed for her brunch date with her mother. At a few minutes passed nine she left to pick her up.

"Good morning, darling." Laura greeted.

"Good morning, Mom." Susannah said.

"You don't look as though you slept very well." Laura commented.

"I didn't. I had another nightmare." Susannah confided.

"Was it bad?"

"Yes, Wayne and father were trying to convince me that people in my life weren't trustworthy and Alexander Arthur was the worst of them."

"It sounds horrible."

"It was, I woke up at three this morning covered in sweat and anxious, so I drank a glass of warm milk."

"Did it help?"

"Yes, I went back to sleep and dreamt I was in a beautiful field of wild flowers in assorted colors. I stood at one end and Alexander stood at the other."

"Tell me how you met him."

"The first time I saw him he was eating lunch at Tilly's. I told you how I met him at Matilda's."

"Yes, Wayne accosted you, but you didn't tell me how Alexander appeared on the scene."

"He saw Wayne bothering me and slid in next to me. He introduced himself to Wayne. They were talking, Alexander asked Wayne how he knew me. Wayne told him we were engaged once. Alexander told him we're engaged now."

"Now Wayne thinks you're engaged to Alexander Arthur."

"Yes, but he keeps calling."

"That's why you aren't sleeping well and having nightmares."

"Partly, it's also from the stress of a heavy workload."

"Does Nathan know you're overworked?"

"Yes, he put an ad in the classified section for a part-time assistant. It should be in today's paper."

"That should take some of the burden off of you. Now about your father."

Susannah sent a silent prayer Heavenward that they had arrived at the restaurant. She could forestall talking about her father.

They went in and were seated by the host.

When they were seated and had ordered beverages Laura brought up her ex-husband again.

"About your father." She began.

"What about him?" Susannah said.

"He wants to get to know you." Laura told her.

"Why now?" Susannah asked.

"His wife recently passed away."

"What does that have to do with us?"

"She bequeathed a good deal of her money and property to him stipulating he contact you and tell you what she'd done to him."

"He doesn't really want see me, the only reason he's here is to collect his inheritance? Why should I even bother? He'll just fulfill his obligation and leave again. What could she have done to him to make him leave his family, then reappear twenty-six years later?"

"She blackmailed him. They have three children. At the reading of her will, her attorney played a DVD explaining to her heirs what she'd done. She fell in love with your father. Maybe I better start at the beginning. You were conceived at the beginning of the affair."

"He was having an affair with her, he left you for her and you expect me to give him a chance."

"You have to know we had been married five years and weren't getting along at the time."

"So it is acceptable to you that he gave up on your marriage and had an affair? You can't expect me to believe you condoned the affair."

"I didn't know about it until five months into the pregnancy. At the time we were living more like roommates than husband and wife."

"You may have worked things out. Who knows what might have happened?"

"Only Heaven knows what might have happened."

"We can talk after we get some food." Susannah said.

Susannah and Laura went up to the buffet to fill plates with food.

When they were back at their table Laura began again.

"After I learned of the affair I tried to make him happy. I realized my efforts were to no avail and agreed to an amicable divorce making one stipulation."

"Nice guy, you should have just let him leave. What stipulation?"

"I really loved him, or at least I thought I did. I couldn't give him up without a fight. The stipulation was between your father and me, nothing you should concern yourself with."

"Why try to keep a man who obviously didn't want you?"

"I think he really loved me, he just didn't know how to be a husband and father. I made a promise to love, honor, cherish in sickness and health, in good times and bad until death do us part."

"Obviously those were just words to him, they didn't mean anything."

"They weren't just words to him, Susannah. He honestly meant them at the time."

"Why didn't you ever marry again?"

"I didn't meet anyone I wanted to share my life with. I hate to think your father leaving has made you cautious in your view of men."

"From my experience I have no reason to trust men. They take what they want from a woman or they can't get what they want and they dump her."

"Not all men are alike. I've been seeing a man for about a month."

"Mom! Why didn't you tell me?"

"I didn't want to upset you."

"Upset me, Mom I think it's wonderful. Who is he? Where did you meet him? What does he do?"

"Whoa, slow down Susannah. His name is Blaine Smith. I met him when I was doing volunteer work at the hospital. And he's retired from Western Chemical."

"What's he like?"

"He's a kind, caring and wonderful man. He'll do anything for you, no matter how trivial."

"Are you in love with him?"

"I may be, but it will take time to find out."

"It's taken you twenty-six years to get involved with a man. It's only been four years since my break up with Wayne then Alexander walked into my life. Do you think he could be the one for me?"

"I don't know. You'll have to be willing to give him a chance."

"That's the hard part, Mom. How do I trust him when the men in my life have abandoned or betrayed me?"

"You were too young to know your father abandoned you and Wayne isn't self-confident enough to be honest when he fails. I'm guessing Alexander isn't like that."

"I'm afraid to take a chance, Mom. It hurts too much."

"I suggest we not talk about your father, Wayne or Alexander. I can almost feel the tension pouring out of you."

"How is your volunteer work going?"

"Good, I love working with the children. It reminds me of when you were in school and I volunteered in your classroom."

"I don't understand, I thought that was your job. How were you able to spend so much time volunteering when all the other kids' moms were working?"

"We agreed not to talk about your father, Wayne or Alexander."

"How could father afford to support us so you didn't have to work?"

"It wasn't your father, it was Glenda. Your father has a DVD for you from her."

"I'm not sure I want to see it."

Susannah and Laura had eaten while they talked.

"I'm through eating. Shall we go?"

Susannah looked at her plate. It was empty.

"I'm ready whenever you are."

They went to pay their bill and left.

"Are you going to come in to meet your father?" Laura asked.

"Yes, I'm curious about him and I think I'm ready. What do I to say to the man who abandoned us when I was born? What do I call him?"

"Take one step at a time."

They rode the rest of the way to Laura's in silence, both lost in their own thoughts.

When they arrived Susannah's heart pounded loudly. Parked outside the house that she grew up in, knowing that her father was inside made her feel...

Susannah took a deep breath, got out of the car and said, "Let's get this over with."

"You don't have to act as though you're going to your death." Laura told her.

"It feels like death then slowly being resurrected." Susannah answered.

"Your father really has changed. He loves you and regrets walking out on us, we can't change the past."

"That doesn't help, Mom. I can't change the way I feel just like that." Susannah said snapping her fingers.

"All I ask is that you try."

They walked up to the house. Laura opened the door.

"Ready?" She asked.

"As ready as I'll ever be." Susannah answered.

Going into the living room she saw a broken old man. Her resolve to hate her father almost crumbled.

He stood.

"Hello, Susannah." Thomas Roberts greeted.

"Hello." Susannah said.

They stood staring at each other.

"Are we going to stand around or are we going to make ourselves comfortable?" Laura asked.

Susannah made the first move to sit down. She chose a spot as far away from her father as she could get.

"Would anyone like coffee?" Laura inquired.

"Yes." Susannah and Thomas answered together.

"I'll make a fresh pot. I'll just be a moment." Laura told them.

Susannah and Thomas sat in an uncomfortable silence.

"I'm sure you're wondering why I'm here." Thomas stated.

"Mom told me your wife stipulated in her will that you contact me in order to collect your inheritance." Susannah said bluntly.

"That's only part of it." Thomas told her.

"Why else would you contact us after all these years, if not to collect your inheritance?" Susannah asked.

"I understand your bitterness. I'd like a chance to explain."

"I'm listening."

"I met Glenda when I worked at Western Chemical. It's her family's business. They worked hard to get it up and running."

"I'd rather not hear about Western Chemical. All I want to know is how you could leave your family."

"When I met Glenda your mother and I were having problems. In a weak moment I turned to Glenda and started an affair. Shortly after, I learned you were on the way."

"You continued the affair knowing I was on the way."

"I wasn't happy in the marriage, Glenda convinced me that leaving your mother was best for everyone. I believed Glenda really loved me."

"After only a few months, that's hard to believe."

"At the time Glenda was only interested in getting what she wanted. She didn't care how she got what she wanted as long as she got it. Her mind was made up to have me and she blackmailed me."

"How? What did she have over you that would make you leave your family"?

"She said she'd have me fired and make it difficult for me to get a job in this town. On top of it, she threatened to have me charged with rape."

"You couldn't move away and take Mom and me with you."

"That was not an option for us. She still would have made good on her threat to have me charged with rape."

Susannah recoiled at that.

Laura walked in carrying a coffee tray and refreshments.

"Fresh coffee and refreshments." She announced.

Susannah was reluctant to continue the conversation in front of her mother.

"Don't let me interrupt." Laura said.

"Your mother knows everything." Thomas said.

"How old was the woman you left us for?" Susannah asked.

"Eighteen." Thomas answered.

"You let a virtual child make your decisions for you and put a ring through your nose and lead you around?" Susannah questioned.

Thomas walked to the window to see the trees, flowers and all early spring coming to life outside.

Turning back to Susannah he said, "I had no choice. She would have ruined my life and my family in the process. I left to protect you."

"Where's the DVD Mom said you wanted to show me? I'd like to see for myself how this woman could ruin our lives."

"I'd like to say one more thing before you see the DVD."

"I'm listening."

"I was immature and irresponsible when I left your mother and you. Living with Glenda and leaving my family made me mature quickly, I grew old practically overnight."

"I'd like to see the DVD now."

Thomas handed the DVD to Susannah. He and Laura left the room so she could view it in private.

Susannah set up the DVD player and popped in the DVD.

The woman who came on the screen looked haggard.

"Hello, Susannah. If you're watching this it means I'm dead." Glenda Hawthorne Roberts said.

Susannah sat still, not moving a muscle. There was something oddly familiar about the woman on the screen.

"I'm your father's wife, Glenda Hawthorne Roberts. I know you're probably sitting there itching to shut off this DVD. For the sake of your family, I beg you not to."

Susannah couldn't imagine this woman to be the cold, hard bitch her father made her out to be.

"Before watching this your father will have told you of the circumstances in which he left your mother and you. I've made this DVD to tell you that it's all true. I fell in love with your father the moment I set eyes on him. I knew he was the one for me."

~ 73 ~

Susannah sat watching and listening to the woman on the tape, becoming more and more appalled as the DVD went on. She couldn't move and hardly dared breathe. Her stepmother was reaching out to her from beyond the grave to tell her the awful things she'd done to break up her family.

"In conclusion as part of my resolve to right as many wrongs I've caused as I could, I've made this DVD to help you better understand what your father had to go through because of me. I've been diagnosed with inoperable cancer and don't have much time left. The doctors say a few years at the most. Please forgive your father for the choices he made all those years ago. It was my coercion and threats that made him make those choices. Your father was broken up by the decisions he was forced to make. I know I have no right to ask, but I'd like to ask your forgiveness also. One last thing before I go, I named you as one of my beneficiaries. I know you probably don't want anything to do with me or the life your father has led all these years, but I'll feel much better knowing I've at least tried to make amends."

The DVD came to an end. Susannah shut off the DVD player. She sat in shock. She couldn't believe what she'd just heard.

Laura and Thomas came back into the room.

"Are you all right Susannah?" Laura asked.

"Oh, Mom." Susannah said, bursting into tears holding her arms out to her mother.

Laura went to her daughter, holding her.

The room was filled only with the sound of Susannah's crying.

Thomas watched his former wife hold Susannah as she cried out years of pain, anger and sorrow.

"She really was awful, Mom. She told me everything, including what she threatened to do to father if he tried to leave her or see us." Susannah said.

"I expected as much." Laura said.

"She was diagnosed with inoperable cancer and realized she wasn't immortal. She set out to right the wrongs she caused all those years ago." Susannah told her.

"She did change the last few years of her life. She went to counseling once a week." Thomas told them.

"Did you love her?" Susannah asked.

"Yes, she wasn't always cold and hard. She had a soft side when it came to our children and me." He answered.

"Did she really love you the way she claimed?"

"Yes, she really did. She had a hard time expressing that love."

"She said she named me as one of her beneficiaries. Are there any stipulations to my inheriting anything from her?"

"Only that you be happy. She left you money, the family home here in Camille and stock in Western Chemical."

"Suppose I don't want to accept anything from her?"

"It will be held in trust for your children should you have any. In the event you don't have children at the time of your death all of your inheritance will go to charity. Her will is iron clad; no one can contest it, including your brothers and sister. Not that they would of course."

"Mom said you have three children. I have two brothers and a sister?"

"Yes, they're anxious to meet you. They couldn't come up with me because of business and school, but they would like to come to meet you soon or you could come home with me."

"I'd rather they come to Camille. I can't take time off of work right now; I have too much work to do."

"I'll arrange for them to come here then."

"What are their names, what are they like?"

"In order of birth there's Phillip, Martin and Jennifer. I'll let you decide for yourself what they're like when you meet them."

"If you don't mind I'd like to go home now. I'm exhausted."

"That's perfectly understandable after all you've learned today." Laura said.

Susannah stood to go. She hugged her mother tightly and offered her hand to her father.

Thomas took the gesture as a good sign.

"I'll call you later, Mom. Good-bye Father."

Susannah walked out to her car, started the engine, let it idle down and drove home.

When she walked into her apartment the light on her answering machine was blinking.

She pushed the play button.

The first call was from Allie, the next from Alexander and the third from Wayne.

He just wouldn't give up. No matter how many times she turned him down, he just wouldn't take no for an answer.

Susannah left a message for herself to call Allie and Alexander.

Exhaustion overwhelmed her, she went to lie down to nap. She'd learned a lot today and would better be able to deal with it when she was rested.

Her sleep was without dreams. For the first time in four years she slept soundly.

When Susannah awoke she was rested and felt better able to handle the events of the day.

She made coffee. While she waited for it to brew she called Allie.

"Hello." Allie said.

"Hey, Allie, it's Susannah." She said.

"How was the dinner party last night?" Allie asked.

"I had a good time. Alexander's family was welcoming and courteous." Susannah said.

"What are they like?" Allie questioned.

"Normal, common people. They don't flaunt their wealth." Susannah told her.

"Are you going to see Alexander again?"

"I'm not sure, we didn't make plans to see one another again."

"I think he'll be good for you. He has a good reputation around town."

"Don't let your imagination get away from you, Allie. We just met."

"You deserve a good man who cares about you and will be there for you."

"Speaking of being there for me are you free for dinner tonight?"

"Sure why?"

"I have big news and who better to share it with than my best friend."

"What time is dinner?"

"How's five o'clock?"

"Sounds good. Do you want me to bring anything?"

"Dessert, I'll see you at five."

Susannah hung up and dialed the number Alexander had left on her answering machine.

His answering machine picked up.

"Hi, Alexander it's Susannah. I'm returning your call, please call me when you get this message."

Susannah hung up the phone and went to pour herself a cup of coffee. Deciding to have the steaks that she had been saving for a special occasion, she took them out of the freezer.

She took her coffee into the living room sitting down to think over the events of the day.

Her mind whirled. She couldn't believe anyone could be as nasty and manipulative as her late stepmother had been.

How could a teenager wrap a grown man around her finger? And how could a grown man let himself get involved with a young woman several years younger than himself?

The realization of everything she'd learned today hadn't really set in yet. If it had, she was sure she would have been a nervous wreck.

Trying not to think of the events of the day, Susannah busied herself cleaning and straightening, showering and preparing the meal; putting the steaks on the broiler in her oven she put together a salad turning the steaks at intervals.

She peeled the few potatoes she needed and put them on to cook then poured the gravy and corn into pans to warm when the steaks were almost ready. When the steaks were nicely cooked, she turned on the burners beneath the corn and gravy and set the table.

Allie arrived promptly at five o'clock walking in like she had for so many years.

"Hi, what's the big news?" Allie asked, rushing in.

"I'll tell you over dinner. What did you bring for dessert?" Susannah said.

"Chocolate, double layer cake. When's dinner, I'm starved." Allie answered.

"As soon as I put everything on the table." Susannah told her.

Susannah and Allie quickly placed the food on the table.

"The steak looks delicious." Allie commented.

"Thank you, I thought they'd go well with my news." Susannah said.

"Are we celebrating something?" Allie asked as she sat down.

"My father came to town last night." Susannah told her.

Allie gasped "You're kidding." She said in disbelief. "I thought you hated your father."

"I've learned a great deal today that explains why he left."

"I'm anxious to hear the details."

Susannah began at the beginning, telling Allie everything she'd been told, including the information she'd learned from the DVD. When they came to dessert Allie was enraged.

"How could your father let a teenager control him like that?"

"I've asked almost the same question. Apparently she was serious enough in her threats that he had to do what she said. Otherwise she would have caused him a lot of trouble."

"I can't imagine being that nasty and manipulative."

"She decided whatever she wanted she'd get no matter what the consequences were."

"Too bad she's dead, I'd like to give her a piece of my mind."

"She thought well how to handle things. She waited until she learned of her impending death to rectify things."

"A lot of good that does you now."

"She actually put me in her will. I am one of her beneficiaries. Along with money, I've inherited the Hawthorne family home and stock in Western Chemical."

"Your father was married to Glenda Hawthorne?"

"Yes, why do you know her?"

"Do you know how much money that family has made over the years? And how well Western Chemical is doing?"

"No, should I?"

"Where have you been living? In a box? You haven't heard the rumors around town?"

"What rumors?"

"The ones that tell of Glenda Hawthorne seducing a married man and stealing him from his family, but no one knows for sure who it was and how she did it."

"You know I don't listen to idle gossip or rumors."

"Now that you've inherited Hawthorne Manor the rumors are going to start again."

"You really think so?"

"Of course, this town isn't so big that people won't think it odd you inherited that house."

"That's just great, my life isn't complicated enough now that my father has reappeared I have to deal with rumors too."

"Are you going to claim your inheritance?"

"I don't know. I'll have to ask Nathan for legal advice."

Allie looked at her watch. "It's getting late, I told John I'd be home by seven. I'm going home, if you need to talk give me a call."

"I will. Thanks for listening."

"What are friends for?"

Allie kissed Susannah on the cheek gave her a gentle squeeze, then let herself out.

CHAPTER FIVE

While Susannah cleared up from dinner she thought over what Allie had said.

What would people say and think when they learned she'd inherited Hawthorne Manor? Was Allie right, would her inheritance of Hawthorne Manor stir up old rumors?

Should she accept the inheritance or let it go into trust for her children if she had any?

That was another kettle of fish to fry. One certainly can't have children when one is alone.

She'd have to talk to Nathan and ask him to represent her.

The rest of the evening Susannah made up a list of things she wanted to discuss with Nathan.

She was tired, so went to get ready for bed. She brushed her teeth, brushed her hair, put on her pajamas and climbed into bed.

As she lay down the phone rang.

"Hello." Susannah answered.

"I'm not calling too late am I?" Alexander asked.

"No, I was just getting ready for bed. You called earlier today, did you want something?" She said.

"I won't keep you then. I was wondering if you would like to have dinner with me on Friday." He said.

"Yes, I'd like that."

"I'll pick you up at seven."

"Okay."

Not wanting to let her go just yet and wanting to hear her voice. He asked, "How has the rest of your weekend gone since the dinner party?"

"Hectic."

"Would you like to talk about it?"

"Alexander, I don't know you well enough to burden you with my problems."

"In case you hadn't noticed, I've been trying to get better acquainted with you."

"I've noticed, there are some things you don't know about me that could change your opinion of me."

"What did you do, pose nude for Playboy, or another men's magazine? Or did you get arrested for jumping into the downtown fountain nude?"

"Nothing like that. It has something to do with your construction company. I was involved in something I had no control over, if you knew of my involvement you may not think it wise to get better acquainted with me."

"I'll take the news easier coming from you than I will learning about it from someone else."

Afraid of what Alexander might do and how he'd feel about her when he learned what Wayne did to his family's reputation Susannah said, "Maybe we shouldn't have dinner Friday and not further our acquaintance. That would be best anyway. Good night, Alexander."

Susannah hung up the phone. She felt bad about having hung up on Alexander the way she had; it was better than having to explain to him what Wayne had done to his family.

The phone rang. What she wouldn't do to have caller ID so she'd know who was calling.

"Hello?" She said.

"I don't like it when people make up my mind for me, I'd rather make my own decisions. I also don't like being hung up on." Alexander said.

"If you want to know what happened in the past, find out yourself. I can't stop you, nor would I try." Susannah told him.

"I'll pick you up at seven Friday and we'll discuss it." He said.

"I'm of the opinion we shouldn't see each other."

"I would respect your opinion normally but I think you are wrong this time. I'd like to know why you're so afraid of letting me get close to you."

"Alexander, it's late, I've had an emotionally exhausting day and I have to work tomorrow. If you want to discuss this I'll see you Friday at seven."

"All right, sleep well. I'll see you Friday."

Susannah hung up. She was exhausted and only agreed to meet with him so he would hang up. She was not looking forward to dinner with Alexander on Friday.

The nightmare began again. It was as hurtful as when they began. Scenes of Wayne's lies played before her while her late stepmother cackled the torment she'd put Susannah's family through.

Alexander came next telling her he knew what had happened in the past and that he wanted nothing to do with her.

All the people from her past were jumbled together. Not one thing made sense to her. All of her problems seemed to be in the nightmare.

Susannah did something she'd never done before. She tried what her therapist suggested, she took control of the nightmare.

First, she separated everyone and everything into individual groups. Second, she began dealing with each individual problem.

When she awoke, Susannah made an oath that she wasn't going to let anyone or anything hinder the progress she'd made.

She'd learned to live with herself and the consequences of Wayne's betrayal and her father's abandonment, if not forgive.

She was grateful she had an early appointment with her therapist. She dressed for work as usual and went to her appointment.

Susannah checked in at the front desk, sat down and began reading a magazine while she waited for Linda to come out.

"Susannah." Linda said.

Susannah looked up, put down the magazine she was reading, picked up her purse and followed Linda to her office.

"How are things going?" Linda asked.

Susannah closed the door, walked to a chair and sat down.

"My father came to town Saturday, I had brunch with my mother yesterday then met and talked to my father." Susannah told her.

"How did that make you feel?" Linda asked.

"At first I was reluctant to talk to him; he explained what happened when he left mom. His wife recently passed away. She left a DVD for me to view explaining the past." Susannah said.

"How do you feel?"

Susannah told Linda what she'd learned the previous day.

Linda interrupted occasionally to ask questions or make comments.

By the end of her session Susannah was crying and exhausted. The events of the day before had finally caught up with her and the reality of her situation set in.

"How do you feel about your father now?" Linda asked.

"I'm still angry with him, but I understand why he did what he did. I don't understand how he let a young woman several years younger than himself control him." Susannah said.

"I'd like you to try an exercise at home. Sit down and write your father a letter asking him the questions you have and although you can't give it to her I'd also like you to write a letter to your late stepmother." Linda said.

"Okay. How should I write it?" Susannah asked.

"As though you're writing to a friend you've had a quarrel with. Tell your father and stepmother how they've made you feel and demand they answer your questions."

"I don't know if I can do that. I'm not good at confrontations."

"I want you to write the letters; you may not need to confront your father but at least you'll know why you're angry and you'll have released your feelings about your stepmother."

"Okay, thank you."

"Our time is up for today. I'd like you to come back in a couple weeks." Linda said.

"All right, bye." Susannah answered.

Susannah went to the front desk to make her next appointment. She was thankful that Nathan provided her with insurance coverage to see Linda.

When she arrived at work Nathan was in his office hard at work.

"Nathan." Susannah said.

"Yes." He said looking up from the papers he was working on.

"I just wanted to let you know I'm here." She told him.

"Fine, how was your session today?" He asked.

"Good, I need to talk to you when you have time."

"Personal or legal?"

"Legal, it will take a while to explain."

"Are you free for dinner tonight? We can have a business dinner at Matilda's."

"That sounds good. We'll go right after work."

Susannah went to her desk to get busy with the work there. She'd be glad when Nathan hired her assistant.

Susannah wasn't aware of the time passing as she worked. Her watched alarm sounded at noon. She told Nathan she was leaving, went into the bathroom to check her hair and make-up and left for Tilly's.

While Susannah waited for her order she looked around, seeing Alexander she smiled, feeling giddy.

He threw her a salute.

When her order came up she walked over to his table.

"May I sit down?" She asked.

Alexander stood, "Yes ma'am." He said.

Susannah sat down.

He sat down.

"How are you?" He asked.

"As well as I can be." She answered.

"How is that?" He inquired.

"I'm not sure. Besides the problem with you I have a personal problem I'm dealing with." She told him.

"If you tell me your problems you may feel better."

"Alexander, I don't know you well enough to trust you with anything."

"Trust, is that what this is about?"

"And suspicion."

"Trust and suspicion. Those are big problems."

"Those aren't my problems, Alexander. My problems are bigger and you aren't going to trick me into telling you what they are." She felt herself getting angry.

"Why did you join me for lunch?"

"To tell you I don't think it's a good idea for us to date."

"We've had one date, I wouldn't say we are dating."

"You know what I mean, don't twist my words, Alexander."

"I'm trying to understand you. I've never met a woman so set on staying single."

"I'm not set on staying single. You want to know my problems? I don't have faith in anyone or anything and I believe in an eye for an eye. If someone hurts me I want to hurt them worse." She blurted out.

Alexander sat looking at her. She couldn't tell if he was stunned, in shock or what he was thinking.

Finally he spoke, "So you have a few problems that seem insurmountable."

"Insurmountable? Alexander those are pretty hard things to overcome."

"Not with faith in God and love."

"Like I said I don't have faith in anyone anymore." She said remorsefully.

"Faith doesn't come in an instant, it's learned."

"How do I learn to have faith when I don't trust anyone?"

"Take one day at a time. Let go of your fear, believe in me, Susannah."

Susannah looked at her watch.

"I'm going to be late. Sorry to have to rush off." She said.

"I'll see you Friday at seven." Alexander said to her back.

Susannah picked up Nathan's lunch, paid for it and went back to her office.

"Here's your lunch, Nathan. Sorry I'm late." She said.

"Thanks, I'm sure it was for a good reason." He answered.

"I was talking to Alexander." She told him.

"You've been seeing a lot of him." Nathan said.

"We've had one date at his mother's and had dinner together at Matilda's. Sometimes I see him at Tilly's."

"It's nice to see you dating again. I wish I'd known you were ready, I would have introduced you to Alexander long before now."

"Playing matchmaker, Nathan?" She said sarcastically.

"You couldn't have picked a better man."

"I have that legal problem I am anxious to discuss with you."

"The sooner you get back to work, the sooner it will be quitting time."

"Yes, Nathan."

Susannah went to her desk. The rest of the afternoon went by quickly as she worked on the paperwork on her desk.

"Ready for that dinner I promised you?" Nathan asked at five o'clock.

"Yes, I'm famished." Susannah answered.

"Let's go." Nathan said.

"I'll close up and be right behind you." Susannah said.

After she checked the coffeemaker, straightened her desk and called the answering service she followed Nathan out the door.

They pulled in front of Matilda's, stepped out of their cars and went inside.

The hostess seated them. As soon as she left, their server appeared.

After they ordered, Nathan asked, "Do you want to talk or eat first?"

"I'm hungry and I really need to talk to you as my attorney. Let's get some food, we can talk while we eat." Susannah answered.

"All right." Nathan agreed.

Susannah and Nathan went up to the buffet, filled plates and went back to their table.

"Okay, what's on your mind?" Nathan asked.

"Several things. I'll start with this past weekend. My father came to town." Susannah told him.

"Your father is in town? What does he want?" Nathan politely inquired without judgment.

"It's a long story. That's why I want to talk to you." Susannah replied.

"Start at the beginning and work your way from there." He suggested.

She told him what she had learned over the weekend.

"What I need to know is if there are any strings attached to my inheritance, if my siblings can contest the will, things like that." She finished.

"I'll have to read the will, check to see if the money is tied up, if there are any back taxes owed on the property, how much stock you own and the price of the stock." Nathan told her.

"How long will that take?" She asked.

"Depends on how long it takes me to get a copy of the will and do the research. I'll also need to see the DVD your late stepmother left." He said.

"I'll contact my father and ask him for the DVD and a copy of the will."

"I may have to leave town, can you handle the office while I'm gone?"

Susannah arched an eyebrow at him.

"I'm sorry, I forgot how efficient and organized you are as well as how overworked you are."

"How soon do you think you can go to Rose Lake?"

"I'll go as soon as we hire your assistant and get her trained."

"All right."

They finished dinner. After Nathan paid the check they walked to their cars and went their separate ways.

When Susannah walked into her apartment she didn't see the usual blinking of the answering machine light.

She was grateful. The only person she wanted to talk to tonight was her mother.

Picking up the phone, she put in her mother's number.

"Hello." Laura answered.

"Hi, Mom." Susannah said.

"Susannah, how are you?" Laura asked.

"As well as can be expected I guess." Susannah answered.

"How was work today?"

"Busy, I talked to Nathan today. He's agreed to represent me in regards to claiming my inheritance from Glenda."

"So you've decided to claim it then."

"I'm thinking about it. Nathan is going to check into things for me."

"How are things going otherwise?"

"Wayne is calling and I've seen Alexander. We have a date Friday night."

"Is that wise? I mean, after all Wayne put you through with that Arthur fiasco."

"I don't think Alexander knows about it. He keeps trying to get me to tell him about it. I finally told him to find out for himself. Is father still in town?"

"No, he went home this morning. He said he'll keep in touch."

"You know there is one thing you haven't told me."

"What's that?"

"How you were able to volunteer so much at school and how you could be a stay at home mom."

"Your father thought it best not to tell you so soon after the things you've already learned about Glenda."

"I'm a big girl, Mom."

"Are you sure you want to know?"

"If I didn't, I wouldn't ask."

"Glenda sent us a monthly allowance. It wasn't enough to make us rich, but we were comfortable."

"She tried to buy you off or tried to make up for her own guilt."

"No, she wanted to, in her own way, make up for the loss of your father."

"So she wasn't as bad as she's been made out to be."

"I don't think so; she didn't want anyone to know she had a kind heart. By the time she met your father she'd been through so much she wasn't going to take the risk of getting hurt."

"How do you know all this?"

"I know Glenda's background."

"This keeps getting more and more complicated. Is there anything else I should know?"

"Not that I can tell you."

"I'm tired, Mom. I'll talk to you later."

"Okay, I love you."

"I love you too, bye."

Susannah hung up. A nice warm shower, a snack and she'd be refreshed. After her shower and while she ate her snack, Susannah mulled over what her mother had told her.

Her situation was complicated enough adding her attraction to Alexander made her cry. She cried for several minutes. Afterwards she wiped away her tears, finished her snack, then went to bed.

Susannah's dreams were nothing out of the ordinary. She slept well, awoke only once to get a drink, and had quickly fallen back asleep.

When her alarms went off she climbed out of bed and got ready for work as usual. She felt good, like she could tackle anything that came her way.

The feeling was rare, so she enjoyed it.

When she arrived at work Wayne was sitting in the parking lot waiting for her.

He stepped out of his car as Susannah parked hers.

"Good morning, Susannah." Wayne said when she stepped out of her car.

"What are you doing here, Wayne?" Susannah asked sharply.

"I came to see you. You haven't returned my calls." He answered.

"We've been over this. I don't want anything to do with you. I don't trust you and I'm suspicious of anything you do."

"I want to change that. I want to show you I've changed."

"Given your track record, nothing could make me believe you've changed that much. Go back to where you came from and leave me alone."

"Why won't you give me another chance?"

"You didn't stick around to face the consequences of your actions. I don't like the way I became after you left."

"What way is that?"

"I became vengeful and vindictive."

"I'm truly sorry for what I did to you. I'd like to make it up to you."

"It's too late, Wayne. The damage has been done and can't be undone. I have to get into the office. Goodbye."

Susannah walked away with as much dignity as she could muster.

When she made it inside her office she turned to see Wayne climbing into his car. He sped away.

She thanked Heaven Wayne hadn't followed her into the office.

She went about business as usual. Nothing about her work day changed. She disliked change, but doing the same thing day after day was making her irritable.

Settling down to work, she thought about him. Her knight in shining armor who would come riding up and take her to ride away into the sunset.

Her daydreams came more frequently now. She knew it was because her life was boring. Nothing exciting ever happened to her.

Nathan came into the office.

"Good morning, Susannah." He greeted.

"Good morning, Nathan." She said automatically.

"Is anything going on this morning?" He asked.

"Nothing out of the ordinary, just the usual." Susannah answered.

"You sound disheartened."

"I am a little. Nothing ever changes and I feel like I'm on automatic pilot. I do the same thing day after day."

"You need a vacation. As soon as we hire your assistant and get her trained you can take a two week vacation."

"I wouldn't know what to do with all that time off. What would I do by myself?"

"Promise me you'll think about it."

"All right, I'll think about it."

Over the next two and a half weeks nothing changed. Susannah processed applications and resumes of the applicants who had applied to be her assistant.

She had to keep up with her regular work as well. There were days she just wanted to leave and not come back.

Other than their date two weeks earlier Susannah hadn't seen or heard from Alexander.

He hadn't done anything to make her feel uncomfortable or threatened. He did let her know he wouldn't be pushed aside because she had been hurt in the past.

Susannah wasn't sure how she felt that he hadn't contacted her. She was relieved, yet she was irritated, her up and down emotions were driving her crazy.

One Monday morning she came into the office as usual finding Nathan hard at work.

"Nathan?" She said.

"Yes." He answered.

"You're in early this morning. Is something going on I should know about?" She asked.

"No, I decided I'd come in early for a while to help lighten your workload." He told her.

Susannah nodded, then went to her desk. She noticed there were papers missing from it.

Nathan must have come in very early to get those papers and be hard at work by the time she arrived.

Yesterday had been the last day for the advertisement for her assistant to run in the paper. She'd have to arrange the applications and resumes according to qualifications, experience and willingness to work part-time as well as other factors.

This coming Friday would be the last day they would accept applications and resumes for the position.

Susannah busied herself reading the materials in front of her. She was thorough making notes for each application.

Lunchtime came, she went to lunch after her usual check of her hair and make-up.

Walking into Tilly's Susannah didn't notice Alexander sitting in a corner.

Tilly came to the counter to take her order.

"How are you today, Susannah?" She asked.

"Well, I'm going through applications and resumes for the assistant Nathan wants to hire to help me." Susannah answered.

"It's about time he hired someone to help you. When I left him to open this place he was dragging his feet about getting that office into the technological age." Tilly said.

"He wouldn't go back to the old way of doing things; with my workload it's more efficient and faster to have the computers, fax machine and other office machines." Susannah said.

"What can I get you today?"

"The sandwich special, traditional cheesecake and iced tea."

"Eating in or to go?"

"Eating in."

"That will be ready soon."

"Thanks, I'll find a table."

Susannah went to sit down.

Alexander came over to her.

"I was a little early, darling. I have a table in the corner." He said.

"What are you doing?" Susannah asked.

"Loomis just walked in. You don't want him to think we've broken up do you?" Alexander said.

"No, of course not." She replied.

They went to Alexander's table.

"How is work today, darling?" Alexander inquired.

"Busy, I'm going through applications and resumes for the assistant Nathan wants to hire to help me." Susannah answered.

Alexander watched Wayne sit at a nearby table. He suspected it was to eavesdrop on their conversation.

Putting his hands on Susannah's face he pulled her close kissing her. His kiss was erotic and sensual.

Susannah gave herself up to the kiss, forgetting it was only for Wayne's benefit.

"Excuse me." Tilly interrupted.

Susannah slowly drew away from Alexander blushing.

Tilly sat her lunch in front of her.

"Enjoy your lunch." Tilly said with a smile.

"This is going to get complicated if we have to pretend we're lovers every time Wayne is around." Susannah whispered.

"Why pretend?" Alexander asked in a low voice.

Susannah looked at him oddly, her mouth hanging open.

He pushed her mouth closed.

"Why pretend, what does that mean?" She asked.

"Don't pretend you don't know what it implies. Why not become lovers, then we won't have to pretend? I can feel the way your body reacts when I'm near you. I feel the same way when you're near me." Alexander said.

"Are you out of your mind? I'm not one of those women who jumps into bed with every man she fancies."

"I wasn't implying you were."

Susannah began eating her lunch.

"Well?" He asked.

"Well what?" She answered.

"Are we going to become lovers or not?" He asked.

"Certainly not. We don't know each other well enough. Besides I've never..." Susannah trailed off.

"You've never been intimate."

"Yes, I have no intention of doing so until I'm married."

"You're beautiful when you blush."

Susannah put her hands up to cover the telltale redness of her face.

"Will you have supper with me Friday and breakfast with me Saturday?"

"All right, pick me up Friday at seven and Saturday at eleven."

Alexander looked at his watch. "I have to get back to work I'll call you later."

He stood up, leaned over and kissed her in the same erotic and sensual way he had earlier.

Susannah watched him walk away. After he left she finished her lunch, ordered Nathan's then went back to her office.

It was cool, almost cool enough to wear a sweater.

She went back to work. Looking through the applications and resumes was tedious.

Her watch alarm sounded at five. Setting the papers aside she set about closing the office for the day.

CHAPTER SIX

Driving home she remembered a few things she needed from the store. Stopping, she made the purchases and went home.

The rest of her week seemed to pass slowly as she continued going through applications and resumes.

Friday dragged on endlessly. Susannah tried to check the excitement she was feeling about her date with Alexander.

Her attraction to him was nothing like she'd ever felt for a man.

Linda said she was managing her life and her negative personality traits came from what Wayne had done to her.

She didn't like knowing part of her personality was harmful to others.

Susannah knew she had to be the one to change, but change was hard for her and she didn't know where to start.

Alexander hadn't done anything to hurt her. Still, she was afraid to let him get close to her.

Wayne wasn't helping by calling and demanding they reconcile. As far as Susannah was concerned he was a liar and she could never be with him again.

On the other hand, she didn't know Alexander well. How could she know he wasn't like Wayne? As she thought about it, she knew the answer. She wasn't sure how, she just knew.

Susannah followed her daily ritual of closing the office and calling the answering service.

Driving home she was lighthearted and excited. She had a date, she wasn't going to let anything spoil her evening.

When she walked into her apartment the familiar light on her answering machine was blinking. She pushed the button to listen to her messages. Her mother and Allie had called.

Susannah called each one talking to them briefly explaining she had a date.

After she hung up she went to take a quick bath. She took great care choosing her dress and to look her best for the evening.

Alexander arrived promptly at seven. He brought her flowers.

"Thank you." Susannah said taking them.

"My pleasure." Alexander said.

"Please come in." Susannah invited.

Alexander walked in kissing Susannah.

Surprised, Susannah said "I'll put these flowers in a vase. Please make yourself at home."

Alexander followed Susannah into her apartment.

While she put the flowers in a water filled vase she thought about the kiss Alexander had given her.

He didn't usually kiss her without the pretense of their engagement. Although the kiss had been a surprise it wasn't unwelcome.

Picking up the vase she carried it into her living room where Alexander waited.

"Do we have time for coffee or should we leave now?" She asked placing the vase on an end table.

"We should go, I made reservations for seven thirty." Alexander answered.

Susannah went to get her purse and wrap. Alexander took the wrap, placing it around her shoulders.

Putting his hand on the small of her back, he escorted her out the door. They walked down to the elevator, rode it down to the lobby went out the front door going to a sleek black Camaro.

"How was your week?" Alexander asked pulling into the street.

"Busy and slow. How was your week?" Susannah said.

"We're trying to get the contract on a new mall. The deal was going fine until the land developer's daughter decided she'd rather have me as her husband rather than a contractor building her father's mall." He told her.

"What did you do?" She asked curiously.

"Told her I'm engaged of course."

"We're not really engaged."

"She doesn't know that, neither does your friend Loomis."

"Wayne is not my friend."

"I have a confession to make."

"I'm listening."

"I know about your relationship with Loomis."

"How?"

"Nathan told me. He thought if I knew I could help you learn to trust again."

"How long have you known?"

"Since we first met. The day I went to see Nathan we didn't talk about business."

"You don't blame me for the things Wayne did."

"Of course not. Why would I? You're not to blame because he's a pathetic excuse of a man. Are you angry that Nathan told me?"

"Surprisingly, no. I'm happy I don't have to tell you. However, I must remind you that I distrust people in general and I believe most people don't tell the truth."

"I remember, Susannah. I'd like to know why. Nathan wouldn't tell me about your childhood. He said that would be better coming from you."

Susannah was thankful they had pulled up in front of the restaurant. A valet opened her door and helped her out.

Alexander turned the keys over to another valet and joined Susannah in front of the restaurant.

He escorted her inside to the maitre d'.

"Table for Arthur."

The maitre d' looked on his list. "Yes, Mr. Arthur right this way."

Alexander escorted Susannah to their table.

The maitre d' pulled a chair out for Susannah, seating her. Alexander sat down across from her.

"Your server will be right with you." The maitre d' said.

"Thank you." Alexander replied.

After the maitre d' left Alexander and Susannah opened their menus. They looked them over silently for a moment.

The waiter interrupted to take their order.

"I'd like to get back to the conversation we were having." Alexander said.

"About my childhood." Susannah said.

"Yes." He answered.

"I'm not comfortable talking about myself to a virtual stranger." She told him.

Alexander took her hand in both of his. "I'd like to be more than a virtual stranger or casual acquaintance."

"Things are going too fast, Alexander. I don't want to be pressured."

"We won't talk about the past or present. What would you like to do with your life?"

"I'd like to get married and have a couple of kids. I'd like to continue to work."

"Suppose your husband doesn't want you to work."

"That's what Wayne wanted, I hope I don't fall in love with a man like that."

"Loomis really hurt you, didn't he?"

"More than I'd like to think about. I've become vindictive and vengeful. If I were to be hurt that way again I don't know what I'd do."

"Nathan said you hadn't dated since your break-up with Loomis, until you went to my mother's dinner party with me."

"There wasn't anyone I wanted to go out with... until now."

"I'll take that as a compliment."

"Just don't let it go to your head."

Their meals arrived. They began eating and were quiet for a time.

Susannah decided she liked spending time with Alexander. He was easy to talk to and listened to what she had to say. He didn't try to push his ideas on her.

Alexander interrupted the silence. "May I ask you a personal question?" He asked.

"Yes, but I reserve the right not to answer." Susannah said.

"How was your childhood, good, bad or indifferent?" He asked.

"Mostly good, we were comfortable, but not rich. My mother was able to spend a lot of time with me. I recently learned that my late stepmother sent us an allowance every month." She said.

"Was there anything you would liked to have changed?"

"I would have liked having a full time father."

"Your mother never married again?"

"My parents were married for five years before I came along. When I was born he left to be with my late stepmother."

"That must have been difficult."

"I only knew my father from what my mother told me. She told me about him and let me draw my own conclusions. I've always been able to talk to her about almost anything."

Their dessert came. They ate silently. When they were finished Alexander escorted Susannah out after paying their bill.

A valet brought his car.

Alexander maneuvered into the flow of traffic.

"What would you like to do now?" Alexander asked.

Feeling more relaxed and that she could tell Alexander anything she said, "Go home, we can have coffee and talk unless you'd like a night cap."

"I'd like coffee and conversation."

Alexander pulled up in front of Susannah's building. He helped her out of the car.

Walking up to the door of her building he put his hand on the small of her back, which sent shivers down her spine.

Going into the building and the elevator they were silent, each lost in their own thoughts.

Susannah unlocked her apartment door and they walked in.

"Make yourself at home. I'll have coffee ready in a few minutes." She told him as she turned on lights.

Alexander took his shoes off at the door, walked to the sofa and sat down.

Susannah made quick work of making coffee. After she had it brewing she went back into the living room.

"I'm going to change into something more comfortable. I'll only be a few minutes." She said.

"Take your time." Alexander replied.

She came back out a moment later wearing baby blue sweats.

She smiled at Alexander as she passed through the living room to check on the coffee.

Minutes later she brought in a tray laden with coffee, cream, sugar and mugs.

"Here we are." She said.

She sat the tray on the coffee table in front of the sofa.

"What would you like to talk about?" He inquired.

"Something interesting and exciting." She said

Alexander told a joke, getting her to giggle. They talked long into the night jumping from subject to subject. They learned more about one another, getting to know each other the way any new couple would.

After receiving his law degree, his father had worked in the legal field for a several years then had given up practicing law.

As an attorney he'd seen that there wasn't adequate and affordable housing for the middle class. He had started his construction company with the purpose of changing that.

As Alexander grew up he had become interested in his father's work. When he'd become old enough he was allowed to work alongside his father, learning the construction business. He'd gotten his contractor's license when he was twenty-six.

Susannah told him how she'd come to want to be a Legal Secretary. As a high school freshman she'd met with a career counselor to discuss her future plans.

She had been advised to take the required freshman courses and come back when she was a sophomore.

She'd gone to summer camp the summer after her freshman year in high school. At the camp there had been occupational classes. After reading several job descriptions she'd become interested in the one for Legal Secretary.

Alexander was building a home of his own on the outskirts of town. He described in great detail what his house would look like when it was finished.

Susannah envied his direction in life. She'd never planned out her life, except college. She had no idea what direction her life would take.

Alexander looked at his watch. "It's four o'clock, I should be going." He said.

"I was having such a good time I lost track of the time. You can sleep on the couch if you'd like. It pulls out into a bed." Susannah told him.

"I'd better go home so I'll have fresh clothes to put on in the morning." He told her.

Susannah was very disappointed that he didn't want to stay. She wanted him to hold her.

She had begun to let her guard down. Alexander had kissed and caressed her while they talked. Her body hummed as they sat together on the sofa.

"Do you want to move the time for breakfast back?" She asked.

"No, we agreed eleven o'clock. I like to keep my commitments."

Reaching into his pocket he said, "Close your eyes."

"Why?" Susannah asked.

"I have something for you." He said.

Susannah cautiously closed her eyes.

"Are they closed good and tight?" He asked.

"Yes. What is it, Alexander?" Susannah asked irritably.

Alexander picked up Susannah's left hand. She felt him slide something onto her finger.

"Open your eyes." Alexander said.

Susannah slowly opened her eyes, looking at the ring Alexander had placed on her finger.

The ring was a two-carat oval red ruby surrounded by a carat of diamonds.

He leaned over to gently kiss her on the lips. When she responded he deepened the kiss.

"Alexander, it's beautiful." Susannah exclaimed when the kiss ended.

"Not as beautiful as you are." Alexander commented.

Susannah blushed. "It fits perfectly." She said, holding her hand up to look at the ring in the light.

Alexander stood to go.

Susannah stood at the same time.

"I'll pick you up at eleven."

"See you at eleven."

Susannah followed him to the door so she could lock it.

After clearing the coffee table, she took everything to the kitchen rinsing them in the sink.

Going to her room she changed into her nightshirt, turned on her fan then climbed into bed.

She fell asleep almost as soon as her head hit the pillow. In her dreams Wayne told her they had to get back together because they loved each other. Alexander was telling everyone they were really getting married. Her father insisted she had to let him be part of her life.

She awoke in a fluster. Her emotions were not something she was familiar with. No man had ever made her feel the way Alexander did. Sexy, cared for, loved, cherished... wanted.

She went to take a shower and get dressed.

Alexander arrived promptly at eleven. She hadn't braided her hair yet. She answered the door, brush in hand.

"Hi, I'll just be a few minutes. I have to braid my hair." She told him.

"Why, I like it down it looks so sexy." He said.

"It usually gets in the way. It's much easier to deal with when it's braided." She said.

"I'd still like you to wear it down." He said.

"Okay, let me get my purse and a sweater."

"There's no hurry."

Susannah went to get her purse and sweater.

They left to get breakfast.

Going inside the restaurant. they were seated by the hostess.

Their server came to take their order.

"What can I get you?" She asked.

"The breakfast buffet with coffee." Alexander said.

"Help yourself, let me know if I can get you anything."

The server left to wait on other guests.

"Why did you buy the ring, Alexander?" Susannah asked.

"Loomis thinks we're engaged and we have to convince my new client's daughter I am not available." Alexander said.

"Wasn't buying a ring extreme? What are we going to do when Wayne leaves town and you finish building the mall?" Susannah asked.

"We'll take things one day at a time."

Susannah decided she wouldn't dwell on the ring. After all, she would be returning it as soon as Wayne left and Alexander finished building the mall.

Finishing breakfast Alexander paid their bill and they left.

They rode back to Susannah's apartment in comfortable silence.

"Would you like to come in or do you have plans for the day?" Susannah asked.

"I'd like to come in." Alexander answered.

She led the way to her apartment. When they went in the red light on her answering machine was blinking.

Susannah played the messages.

Her mother had called sounding upset. Wayne had called demanding Susannah call him back. Allie had called sounding much the way her mother had.

Susannah called her mother first.

"Hello." Laura answered.

"Hi, Mom, it's me. What's up?" Susannah said.

"Wayne was here demanding to know about your engagement." Laura said.

"What did you tell him?" Susannah said.

"Nothing, I told him your engagement is none of his business."

"If you're free for dinner we'll explain tonight."

"I'll be there at five."

"Okay, I have to go."

Susannah hung up from talking to her mother and called Allie.

"Hello." Allie answered.

"Hi, Allie, it's me." Susannah said.

"What's this I hear about your engagement?" Allie said.

"If John and you are free for dinner tonight I'll explain." Susannah said.

"We'll see you for supper at five."

"Okay, see you then." Susannah said.

Susannah hung up and turned to Alexander. "Well this is a fine mess. Wayne went to visit my mother and best friend demanding to know about my engagement." Susannah told him.

"We'll work it out tonight at dinner. Call Nathan and invite him over too, Loomis may try to get in touch with him." Alexander said.

"He doesn't know where Nathan lives or have his phone number. Thank Heaven for small favors, but you're right Nathan should know too." She said.

"What are we having for dinner?" Alexander asked.

"You can't be hungry already."

"Haven't you heard the way to a man's heart is through his stomach?"

"Of course, I thought it was just an old wives' tale. We have to decide what to make for dinner."

Susannah scanned her cupboards then decided that she needed to get more groceries for her dinner party tonight.

"I have to go to the store Alexander. Do you want to go or stay here?" Susannah said.

"I'll go. This will give us the opportunity to be a couple having family and friends over for dinner." He said.

"I'll call Nathan before we leave."

Susannah went to call Nathan.

"Hello." Nathan said.

"Hi, Nathan it's Susannah." She said.

"Is something wrong?" He asked.

"Just a problem with Wayne. Can you come over for dinner at five?"

"If it has something to do with Loomis it's important. I'll be there."

"All right, see you at five."

Susannah hung up the phone.

Alexander took Susannah by the hand leading her out of the apartment down to his car.

Before helping Susannah into the car, Alexander turned her toward him, looking into her eyes he kissed her.

Moaning, Susannah responded, he deepened the kiss.

Alexander pressed her against the car. She could feel him begin to become fully aroused against her.

Susannah clawed at the car for something solid to hang on to as she became as aroused as him.

He trailed hot kisses down her neck.

Susannah cried out her pleasure in small gasps.

"Alexander... yes." Susannah said.

"Yes?" Alexander questioned near her ear.

"I want to go back upstairs." She said.

Alexander felt like cold water had been poured over them.

He stepped away from Susannah.

"What's wrong?" She asked.

"You don't know what you're saying." He answered.

"I know exactly what I'm saying." She said.

Alexander pulled Susannah away from the car, opened the door and helped her in.

Closing the door, he walked around to the driver's side.

"This is not the time to begin an intimate relationship." Alexander said.

"Why not?" Susannah asked.

"Our relationship isn't real, we're only pretending to be engaged." He said.

Stung, Susannah sat silent in her seat.

Alexander reached over to grasp her hand.

She stiffened.

He pulled his hand back, started the car and pulled into the street.

It was a short trip to the store. When they went in Alexander took a cart.

"What's that for?" Susannah asked irritably.

"Groceries." He answered.

"I'm only getting milk, cake and breading mix." She told him.

"I saw what's in your freezer." He said.

"What's wrong with the stuff in my freezer?"

"There's only enough for one person."

"I am only one person."

"Not anymore. Remember, we're a couple, at least until Loomis leaves and I'm finished building the mall."

"This is getting more and more complicated."

"Suppose Loomis decides not to leave? He may stick around for a while."

"I hadn't thought about that. We can't pretend to be engaged indefinitely."

"Why not? It'll be fun."

"I'm sure you have a life you'd like to get back to."

"Work is my life."

"A match made in heaven. Work seems to be the only life I have."

"I'd rather not talk about work. Let's do our grocery shopping."

"Agreed."

Alexander had put items in the cart as they were talking. There were several items in it.

They had been in the store for nearly an hour by the time they went to the checkout.

After making their purchases they went to Alexander's car, loading the items into the trunk.

"I have limited cupboard and freezer space, I hope you planned on taking some of this food home." Susannah said.

"No, I hope to come over for dinner a lot. After all, I am your fiancée." Alexander told her.

"You use that excuse a lot you know." She told him.

"Does it work?" He asked.

"Yes, but it's wearing thin." She told him.

"Yes, dear."

Susannah was quiet on the trip home. She thought about what she and Alexander would tell their dinner guests.

"Alexander." She said.

"Yes." He answered.

"Does anyone call you Alex?" She asked as they unloaded groceries.

"Not if they expect me to answer. I assume you prefer Susannah." Alexander said.

"Yes." She told him.

The next several minutes were spent unloading groceries and taking them into Susannah's apartment.

After the groceries were put away she washed her hands and started dinner.

"What would you like me to do?" Alexander asked.

"Peel potatoes please." She answered.

Alexander and Susannah worked together in comfortable silence.

When he finished the potatoes, Susannah was finished breading the pork chops.

Together they worked on the salad. Afterward Alexander took the corn out of the freezer, letting it thaw a little before preparing to cook it.

Susannah set the table. Afterward she went to check her answering machine for messages. There weren't any.

Allie and John walked in at five.

"We're not too early are we?" Allie asked.

"No, you're right on time. We're waiting for Mom and Nathan." Susannah told her.

Alexander came out of the kitchen drying his hands on a towel.

Allie's mouth dropped open.

"Close your mouth, Allie." Susannah said.

"I haven't seen a man come out of your kitchen in a while." Allie said.

"Alexander Arthur, my best friend Allison Cole and her fiancée John Sanders." Susannah introduced.

"What's this about an engagement between Susannah and you?" Allie asked.

"We'll wait for the rest of our guests to arrive, then we'll only have to explain once." Alexander said.

The doorbell rang again. This time it was Laura and Nathan.

Susannah made the necessary introductions, and then announced that dinner was ready.

When everyone was seated at the table Alexander asked for their attention.

"As you all know we've asked you here because Susannah is being pestered by Loomis." He said.

"Explain your engagement." Laura said.

"I told you Wayne was pestering me at Matilda's one night. Alexander stepped in and pretended to be my fiancée. Wayne has continued to pester me and now he's asking Allie and you about my engagement." Susannah said.

Alexander went on to explain the situation with Wayne and his new client's daughter.

Susannah showed them her engagement ring at Alexander's insistence.

Naturally their guests had questions. Alexander and Susannah answered them, setting their minds at ease.

When they got to dessert everyone knew what was going on and what to tell Wayne if he asked questions about the engagement.

Laura was concerned about her daughter. She wanted to know what Alexander's intentions were.

He assured her he'd never hurt Susannah and would only do what was necessary to protect Susannah and himself from their admirers.

Finally the evening was over. Susannah drew in a sigh of relief when the last guest left.

"That bad huh?" Alexander asked.

"No, it's overwhelming. How long do you think we'll have to pretend to be engaged?" Susannah said.

"We've only just begun construction on the mall. It could be a year or more. No telling how long Loomis is going to stick around." Alexander answered.

"I have my inheritance to think about. No telling what kind of work needs to be done on Hawthorne Manor." Susannah said.

"Hawthorne Manor? What does that have to do with you?"

"I inherited it from my late stepmother. I just remembered Wayne said he was back for good and that he wanted me to give him another chance."

Alexander didn't know what to ask first. How she had a Hawthorne as her stepmother or about Loomis.

Susannah sat down. How was she going to get rid of Wayne and out of this engagement?

"What are you thinking, Susannah?" Alexander asked.

"How I'm going to get Wayne to leave me alone and how I'm going to get out of this engagement with my dignity intact." She answered honestly.

"If Loomis is going to be around for good you may not get rid of him. He might give up if you actually do get married. How did you inherit Hawthorne Manor?" Alexander said.

"My father married Glenda Hawthorne after I was born. She left me the house in her will." She answered.

"I heard rumors growing up about Glenda and a man she supposedly took away from his family." Alexander said.

"My father was the man. I already told you he walked out on us after I was born."

"I was six when that happened. Tell me about it. Maybe I can help you work through things."

"It's personal, Alexander. I'd rather not talk about it."

"If were going to pretend to be engaged you have to learn to trust me."

"Alexander."

"Don't Alexander me."

"All right here goes." Susannah began the story of her father and Glenda.

As she told it she cleaned up from supper.

After she finished telling the story her doorbell rang. She went to answer it.

"Hello, Susannah." Wayne said.

"Wayne what are you doing here?" Susannah asked.

"I was out for a drive and decided to stop by." He said.

Alexander came out of the kitchen at that moment.

"Who is it, darling?" He asked.

"Wayne you remember my fiancée, Alexander Arthur." Susannah said.

Susannah watched Wayne stiffen and pull himself up trying to match Alexander's height. She could see he didn't like the idea of her being engaged to the man he claimed who had gone back on a deal.

The two men shook hands.

Alexander was curious as to why Wayne would stop by knowing Susannah was engaged so didn't encourage him to leave.

"What are you doing here, Wayne?" Susannah asked.

"I'm curious about your engagement." Wayne admitted.

"My engagement is none of your business." Susannah said.

"How about some coffee, Susannah?" Wayne asked.

"You won't be staying that long." Susannah stated.

"Darling, there's no need to rush our guest off. We have all evening and tomorrow to spend together." Alexander said.

Susannah saw Wayne's reaction to Alexander's statement. She could almost have laughed at his thought that she and Alexander were lovers.

"Of course, darling." Susannah said. "I'll have coffee made in a few minutes."

She went to the kitchen wondering what Alexander and Wayne would talk about in her absence.

Busying herself making coffee she wondered what to serve with it. There was the cake from dinner, it would have to do.

Carrying the coffee and cake into the living room she heard the men discussing Wayne's latest project.

"As soon as I get the patent papers filed we can begin production." Wayne said.

"Coffee and cake." Susannah announced.

She sat the coffee on the table in front of Alexander.

"After that delicious dinner you made I couldn't eat another bite, but I will have coffee." Alexander said.

Susannah poured coffee into three mugs and made each cup to each person's liking.

Wayne noticed Susannah's engagement ring as she passed the cups around.

He took hold of her hand to inspect the ring. His reaction was one of dislike. He knew it was real and expensive.

Susannah pulled her hand away.

"I surprised Susannah with her ring last night." Alexander said.

"It's beautiful. What did you do with the engagement ring I bought you?" Wayne said.

"You mean the ring you bought with my money. It's in my jewelry box where it has been since the day I broke our engagement." Susannah said.

"Why did you keep it?" Wayne asked.

"I don't know." Susannah answered honestly.

"Darling, you haven't offered our guest any cake." Alexander reminded her.

"Of course, Wayne would you like cake.?" She asked.

"Yes, please." He answered.

Susannah cut a sliver off handing it to him.

"Thank you." He said.

"What are you doing in town?" Susannah asked.

"I came back to see you. I'd planned to start our relationship over. I was surprised to learn of your engagement." Wayne told her.

"We haven't been engaged long. When I met Susannah I knew she was the one for me." Alexander said.

"That's how I felt when I met her. Congratulations." Wayne said.

"Thank you." Alexander and Susannah said together.

Wayne finished his cake and rose to leave.

Susannah stood too.

"I wish you all the best on your upcoming marriage." Wayne said taking both of Susannah's hands in his.

She pulled them away, putting them in her pockets.

"Thank you, Wayne." She said.

"I hear you know Gina Langley, I ran into her the other day." Wayne said sarcastically to Alexander.

"Yes, I've met her." Alexander said.

"Do you know anything about her?" Wayne asked.

"Not much. I've only met her a few times. My construction company is building her father's new mall." Alexander answered.

"I'm going to look her up." Wayne said.

He headed to the door. Susannah went to show him out.

Wayne leaned over to kiss her cheek. "Good-bye, Susannah. Be happy." He said.

He walked out the door. Susannah couldn't wait to close the door on him and their past.

She went back into the living room. Pouring herself a cup of coffee she sat down. Her hands were shaking so badly she almost dropped the carafe.

Alexander took it from her, sitting it on the table.

She began to cry. Alexander put his arms around her, holding her.

After a few minutes the tears subsided.

"Feel better now?" He asked.

"Better than I have in years." Susannah admitted.

"Are you still in love with him?" Alexander asked.

"No, that's why I was crying. Tears of pure joy and relief after all these years. No, I don't love him, Alexander. Isn't that wonderful?" She said.

More than you can imagine. Alexander thought.

"As long as you're happy it doesn't matter what anyone thinks."

"I can get on with my life and not worry about Wayne trying to interfere."

"What do you plan to do now that Loomis is out of your life?"

"There's still the problem of your admirer. We'll have to pretend to be engaged until you're free of her."

"That will be at least a year. By that time we might just decide to make our engagement real."

"Don't get ahead of yourself, Alexander. One day at a time, remember."

"One day at a time."

Alexander and Susannah settled on the couch to watch television. She felt comfortable, relaxed and secure for the first time in a long time.

She was free of Wayne and she had Alexander. She pulled his arms around her middle holding him to her.

She was happy and in a joyful mood. Alexander enjoyed her mood. She was wearing his ring and he'd do everything he could to keep it that way.

Susannah fell asleep in Alexander's arms. He made himself more comfortable. She turned more firmly into his body, hugging him.

He allowed himself to fall asleep, wrapping his arms more firmly around her.

CHAPTER SEVEN

Susannah awoke to feel steel bands wrapped around her. She looked up to see Alexander sleeping soundly.

She felt good. Wayne was out of her life and Alexander was here with her.

The phone rang. Susannah gently worked her way out of Alexander's arms. She didn't reach the phone before the answering machine picked up.

"Hello, Susannah. If you're there pick up." Laura said.

Susannah reached the phone. "Hi, Mom, sorry I had a hard time getting up." Susannah apologized.

"Your father called. He's coming back next weekend and he's bringing your brothers and sister." Laura told her.

"I'm looking forward to meeting my brothers and sister and introducing Alexander." Susannah said.

"How did the rest of the evening go?"

"Fine for a while. I told Alexander about Glenda then Wayne showed up."

"What did he want?"

"He wanted to talk about things. When he saw my ring he gave up on winning me back. He said good-bye and told me to be happy."

"What did Alexander say about that?"

"He was supportive and helped me get through Wayne's visit. I don't love Wayne, Mom."

"Do you love Alexander?"

"I don't know. It's too soon to tell, but I could."

"Good morning, Susannah." Alexander said.

"Good morning, Alexander." Susannah replied.

"Alexander is still there." Laura said.

"Yes, Mom." Susannah said.

"Be careful you're not getting into something you can't handle."

"I can handle it, Mom."

"I'll let you go. Call if you need anything."

"Thanks, Mom."

Susannah hung up the phone. Turning, she came face to face with Alexander.

"How's your mother?"

"Fine, worried I might be getting into something I can't handle."

"Mothers worry, that's their job."

"Would you like breakfast?"

"You're changing the subject."

"You're very perceptive."

Susannah went to the refrigerator and started taking things out for breakfast. Going to the cupboards, she took out pans to make it.

Busying herself with making their meal, she was aware of Alexander watching her.

"Are you trying to stare a hole through me or are you that interested in what I'm making?" She asked.

"I'm trying to read your mind, but it's closed." Alexander said.

"Didn't your mother teach you a woman's thoughts are private and you shouldn't pry?" Susannah said.

"Didn't your mother tell you men rarely listen to their mother's advice when it comes to women?" He retorted.

"How many pancakes do you want?"

"You know, I could take you out for breakfast."

"And have you miss out on more of my culinary talents. Perish the thought. How many pancakes do you want?"

"What else are we having?"

"Sausage and eggs."

"Six pancakes, three eggs and a few sausage."

Susannah fixed breakfast, keeping the pancakes and eggs warm in the oven while cooking the sausage.

"That was delicious. Your mother taught you to cook." Alexander said after finishing his meal.

"I'm glad you liked it. Yes, mom taught me to cook." Susannah answered.

"She taught you well." He told her.

"I'll pass along the compliment. Besides teaching me that an education was important, mom also made sure I had a well rounded education in domesticity." She informed him.

"What was your life like growing up?" Alexander asked.

"I've told you, normal. Glenda sent an allowance every month so mom didn't have to work. I had friends and mom was able to spend a lot of time with me. How was your childhood?" Susannah answered.

"As far back as I can remember my father worked hard to support us. After he quit practicing law he took construction jobs no one wanted to build his reputation. He made it a priority to put his family first. It seemed like overnight his little construction company grew into the business it is today."

"Did you always want to work in construction?"

"Yes. When I was old enough, and didn't have to go to school, my father would take me on jobs and let me help out. I was fascinated with the way the buildings became houses or places people worked."

Alexander looked at his watch. "I need to go work on my house. Do you want to do anything today?"

"I don't know. Call me later and I'll let you know."

"All right."

Alexander leaned down to kiss her. Susannah accepted and returned the kiss.

She felt as though her life had started at just that moment and things could only get better.

After Alexander left she cleaned her apartment, did laundry, took a shower then settled in front of the television.

Alexander called as promised.

They agreed to get together another time.

Susannah ordered Chinese and had it delivered.

She watched television while she ate.

The phone rang.

Susannah answered it.

"Hello." She said.

"Hello, Susannah, this is your father." Thomas said.

"How are you? Is anything wrong?" Susannah asked.

"No, no everything is fine. I'm calling to let you know we'll be arriving Friday at six. Will you join us for dinner?" He said.

"Of course, where and what time?"

"Matilda's, seven thirty."

"I'll be there, see you then."

"Your brothers and sister are anxious to meet you."

"I'm anxious to meet them. Hopefully the week will go by quickly. Do you still have the DVD Glenda made?"

"Yes, why?"

"My boss would like to see it."

The next morning when she pulled into her usual parking spot she noticed Nathan's car was already there, along with the one she recognized as Alexander's.

Irritably going into her office, she wondered what the two of them were up to. After the situation the day before Susannah wasn't in the mood to deal with Alexander today.

She had only tolerated his presence over the weekend because they'd had to present a united front because of their pretend engagement.

Poking her head into Nathan's office, Susannah was surprised to find her boss and Alexander going over resumes and applications.

"Good morning, Nathan." She said.

Both men looked up.

Alexander smiled at her, she scowled at him.

He wondered why she was annoyed at him.

"Good morning, Susannah. Alexander volunteered to help me go through resumes and applications to pick out the best qualified applicants. I'm happy to tell you your friend from Tilly's is among them." Nathan said.

"She'll be glad to know she has a chance." Susannah said.

"Will you be sitting in on the interviews?" Alexander asked.

"If that's what Nathan wants." She answered stiffly.

"You'll be training and working with her, I think it best you sit in on the interviews." Nathan said.

"All right." Susannah agreed.

"As soon as we choose who to interview I'll give you the list so you can type the letters to send out to the interviewees." Nathan told her.

Susannah nodded.

She went to her desk, putting away her purse. Going to the kitchenette, she went through her usual morning routine. Afterwards, she went to her desk.

An hour later Nathan brought the list of applicants to send notice of interview letters to instructing her to set up interviews for a week from Friday.

Agreeing, Susannah took the papers knowing they'd notify the person chosen the same day of the interviews.

She typed the letters and the corresponding envelopes.

She took them into Nathan to check and sign.

He checked and signed them, then handed them back to Susannah.

She took them back to her desk, folded them into thirds, and readied them for mailing.

She piled together the paperwork that needed Nathan's attention and took it into him.

She went back to work not noticing when Alexander left.

When lunchtime came she put aside her paperwork, went to check her hair and make-up, told Nathan she was leaving and went to lunch.

Walking into Tilly's she was melancholy. Rainy days were gloomy and depressing.

Ordering her lunch, she decided to take it on the enclosed patio even though it was raining.

She enjoyed a leisurely lunch, letting her mind wander to Alexander.

He was tall, handsome and caring. She could easily fall in love with him, if she'd let herself.

"Penny for your thoughts." Tilly said.

"I was thinking." She said.

"Instinct tells me you were thinking about your fiancée." Tilly stated.

"I was a little." Susannah admitted.

Tilly's arched brow told Susannah she thought it was more than a little.

"Okay, a lot." Susannah confirmed.

"Have you set a date yet?" Tilly asked.

"No, Alexander wants to wait until after he finishes the mall he's building so we'll be able to spend time together after we're married." Susannah told her.

"I wouldn't wait too long. Alexander is a handsome, virile man. There are a lot of women who'd like to take him away from you." Tilly advised.

Susannah looked at her watch.

"Wow, look at the time. I have to go. It's been nice talking to you, Tilly." She said.

She picked up her trash, took it inside, threw it away, picked up Nathan's lunch and went back to her office.

Enjoying the rain she nearly walked past her office.

"Are you planning to let me go hungry this afternoon?" Nathan asked from the doorway.

Susannah looked down the street, then at Nathan.

"I guess I let my mind wander and forgot where I was going." Susannah admitted.

"You really do need a vacation. I promise as soon as we hire your assistant you'll have two weeks off to rest and relax." Nathan told her.

"How long have you worked without a vacation?" Susannah countered.

"More time than I'd like to count. We weren't talking about me."

They had moved into the office. Susannah handed Nathan his lunch.

"Eat your lunch." She said.

"Yes, mother." Nathan said taking the bag.

She went to her desk. Getting back to work, she became absorbed in her work. Susannah was surprised when her watch chimed at five.

Her personal problems hadn't plagued her during the afternoon as they normally did and she was able to get more work done.

Even so, she'd be glad when Nathan hired her assistant.

"Good night, Nathan. See you in the morning." Susannah said as she left.

Susannah spent the rest of the week working and getting ready for her father and siblings' visit.

When Friday arrived Susannah was nervous. She hadn't talked to or seen Alexander since Monday and her father was arriving tonight.

"Susannah, go home early today." Nathan suggested.

"Why?" She asked.

"You've been staring at your computer for the last five minutes as though it were an alien being." Nathan informed her.

"Have I? I wasn't aware." Susannah admitted.

"Precisely my point. Go home, relax before your family arrives."

"All right, but only because I know you'll stand over my shoulder until I go."

"I knew you'd see it my way."

Susannah snorted and went about her daily closing up chores. When she was finished she called the answering service to take messages.

When she arrived home she treated herself to a midday pampering bath.

Susannah stepped out of the bath just as the phone started ringing.

She quickly put her robe on, tied it at the waist and reached the phone before the answering machine picked up.

"Hello." She answered.

"Hello, Susannah." Alexander said.

"Alexander, how did you know I was home?" She asked.

"I called your office. The answering service told me you'd left early. Are you ill?" He said.

"No, Nathan sent me home early. My father and siblings are coming into town tonight and I wasn't getting much work done."

"Were we supposed to have a date tonight?"

"No, but I'd appreciate the moral support tonight. I know the invitation is last minute, so don't feel obligated."

"I don't have plans for the evening; I'd be honored to go with you."

"Thanks, I really appreciate it. I'm meeting my father and siblings at Matilda's at seven thirty."

"I'll pick you up at seven."

"Okay, see you at seven."

Susannah hung up. She went back to the bathroom to finish drying and to blow-dry her hair.

When she finished she went into her bedroom to look through the closet.

Choosing her pink cotton dress, she knew it made her look demure, yet confident. It went to the floor, covering her shapely legs.

Although she wanted to look nice for Alexander, she also wanted to look just right to meet her father's children.

"I have to remember these are my half-siblings." She reminded herself aloud.

Time was going quickly. Alexander would be there in three quarters of an hour.

When she put on the dress and smoothed it down, there was a slight hint of her curves underneath.

Looking at herself in the full-length mirror, on the back of her bedroom door, she was glad she chose the dress.

Going back into the bathroom, she put just a hint of make-up on. Her hair was another matter. Should she wear it up or down?

The image she wanted to project demanded it be worn up; her instinct told her to leave it down.

It took all of two seconds to decide. Her instinct won. She told herself she hadn't made her choice because Alexander preferred her hair down.

He would be there in half an hour.

Susannah had butterflies in her stomach. She knew the butterflies weren't due to Alexander's forthcoming arrival. Although he made more than her pulse race, her nervousness came from her upcoming meeting with her father and half-siblings.

She paced back and forth across her living room. No matter how many times she told herself to calm down, she just couldn't still the fluttering in her stomach.

When the doorbell rang at seven, Susannah jumped.

Realizing it was the doorbell, she went to answer it. Opening the door, she stepped back.

Alexander was wearing a blue pinstripe suit, a baby blue dress shirt, matching socks, white dress shoes and a blue tie decorated with Disney characters.

"Do I pass muster?" Alexander asked.

Susannah nodded and giggled.

"Did I say something funny?" He said.

Susannah brought her laughter under control.

"No, I was laughing at your tie." She told him.

"What's wrong with my tie?" He asked in mock indignation.

"Nothing it's very... cute." She said

"Cute. If I'd wanted cute I'd have worn my feet pajamas."

"You wear feet pajamas."

"That's for me to know and you to find out."

"I'll pass thanks. If not cute, how about charming."

"Is that the best you can do?"

"Fishing for compliments, Alexander. I thought you were more self-assured."

"I am, but I stopped being cute and charming when I was five. Puppies, kittens and children are cute."

"All right, you're very handsome. Is that better?"

"Excellent."

Taking her hand, Alexander spun Susannah around in a circle. Her dress flared out hoop like.

"You my dear, look beautiful, if not a bit modest."

"Shall we go? I don't want to be late."

~ 135 ~

Susannah went to get her wrap. Alexander put it on for her.

"Ready?"

"Let me check to make sure everything is off."

She went into the kitchen and checked all of the appliances. Satisfied that things were in order, Susannah went back to Alexander.

He escorted her out the door, to the elevator, through the lobby and into his car.

Opening her door, he assisted her into the car and shut the door. Walking to the driver's side, he opened the door sliding behind the wheel.

Susannah put her hand on her stomach to calm the fluttering.

"Are you okay?" Alexander asked, observing her nervous gesture.

"Butterflies, this will be the first time meeting my siblings. This will also be the second time I've seen my father in twenty-six years." She said.

Alexander took her hand, put it to his mouth and kissed the back.

"Relax, I'm sure they're as nervous as you are." He told her.

"Tell that to the butterflies in my stomach. I suppose you're right though. Let's go." Susannah said.

He pulled into the street driving them to Matilda's.

"We're early. Should we go in to get a table?" Susannah said.

"What would you like to do?" Alexander asked.

"Turn around and go back home." She said.

"At this point I don't believe that's an option." He told her.

"Let's go get a table. I'll relax once we're inside, I hope."

"Lead the way my love."

Shocked at his use of the phrase 'my love', Susannah opened her door and stepped out into the warmth of the night.

Alexander joined her on the passenger side of the car.

As they walked into the restaurant he linked his fingers with hers.

The hostess greeted them.

Susannah pulled her hand from Alexander's.

"Hello, Alexander, Susannah. How are you this evening?" April asked.

"Fine." Alexander answered.

"Would you like a table for two?" April inquired.

"We're meeting Susannah's family. There will be six of us." Alexander told her.

"I have a table at the back or one in the center. Which would you prefer?" April said.

"At the back." Susannah said.

"The center table will be fine." Alexander stated firmly.

"Right this way." April told them.

Susannah ignored Alexander's outstretched hand as they walked to the table April indicated.

"I'll bring your party over when they arrive." She said.

"Thank you." Susannah said.

April left to go back to her duties.

Alexander pulled a chair out to seat Susannah. She stubbornly chose to seat herself elsewhere.

He chose a seat at the head of the table next to her.

"Are you going to be angry with me all night?" He asked.

"Only until you take me home." Susannah snapped.

"What will your family think?" He asked, trying to pacify her.

"Don't patronize me, Alexander." She said.

"What's wrong, love?" He asked.

"I would have preferred to sit at the table in back." She said angrily.

"You really are nervous. You're usually not easily angered."

"You're right, I'm sorry."

"Apology accepted. I believe our dinner companions are on their way over."

Alexander stood as Susannah's family approached.

"Hello, Susannah." Thomas greeted.

Susannah looked at her father. "Hello, Father. How are you?" She answered.

"I'm well, thank you. These are your brothers Phillip and Martin and your sister Jenni." Thomas introduced.

Phillip was a younger version of Thomas. Susannah guessed his age to be twenty-three, he was dressed casually business like, his disposition alert and on edge.

Martin resembled his mother, was twenty-one wore clean jeans and a western style shirt and seemed to have a more laid back attitude.

Jennifer looked a little like both of her brothers, she looked to be anywhere between sixteen and twenty, she wore a peasant blouse and skirt, her surface manner seemed to be haughty.

Susannah stood extending her hand to each of her siblings.

"I'm pleased to meet you. This is my fiancée, Alexander Arthur." She said, including Alexander in the introductions.

Everyone shook hands, then sat down.

"What can I get you folks to drink?" Michael, their server asked.

"We'll need a few minutes to decide." Alexander told him.

"Yes sir. Let me know when you're ready." Michael said.

"Thank you." Alexander said.

"Daddy told us you work in an attorney's office." Jenni said to Susannah.

"Yes, I was just made an associate." Susannah answered.

"But you're so young." Jenni exclaimed.

Susannah swallowed the sharp retort on the tip of her tongue. Instead she said, "I've been working for Nathan since I graduated from the university."

"What do you do, Alexander?" Thomas asked.

"I own a construction company." Alexander said.

"You can help Susie decide if she wants to claim Hawthorne Manor." Phillip said in a too familiar manner.

"Susannah," Alexander emphasized her given name, "hasn't told me what she wants to do."

"We haven't seen the house, but mother always told us it's beautiful. I'm sure you'll love it, Susannah." Martin stated.

"My boss has agreed to represent me. He'll help me decide whether or not to claim the inheritance." Susannah said.

"You've retained an attorney?" Thomas asked.

"Yes, Nathan will look into the legal aspects of the inheritance and advise me what to do. That's why I asked you to bring the DVD Glenda made." Susannah answered.

"I have it at the hotel." Thomas said.

"What would everyone like to drink?" Alexander asked.

The group discussed drink orders for the next few minutes. When they decided Alexander motioned for Michael.

"Yes sir what can I get you?" He said.

Alexander gave Michael their drink order.

When he finished the conversation turned back to Susannah's inheritance.

"Susannah if you don't claim your inheritance Hawthorne Manor will sit empty. It would be a shame to have such a beautiful house sit empty." Phillip stated.

"I can't make a decision just like that." Susannah said, snapping her fingers. "I have to look at the house and see what condition it's in."

"Mother retained a cleaning service to keep it clean and had repairs done as necessary." Martin said.

"I'd like to have my crew go to check the foundation." Alexander offered.

"Won't that delay construction on the mall?" Susannah asked.

"No, some of my crew is standing idle right now. A couple of days won't make a difference." Alexander told her.

"All right, if you're sure." Susannah accepted.

"Very sure." Alexander said, leaning over to kiss her.

The kiss was light and short, too short, but Susannah felt it down to her toes.

Michael brought their drinks and then took their dinner order.

"What do all of you do?" Susannah asked her siblings.

One by one they told her what they did.

Phillip had started working in Business Administration at Western Chemical, Rose Lake Division a year earlier after graduating from college. Martin was learning the business of raising and training horses and Jennifer had just completed her first year of college.

Susannah held her animosity toward her father's abandonment in check as the evening progressed. She would not let her siblings have the satisfaction of knowing how hurt she was that they'd had both a mother, father and money growing up.

Susannah's siblings brought up her inheritance frequently poorly hiding their resentment that she had inherited the family home in Camille; they'd never seen Hawthorne Manor because they'd been born and raised in Rose Lake.

Susannah avoided discussing her inheritance when the subject came up realizing her brothers and sister were resentful that they had to share the inheritance with her.

Phillip, Martin and Jenni asked what it was like growing up in Camille. In turn they reciprocated by telling her what it had been like growing up in Rose Lake.

There were several invitations extended to Alexander and Susannah to visit.

Susannah accepted explaining it would be a month or more before they'd be able to visit.

By ten o'clock she couldn't hide her yawns behind her hand.

"It's time I took Susannah home. She's too polite to let anyone know she's tired." Alexander said.

"Alexander!" Susannah reprimanded.

"He's only speaking the truth, child." Thomas said.

"I'm not a child father." Susannah reminded him.

"I know. It's hard to believe you're a grown woman." He told her. "You two go on, I'll get the check."

Alexander stood, helped Susannah out of her chair and bid their good nights.

"I'll call you tomorrow." Jenni promised.

"I'll look forward to it." Susannah replied.

She allowed Alexander to escort her out to his car.

When they were inside, Alexander inserted the key into the ignition and turned towards Susannah.

"Did you enjoy yourself?" He asked.

"Surprisingly, yes. I half expected my father's children to be like their mother." Susannah answered.

"Would you like to be at the manor when my crew goes over?"

"No, I trust your judgment."

"All right, I'll send my crew in the next day or two."

"Thank you, Alexander, I appreciate your help."

They rode the rest of the way to Susannah's in silence. Alexander pulled up in front of her building.

"Would you like to come in for coffee or a night cap?" She asked.

"No, it's late and you're tired." Alexander said.

"Thank you for your help tonight." She said.

"You can count on me, Susannah. Remember that."
He told her.

"I will, good night, Alexander."

He leaned over and kissed her. Susannah responded hungrily.

"Good night, Susannah." He said when he was finally able to make himself pull away. "Sleep well, my love."

Stunned again by his use of the phrase 'my love', she opened her door, stepped out of the car and closed the door. Alexander watched her get safely into the building then drove off.

When she unlocked her door and turned on the lights, Susannah looked at the light on her answering machine, it wasn't blinking.

Susannah performed her nightly rituals of getting ready for bed, went to her bedroom, turned off the light, turned on the fan and television, then climbed into bed.

Closing her eyes she was asleep almost instantly. She dreamt of Alexander making love to her.

While she did, she tossed and turned in her bed, kicking the blankets this way and that.

Susannah freed herself from the dream.

The television was still on, she hadn't set the sleep timer.

She couldn't remember the last time she'd had an erotic dream like the one she'd just had.

Turning off the television, she rolled over hoping to go back to sleep. Susannah didn't wake up again until after ten the next morning.

CHAPTER EIGHT

Saturdays were her errand and chore day. Anything she hadn't been able to do during the week was done on Saturday.

Dressing she hurried through her routine because she'd gotten up late.

When she came in from shopping the red light on her answering machine was blinking.

Whoever had called would have to wait until she'd taken care of the groceries.

After making one more trip to her car and putting away the reusable grocery bags Susannah went to the answering machine pushing the play button to listen to her messages.

Alexander called, he was sorry he'd missed her, but would call later. Allie called asking that she call back. Her mother called asking her to Sunday brunch.

Susannah called her mother first.

Laura picked up the phone on the second ring. "Hello." She said.

"Hi, Mom, it's me." Susannah said.

"I was wondering how dinner went last night." Laura said.

"Fine, I was nervous, having Alexander there supporting me helped." Susannah told her.

"Is that it, just fine?" Laura asked.

"It wasn't supposed to be the most exciting night of my life, Mother." Susannah said.

"I know, I expected you to be happier."

"I had dinner with a father I've seen twice in my life and two brothers and a sister I didn't know I had until a few weeks ago. Those people are strangers to me Mom."

"I expected too much I suppose. Can we go to brunch tomorrow or do you have plans with Alexander?"

"I don't have plans with Alexander, I'd love to go to brunch."

"All right, pick me up at nine thirty."

"Okay, see you tomorrow. Bye Mom."

Susannah hung up. She was confused. Why would her mother expect her to be more than mildly excited about dinner last night?

Ignoring the nagging feeling, she called Allie.

"Hello." Allie said.

"Hi, Allie, it's Susannah." She said.

"I thought you'd gotten lost." Allie admonished.

"I know I've been neglectful. I'm sorry, I've been busy." Susannah apologized.

"Apology accepted. What have you been up to?"

"Working, spending time with Alexander and last night I had dinner with my father and siblings."

"How was dinner? What are your siblings like?"

"Dinner was okay. I haven't spent enough time with my family so I'm reserving judgment until I know them better. What have you been doing?"

"Working and we've been trying to make our families understand we don't want a big elaborate wedding. John and I have set a wedding date."

"That's wonderful, when is the big day?" Susannah asked.

"A month from now." Allie told her.

"A month? We can't put a wedding together in a month." Susannah said.

"We don't want a big wedding." Allie said.

"I should be able to take time off from work in a month. Nathan is interviewing applicants for my assistant on Friday."

"How are things going with Alexander?"

"Okay, we haven't set a wedding date. Of course we may not have to. Hopefully his admirer will see how devoted he is to his fiancée and back off."

"Don't bet on it. I've heard stories about Gina Langley. She doesn't sound like the type to give up easily."

"Great, Alexander said it would be at least a year before the mall is complete."

"What are you going to do?"

"I don't know. Alexander and I have agreed to take one day at a time."

"That's sensible. I hate to cut you off, but John should be home soon and our parents should be here shortly. We're going to tell them all again that we want a small ceremony."

"Good luck. I'll talk to you later."

Susannah hung up.

Going into the kitchen, she made a late lunch. While she was eating the phone rang. She went to answer it.

"Hello." She said.

"Hello, Susannah, it's Phillip." He said.

"Hello, what can I do for you?" She asked.

"We're wondering if you're free today. We'd like to show you Hawthorne Manor." Phillip told her.

"I'm eating lunch right now. I can be ready in an hour." She said.

"All right, we'll pick you up."

"Okay, see you then."

"Good-bye."

"Good-bye."

Susannah dialed Alexander's number to see if he wanted to accompany her to see the house she'd inherited. He wasn't home so she left a message.

Susannah went back to her lunch after hanging up.

She hadn't been looking forward to being alone for the weekend. Going to see Hawthorne Manor would get her out of her apartment and give her a chance to look over the house she'd inherited.

Finishing lunch, she cleared up and waited for her father and siblings to pick her up.

Susannah wouldn't allow the butterflies in her stomach to surface. She concentrated on looking forward to seeing the house.

She went down to the lobby to wait.

When her father pulled up out front she went to the car.

"Good afternoon, Susannah." Martin said as he held the door open for her.

"Good afternoon, Martin. Hello everyone." She said.

"Hello, Susannah." Thomas and Phillip said.

Jennifer was pouting in the backseat.

"Good afternoon, Jennifer." Susannah said.

"What's so good about it?" Jenni asked.

"The sun is shining; it's a beautiful day." Susannah told her.

"We're going to look at an old house. It's not even our house, it's yours." Jenni answered.

"It's not mine yet. We're going to look at it so I can decide if I want to live there."

"I wanted to go shopping."

"I'm sure father will take you shopping afterward."

"He doesn't like shopping."

"Stop acting like a spoiled child, Jenni. Susannah will think you're selfish and always want your own way." Phillip said.

"I'm sorry, Susannah. I'm not feeling well today." Jenni apologized.

"Apology accepted. I'll go shopping with you." Susannah said.

"Would you really?" Jenni asked.

"Of course. I love to shop and don't like shopping alone." Susannah said.

"All right, thanks."

"You're welcome. Now on to Hawthorne Manor."

The trip to the manor was short. They were there before Susannah could tell Thomas she'd changed her mind.

When she saw the house she gasped, her mouth hung open.

Thomas stopped the car. "What's wrong? Are you all right, Susannah?" He asked.

"What? Oh, I'm fine. I didn't realize the house was so big." She answered.

He pulled up in front of the house.

Walking into the foyer Susannah noted it was light and airy, not at all like her small, cozy apartment.

Thomas led them into the parlor. Cream colored walls were complemented by white pine furniture which had been handed down through many Hawthorne generations. There were two settees, wooden rockers and other durable, useful furniture. There was also a white pine side table which could be used to serve guests an assortment of liquid refreshment.

Everything looked freshly dusted.

"This is where your grandfather entertained small groups of guests." He said.

"That would be my step grandfather?" Susannah asked.

"Yes." Thomas said.

"It's a beautiful room. How long has it been since anyone has lived in the house?" Susannah questioned.

"About a year. It has been occupied by several Western Chemical managers over the years, not on a permanent basis of course." Thomas said.

"Why did Glenda leave the house to me?" Susannah questioned.

"She wanted the manor to be a permanent residence for a Hawthorne family member."

"Since we were all born and raised in Rose Lake and none of us wants to move to Camille you're the logical choice to inherit the house." Phillip said.

"Why were you all so resentful of my inheriting the manor when we met?" Susannah asked.

"I apologize for our rudeness. We hadn't met you and had just recently learned of your existence. We were afraid you might be an interloper." Martin said.

"You had your mind made up about me before you met me." Susannah said angrily.

"As Martin said we'd just learned of your existence and didn't know what to expect, we didn't know if mother was forced to include you in her will or if it was of her own free will." Phillip said.

"I'd like to see the rest of the house." Susannah said.

Thomas inclined his head so that his children would follow.

The next room they came to was the dining room. It was also furnished in white pine from previous generations. It contained a table large enough to seat six which was set as if expecting company.

A china cabinet stood in one corner displaying dinnerware from previous Hawthorne family members. The walls were covered in clear pine real wood paneling.

Susannah smelled paint and something else she couldn't readily identify. After several minutes she decided it was furniture polish. That confirmed the house had recently been cleaned.

"I had the house freshly painted, cleaned and newly carpeted." Thomas said.

"Because the house needed it or to make my inheritance more appealing?" Susannah asked wryly.

"Are you always so cynical, Susannah?" Phillip asked.

"During the last few years I've become suspicious and cynical of everything. I don't intend to be manipulated again." Susannah answered honestly.

"We're not trying to be manipulative. We believe you deserve the house." Martin told her.

"I promise to try being less suspicious and stop looking for ulterior motives if you promise not to try influencing my decision."

"Deal." Jennifer said extending her hand to Susannah.

Susannah took Jennifer's hand in hers. The two ladies shook on the deal.

Walking through the house, Susannah saw the renovations that had been done to the house.

When they came to the kitchen Susannah stopped dead the room glistened with the brightness of the appliances that were in the room.

She recognized the products her step grandfather's company made. Everywhere she looked there was an appliance that made life easier and more efficient. The kitchen had been set up so no space had been wasted; it had all been used to advantage.

Next Thomas led them to the laundry room. There was an energy efficient washer and dryer, a place for detergent and everything else you'd need to do laundry. There was even a large space for folding laundry to place in baskets to cart off to be put away.

Susannah became excited. The house might help cure the melancholy she'd been experiencing. Of course she knew a house couldn't cure what ailed her, but it would give her a new perspective in which to look at her problems, she hoped.

How would she afford the upkeep? Of course there was the rest of her inheritance, the money and stock in Western Chemical. Susannah fell in love with the house. She couldn't help herself. She knew Nathan would advise her.

She'd made mental notes as they walked through the house.

"Hold on, Father let me catch my breath." Susannah said.

"Is something wrong?" Thomas asked.

"I'm a little overwhelmed. I've never seen a house this large before." Susannah said.

"I'm sorry, Susannah. I hadn't thought about that. Let's go back to the parlor and sit down" Thomas said.

Everyone agreed to go to the living room.

When they were seated Thomas asked, "What do you think, Susannah?"

"It's too large of a house for one person." Susannah said.

"Once you fill it with children it won't seem so." Thomas said.

"You're putting the cart before the horse, Father." Susannah told him.

"We shall see." Thomas said. "We shall see."

"Don't you want children?" Jenni asked.

"Alexander and I haven't discussed children yet. We're concentrating more on the engagement aspect right now." Susannah told her. "Did you bring the DVD from Glenda, Father?"

"Yes, it's in the car. I'll give it to you when we get back."

"All right."

"Do you have plans for the rest of the day? Your brothers and sister would like to look around Camille."

"You used to live here, you're as capable of showing them around as I am. Besides, I promised Jennifer I'd go shopping with her."

"We can go shopping tomorrow. I'd like to see your hometown." Jenni said.

"All right, but there isn't anything special about Camille." Susannah stated.

"Let us be the judge of that." Martin said.

They went out to the car; Thomas handed Susannah the DVD from Glenda.

Susannah showed her family around Camille. Thomas and Susannah's siblings enjoyed their tour of the small town. Thomas's memories were bittersweet. He enjoyed seeing things and places that were familiar and saddened by the loss of old things which had been replaced.

They arrived back at Susannah's apartment. Wanting to get to know her family better she asked, "Would you like to come up for coffee?"

"We'd like that." Thomas accepted.

Going up to her apartment Susannah unlocked her door, leading the way inside. She put the DVD Thomas had given her on a stand next to the TV. The Roberts looked around the apartment, finding it homey and cozy.

"I'll just be a few minutes making the coffee. Make yourselves at home." Susannah said.

She went into the kitchen to make coffee. While she was waiting for it to perk, she found cheese and crackers, sliced apples, putting them all on a platter.

While the coffeemaker completed its cycle Susannah let her mind wander to the people in her living room. She thought about her siblings' reaction after learning of having an older sister. She didn't blame them for being cautious after having learned of her existence.

The coffeemaker stopped. Susannah set up a tray with mugs, cream, sugar and the platter. She also put the coffee carafe on the tray, taking it all into the living room.

"Here we are coffee and snacks." She announced.

"Are these pictures of your mother and you?" Jennifer asked, nodding toward the desk.

"Yes, mother likes us to have our picture taken together every year. I have several from over the years." Susannah told her.

"You favor your mother. She's a beautiful woman." Phillip said.

"Thank you, people think I resemble both mom and father." She commented.

The phone rang.

"Excuse me." She said. "Hello."

"Hello, Susannah, it's Alexander." He announced unnecessarily.

"Yes, I know. I recognize your voice." She told him.

"I was wondering if you're busy this evening. I miss you and want to see you." He said.

"Father and my siblings are here right now. You're welcome to join us." Susannah invited.

"I'll be there in ten minutes."

"All right, see you then, bye Alexander."

Susannah hung up the phone.

"Alexander is on his way over." She told her family.

"Would you like us to leave? We wouldn't want to intrude on your time with your fiancée." Thomas said.

"Don't be silly, Father. I'm sure Alexander is looking forward to getting better acquainted with all of you." She said.

"If you're sure." Phillip said.

"I'm sure.

"I'm hungry." Jennifer said.

Susannah and Jennifer were looking over takeout menus when the doorbell rang.

"I'll get it." Martin offered.

"Thanks." Susannah accepted.

Martin walked to the door and opened it. "Hello, Alexander." He said.

"Hello, Martin." Alexander said.

"Jenni and Susannah are looking at take out menus." Martin said.

"I'm partial to Mexican food." Alexander hinted.

"Who said anything about feeding you?" Susannah teased.

"You wouldn't want me to whither away to nothing would you? I'd lose this great physique you're so fond of." Alexander baited, leaning down to kiss her.

The kiss was tempting. Susannah gave herself up to the seduction Alexander promised.

Thomas cleared his throat to remind them they were not alone.

Embarrassed, Susannah reluctantly pulled away.

"Alexander has made his suggestion for dinner. Does anyone else have a suggestion?" She said in an unsteady voice.

"Mexican sounds good." Thomas said.

Ignoring Susannah's unsteady voice, the rest of her family agreed on Mexican.

"I'll order a variety." Susannah said, her voice steady once again.

She went to the phone placed the order, then rejoined her family.

Phillip began telling her about Rose Lake and Western Chemical. Thomas, Martin and Jennifer added their own thoughts to Phillip's telling.

Susannah was charmed. She hadn't been aware her late stepmother's family had been so influential in environmentally friendly progress.

Western Chemical had nothing to do with chemical processing. It produced a variety of products. Some Susannah recognized as the ones she owned and used on a daily basis.

No one could remember where the name Western Chemical had come from. As long as the company had been in existence it had made products it now boasted made life easier. As times changed, so had the products.

While her family talked Susannah could tell they were proud of their home and company. She wondered what it felt like to be part of something so special.

Not having grown up in a conventional family, she'd always thought there was something missing in her life. Her mother had given her a good childhood bringing her up to have values and principles.

Her maternal grandparents had been a big part of her life. Susannah's paternal grandparents had passed away before her parents had met.

The doorbell rang.

"That will be dinner." Susannah said standing.

She walked to the door opening it.

The delivery person gave Susannah the food taking the money she held out and left.

Susannah took the food to the coffee table, then went to get plates, flatware and serving utensils. Everyone helped themselves.

"How did you meet Alexander, Susannah?" Jenni asked.

"We saw each other at Tilly's, a little café downtown, one day when Susannah was having lunch. We were properly introduced at Matilda's when we met each other again. As I recall you were being pestered by Loomis." Alexander said.

"That doesn't sound very romantic." Jenni said.

"If a man isn't falling over himself to get Jenni's attention she won't go out with him." Phillip told them.

"That's not true!" Jennifer vehemently denied.

"Close enough." Martin joined in.

"Children, Alexander and Susannah don't want to hear your squabbling." Thomas said.

"It's all right, Father. I missed out on sibling relationships growing up." Susannah said.

"You didn't miss anything. Sibling relationships aren't easy. You're lucky you didn't have to go through it. We'd quarrel and fight then one of us would say something we later regretted." Martin told her.

"When I was growing up if my siblings and I fought my parents put whoever was fighting in a room together. We couldn't come out until we'd apologized and made up." Alexander said.

"If everyone is through, I'll clear this food out of the way." Susannah said tension in her voice.

"I'll help." Jenni offered.

"I can get it, but thanks for the offer." Susannah said.

She began picking up Styrofoam containers to take to the kitchen. Alexander picked up the ones she couldn't carry.

Susannah went back into the living room.

"Who wants more coffee?" Susannah asked.

Thomas looked at his watch and said "It's getting late, we have to go."

"Yes, we've taken up enough of your time." Martin said.

"I've enjoyed spending time with all of you." Susannah told them.

"We've enjoyed spending time with you. I'll call you tomorrow to set up a time to go shopping." Jenni said.

"I'll see you tomorrow." Susannah said.

Each of Susannah's family members kissed her on the cheek and left.

When they were alone Alexander asked "Are you all right?"

"Yes, fine." She answered.

"Why don't I believe you?" He said.

Susannah turned to him, eyes moist with tears. "I don't care whether you believe me or not." She stated bitterly.

"Tell me what's wrong, Susannah." Alexander demanded.

"Maybe I don't want to tell you what's wrong." She said.

"I'm sure you'll feel better." He said.

"You have an answer for everything, don't you? First you pretend to be my fiancée to get Wayne out of my life. Now you think you can help me with whatever is wrong, assuming something is wrong." She said.

"I can tell when you're upset, Susannah." He stated.

"Excuse me."

Alexander followed her.

"Are you going to tell me what's bothering you?" Alexander asked.

"Who said anything is wrong?" Susannah countered.

"Don't play games with me, Susannah." He said.

"I get upset when I think about or have to deal with my father's abandonment of mother and me." She told him.

"Why couldn't you just tell me that?"

"I don't like talking about it."

"You have a right to be upset. You need to deal with the problem."

"How do you propose I do that without biting someone's head off?"

"I'm not a therapist, but I think you need to discuss your feelings with your father."

"Oh, right, I'm going to confront my father. I'm not good at confrontations, Alexander."

"You know what I think?"

"What."

"I think we should sit on the couch, snuggle and spend the rest of the night relaxing."

"How's that going to help?"

"I didn't say it would, what's the harm in trying?"

"First I want to clean up this mess."

Susannah began picking up dirty dishes. Her hands trembled and she dropped them.

"Sit down, Susannah." Alexander said gesturing for her to sit on the couch.

"I don't want to sit down, Alexander. Maybe I want to be angry and upset. I haven't let my emotions out in such a long time. They've been bottled up so long; if I don't let them out I'm going to explode."

Susannah picked up a pillow and threw it across the room. She picked up another one and threw it too.

Alexander watched her release the anger and resentment that had built over the years. He didn't try to stop her outburst.

Her fit of temper lasted for a quarter of an hour. All the while she sputtered offensive and disparaging remarks about men.

He couldn't make out what she said and was sure he didn't want to know what she was saying.

When she was through tears were rolling down her cheeks. Her eyes were puffy and expressionless.

"Do you have any idea how difficult it is growing up without a father? All the kids teased me. They called me all sorts of names. I wanted to lash out and hit them, but mother said that would only make things worse."

"Kids can be cruel."

"That phrase gets overused, and it doesn't help when you're a little girl who gets hurt easily. Being kind and gentle wore thin after a while. I had friends, they didn't grow up without fathers and didn't get teased by the other kids."

"Why don't we sit on the couch? I'll hold you so you can relax and pull yourself together."

"I don't want to relax and pull myself together. I want to feel better, I want to heal. I don't want to feel abandoned anymore. I want someone to love me who won't hurt me. I want a strong, self-assured man to love me for who I am, not for who he wants me to be."

Susannah burst into tears again. This time Alexander didn't let her alone. He took her in his arms and held her telling her he loved her.

"Alexander, I am just so tired of paying for others' mistakes. I have my own mistakes to pay for. I'm afraid to let another man get close, I may end up paying for his mistakes." She said calming down and leaning into Alexander's arms.

"Did you hear me, Susannah?" Alexander asked painfully.

"No, I'm sorry I was lost in my own thoughts." She told him.

"I said I love you, I love you for who you are." He repeated.

Susannah withdrew from his arms, looking up at him. "Excuse me."

"Surely you're not trying to tell me you didn't hear or understand."

"Oh, I heard and understand very well. Why tell me now, Alexander? Wouldn't it have been more appropriate to tell me after you'd gotten me into bed?"

"I'm not a cad, Susannah. I've wanted to tell you for a while. There never seemed an appropriate time. I know my timing is bad, but I am sincere and I am telling the truth."

She looked into his eyes which told her he was being truthful.

"Dear Heaven, you are telling the truth. Just exactly when did you realize you love me?"

"The first time I saw you. At Tilly's remember. I saw you standing at the counter placing your order. When you saw me watching you, you blushed."

"How could you have known then? We hadn't met."

"My father fell in love with my mother the first time he saw her. My grandfather fell in love with my grandmother the same way and so on. We Arthur men have a unique way of falling in love. I don't expect you to tell me that you love me right now."

"We take things one day at a time, slow and easy. We get to know each other better. We have other things in our lives to work out before we make a permanent commitment to one another."

"I have to confront my father about my feelings of abandonment. I have to help hire my assistant. I have to get the office organized so Nathan can go to Rose Lake to look into my inheritance."

"Yes, and I have to finish the mall, my house and wait for you to feel whole enough to come to me on your own without feeling coerced."

"All this working out is going to take a lot of time and energy."

"One day at a time, Susannah."

"One day at a time. I'll call father, maybe I can start healing by talking to him."

"That's my girl. I'll call you later to see how you're feeling."

"All right."

Alexander bent to kiss her.

Susannah kissed him back.

He knew it would take more than talking to him to help Susannah start to heal, but he was patient.

Walking to the door, he looked back to see Susannah picking up the shattered pieces of her broken heart. Letting himself out, he smiled. She would heal and when the time was right, he'd propose properly.

Susannah looked up just as the door closed. She'd never been that verbal about her innermost feelings, not even with her own mother.

She knew Alexander was being honest and she could trust him. Confronting her father was going to be hard, but she had to rid herself of the feelings of abandonment.

She cleaned up the mess she'd made during her outburst. She didn't mind she had needed an excuse to change things.

Susannah called her father.

Thomas picked up on the third ring.

"Hello." He said.

"Hello, Father, this is Susannah." She stated.

"How are you? Is anything wrong?" Thomas asked.

"After you left I had a long talk with Alexander. We need to talk." She said.

"You sound serious. Would you like me to come over?"

"Yes, but I'd like to talk to you alone."

"All right, I'll be there in a few minutes."

"See you then."

Susannah hung up the phone. While she waited for her father to arrive she paced.

Thomas arrived.

Susannah answered the door after the first knock.

"Hello, Father, please come in."

He walked into the living room with Susannah following behind. They sat on the couch.

"This may not be pleasant, but it has to be said. I'd like to clear the air about your leaving mother and me."

"This is serious. What would you like to know?"

"I've felt abandoned for as long as I can remember. I want to rid myself of the feeling. No, I need to rid myself of the feeling. I can't begin to heal and get on with my life until I do. Do you understand?"

"Yes, I won't repeat what we both know you're already aware of."

"Start at the beginning."

"I met your mother when I was young. We dated for about three years. We were in love so decided to marry and eloped. We thought it best if we didn't start a family right away."

"I was working at Western Chemical making products. Your mother was a secretary working in the administration office. We were married five years and weren't exactly living a life of wedded bliss."

"I'm not going to make excuses. I wasn't happy in the marriage. I wanted excitement and a better future. Your mother and I were barely making ends meet with the mortgage and other living expenses. Glenda came along and offered me a better future I fell in love with her."

"You're a cad. You abandoned your marriage vows. Mother told me how she tried to fight for you. Do you know how hard it was for me to grow up without a father?"

"I know I made bad choices. I regret them, but you saw the DVD Glenda left for you. She would have made life difficult for all of us if I had tried to work things out with your mother. That's why I'm here now. All of us, your brothers, sister and me want to rectify the past."

"Do you even know how hard it is to listen to your other children telling stories about their childhood with you in it when I have none of those memories? You think by showing up now with an inheritance will make things all right. Think again. I may just accept the inheritance and tell you all to go to hell."

"Don't take the inheritance out of spite, Susannah."

"Who are you to come into my life after twenty-six years and tell me what to do? I've gotten along just fine without you and I'll get along just fine when you go back to Rose Lake. No one is indispensable, Father."

"We won't disappear, Susannah. We're your family and whether you like it or not we're part of your life now."

"Did you ever love me, Father?"

"I've always loved you, Susannah. Remember, Glenda wouldn't allow me to keep in contact with you or see you while she was alive."

"Do you mean it or are you just saying the words?"

"Susannah, say what you have to say and get it over with."

"I need to get things off my chest. If you didn't love my mother anymore why did you have me?"

"Your conception and birth are complicated situations, Susannah."

"You couldn't stand being here making peanuts when you could go to Rose Lake with Glenda and live a life of luxury. She didn't have to do much to coerce you into going."

"You're right, Susannah. I wanted a better life."

"You wanted a better life for yourself and never thought about me at all?"

Thomas broke down then and confessed to his daughter that he left her to be raised by her mother because of pressure from Glenda's family. He couldn't tell her the truth about her conception and birth, he'd been sworn to secrecy. After he was finished, he held the little girl Susannah had been while growing up without him.

Pulling away, Susannah said, "Thank you, Father. I feel better than I have in years. Now I can begin healing."

"Will you be okay if I leave?"

"Yes, Alexander should be calling soon. He said he'd call later."

Thomas leaned over, kissing Susannah on the forehead.

"Good-bye, darling."

"Good-bye, Father. Tell Jennifer I'll look forward to her call to go shopping tomorrow."

Thomas stood, walked to the door and let himself out.

As the door closed behind him the phone rang.

"Hello." Susannah said hoarsely.

"Susannah?" Alexander asked.

"Hello, Alexander. What are you doing?" She said.

"Calling to see how you're feeling." He answered.

"Much better, father just left. We talked a lot. We argued and cried. I finally understand my father. I can begin healing now."

"Do you want me to come over?"

"Yes, I'd like that. See you in a few minutes."

"Bye, love."

Susannah sat down to watch television until Alexander arrived.

When he knocked on the door, she practically jumped off the couch to answer it.

Opening the door, she could hardly keep herself from falling into his arms. Instead she hugged him tightly.

"Hey, what's this about?" He asked.

"I'm glad to see you. It's been a rough day." She told him.

"I'm here now. We'll snuggle on the couch and fall asleep in each other's arms." Alexander said.

"Sounds good to me, get in here." She urged.

Taking his hand, Susannah led Alexander to the couch after closing the door. Lying on the couch, they cuddled and watched television.

Susannah could feel herself falling asleep. She tried in vain to stay awake.

CHAPTER NINE

The following morning she woke up to find herself trapped between Alexander's hard body and the soft couch.

"Good morning, love.   Did you sleep well?" Alexander asked.

"Good morning, darling. Better than I have in years. How did you sleep?" Susannah responded.

"It's been a long time since I fell asleep with a beautiful woman in my arms. I've fallen asleep with you in my arms twice since we met." He answered.

She arched an eyebrow at him.

"I don't sleep around, Susannah. I'm as choosy in my personal life as I am in my professional life. I'm careful who I get involved with."

"I'm sorry, it's going to take time for me to have faith in you."

"One day at a time is all it takes. I'm patient, but you have to talk to me."

"Deal, how about breakfast?"

"Sounds good."

Alexander stood, helping Susannah off the couch.

They made breakfast in a comfortable silence. When everything was on the table they ate silently.

Susannah and Alexander didn't need words to communicate. He touched her hand, she caressed his cheek.

When they were through with breakfast, they quickly cleaned up.

"What plans do you have for the day?" Alexander asked.

"I promised Jennifer I'd go shopping with her." Susannah answered.

"While you're shopping I'll work on my house. I'll call you later." He said.

"Okay, I'll talk to you later." She said.

Alexander kissed her.

Susannah enjoyed kissing him back.

He let himself out.

She went to shower, afterward she occupied herself until she was dry. Taking the towel off of her head she rubbed her hair dry.

She went to get dressed, After dressing and unable to wait, she called Jennifer.

Phillip answered the phone.

"Good morning, Phillip. Is Jennifer awake?" Susannah said.

"Yes Susannah, she thought it was too early to call, here she is." Phillip said.

"Hello, Susannah, are you ready to go shopping?" Jenni asked.

"Yes, I can be there in a few minutes." Susannah said.

"I'll be ready. I'll meet you in the hotel lobby." Jenni said.

"See you soon." Susannah said.

"See you soon, bye." Jenni said.

Susannah hung up. She picked up her purse, checked that she had her keys and credit cards, then left.

On the drive to the hotel, Susannah thought about which shops Jennifer might like. She thought Jennifer might want to look around the more expensive shops in town.

In the hotel parking lot Susannah found a parking spot, then went in to find Jennifer.

Jenni came over, hugging her. "I thought you'd never get here. I'm excited about exploring the shops in Camille." She said.

They walked to Susannah's car.

"We may not have the range of shops you're used to." Susannah told her.

"I'm not a spoiled child, Susannah." Jenni said angrily.

"I wasn't implying that you are. Not having grown up in Rose Lake, I don't know what types of shops you're used to having access to." Susannah said.

Getting into the car, Jennifer said, "I'm sorry. That was uncalled for. I guess I'm a little testy today. Please forgive me."

"You're forgiven. There is one shop we have to stop at first."

Susannah slid in behind the wheel, started the car and wove through the parking lot to the street.

She drove about a quarter of a mile to the Chocolate Hut.

"Here we are, the Chocolate Hut. Garth has any kind of chocolate you want." Susannah said.

"Chocolate?" Jenni asked.

"Yes, chocolate. It's a girl's best friend when that time of the month comes." Susannah said.

"How did you know?" Jenni asked.

"I recognized your symptoms. Chocolate always helps me."

Jenni hugged Susannah. "I wish mother hadn't kept you away from us. I could have had a big sister all these years to share secrets and things with."

"We can't dwell in the past. We have each other now. Look out Chocolate Hut, the Roberts sisters are in town and we take no prisoners."

Jenni giggled and walked along side Susannah as they made their way to the chocolate factory.

Once inside Jenni gasped at all the chocolate confections to choose from.

"Bonjour, ma cherie. What brings you in today?" Garth asked, kissing Susannah on both cheeks.

"Bonjour, mon cherie. This is my sister Jennifer. I thought she might like to meet the best chocolatier in the world." Susannah answered.

"Pshaw, you come for the chocolate, not to see me." Garth teased.

"You found me out. Jennifer would like to try a small sample of Susannah's Buttons."

"Susannah's Buttons? The Little One has the woman's condition, no?"

"Oui, may we have a small sample to go please?"

"You may have a medium sample and we give it to the Little One."

"No, Garth you can't do that."

"It's my shop, no. I give gifts to my special customers."

Susannah knew better than to argue with him, so kissed him on the cheek. "Thank you."

Garth picked up Susannah's left hand. "Who this from? Why you don't bring him to meet Garth?"

"His name is Alexander Arthur. I'll bring him in when he can get away from work."

"Garth must approve of the man who is to take my Susannah away."

Susannah giggled. "Yes, Garth. We'll be in again soon."

Garth motioned for one of his clerks. When she came over he spoke rapidly in French, telling her to quickly make up a medium sample of Susannah's Buttons for his special Little One.

The clerk nodded and hurried away to do his bidding.

Garth turned to Jenni, taking her hands in his, he said, "Now Little One, you do how Susannah tell you when your chocolate come. In no time you feel much better."

Jenni looked at Susannah.

Susannah nodded her head.

"Yes, Garth." Jenni said.

Garth patted Jennifer on the cheek. He turned back as his clerk was bringing the chocolates. Handing it to Jennifer he kissed her on the cheek.

"Now off with you. I have work to do." He said gruffly.

Susannah kissed him on both cheeks and promised to come back again soon with Alexander.

Garth nodded and pushed Susannah toward the door.

When Susannah and Jennifer were outside the chocolate shop Jennifer asked "How did he know?"

"I asked him for Susannah's Buttons. It's a special mix of chocolates he made up just for me when my time of the month comes." Susannah said.

"Why did he call me Little One?"

"You're my little sister."

"Is everyone in Camille like him."

"Not everyone. Let's get back to the car and try the chocolate before it melts."

Susannah and Jennifer walked back to the car and climbed inside.

Jennifer opened the package Garth had given her. She looked at Susannah as if to say now what.

Susannah pointed out each piece she should eat in succession. Jennifer obeyed. As she sat eating she shared with Susannah.

A short time later she could feel the chocolate go to work.

"Feeling better?" Susannah asked.

"Yes, much. What's in those?" Jennifer asked.

"I don't know, but chocolate supposedly has the same endorphins we produce when we fall in love." Susannah answered.

"Is that really true?" Jennifer asked.

"I don't know, but it works so I'm not going to question the old wives' tale. Now, what did you want to shop for?"

"I don't know. I'd like some new dresses and under garments, something feminine."

"I know just the place." Susannah said starting the car and pulling out of the parking spot.

She turned into a modestly priced shopping mall.

"This is charming. You wouldn't find anything like it in Rose Lake, it would be too plain." Jenni said.

"Does that mean you'd prefer to go somewhere else?" Susannah asked.

"No, please don't take offense. I love it, it's quite charming. Let's go spend mother's money." Jenni insisted.

"I'm glad you like our shops. I have my own money, Jennifer." Susannah stated.

Susannah and Jennifer went into a lingerie shop walking over to the racks of brightly colored lingerie.

Both women found lingerie they liked. Susannah and Jennifer looked for over an hour, finding several things they liked. Soon they went to another shop where they purchased dresses and outwear.

"How about lunch, I'm starved. Shopping always makes me hungry." Jenni said.

"Sounds good. We can go to Tilly's or Matilda's." Susannah answered.

"Something light." Jenni suggested.

"Tilly's it is." Susannah decided.

When they walked in Tilly greeted them. "Hi, Susannah, we don't often see you on Sunday." She said.

"Hi Tilly we were shopping and decided to have lunch. This is my sister Jennifer. Jennifer this is Tilly." Susannah greeted Tilly.

"Nice to meet you, Jennifer. Tilly said.

"It's Jenni, I'm pleased to meet you." Jenni said.

"Have a seat. I'll make you the special." Tilly offered.

Susannah and Jenni found a table and sat down.

"How do you like your work?" Jenni asked.

"I love it. It's interesting and has been a wonderful experience. What are you majoring in at school?" Susannah answered.

"Marketing, I have new marketing ideas for Western Chemical." Jenni said.

"Do you enjoy your classes?" Susannah asked.

'Yes, they're interesting and challenging. I've always liked learning. How long have you worked at your job?"

"Since graduating from the university five years ago."

Tilly brought their food, sat it down and left.

Susannah and Jenni dug in.

"How do you like Tilly's soup?" Susannah asked.

"It's delicious, what is it?" Jenni replied.

"Chicken dumpling containing a special ingredient Tilly won't share." Susannah told her.

Jenni took a bite of her sandwich. "This is good." She said.

"Another of Tilly's specials. She had my job, but always dreamed of opening a café. She's been here for five years. Everyone loves Tilly. She's personable and a great cook."

"I can see why everyone loves her. I've been watching her. She has a pleasant personality."

While they ate Susannah and Jenni got to know each other better. They learned each other's likes and dislikes.

Jenni shared with Susannah what she looked for in a man. Susannah reciprocated by telling her about Alexander.

Lunch finished, Jenni insisted it was her treat.

"What would you like to do now?" Susannah asked.

"Go back to the hotel and take a nice long, hot bubble bath. Shopping and lunch wear me out." Jenni answered.

"Back to the hotel it is. I think I'll take a nap when I get home." Susannah said.

They were silent on the way to Jenni's hotel. Susannah pulled in front.

Jenni leaned over and kissed Susannah's cheek. "Thank you for a lovely day and the chocolates. I haven't had such fun in long time. I'm glad we finally met." She said.

"I had fun too and I'm also glad we met. See you later." Susannah said.

Jenni opened her door, stepped out of the car, gathered her packages from the back and went into the hotel.

Susannah watched as she safely got inside, then drove home. This had been one of her best days in a long time.

When she opened the door to her apartment she saw the light blinking on her answering machine.

Going to her room, she dropped her packages and purse on the bed.

Walking into the living room, she pushed the play button on the answering machine.

"Hi, Susannah, it's Allie. John and I are getting married next Saturday. Call me when you get home."

The machine beeped.

"Susannah it's your mother, call me."

That was the end of the messages.

Susannah called her mother first.

Laura picked up on the second ring. "Hello." She said.

"Hi, Mom it's me." Susannah said.

"Where have you been? We were supposed to have brunch today." Laura said.

"I'm sorry, I forgot. I went shopping with Jennifer then we had lunch. What's up?" Susannah said.

"I'd like you to come over for dinner tonight if you're free. I want to introduce you to Blaine."

"What time?"

"Six o'clock and bring Alexander."

"I can come at six, but I don't know what plans Alexander has. When he left this morning he was going to work on his house."

"I'll plan on you both so there's enough food. See you at six."

"Okay, I love you."

"I love you too."

Susannah hung up the phone and called Alexander.

"Hello." Alexander said gruffly.

"Alexander what's wrong?" Susannah asked.

"Nothing, I was drying my hair when I answered the phone." He said.

"Mother invited us over for dinner at six o'clock to meet her friend Blaine, are you free?" She said.

"I'll pick you up at five thirty."

"Okay, I'll see you at five thirty."

"I love you, bye."

The line went dead.

"The least you could have done is wait for a response." Susannah said to the buzzing in her ear.

She called Allie.

"Hello." Allie answered.

"Hi, it's me. What's with the message you left on my machine?" Susannah asked.

"John and I want to be married as soon as possible. We don't want to give our parents a chance to change our minds. Will you still be my maid of honor?" Allie said.

"Of course, what time and where? What happened to waiting out the month?" Susannah replied.

"At my parents' house, two o'clock and bring Alexander. We can't wait a month. Our families are pushing for a big, formal ceremony."

"All right. Do you need me to do anything?"

"No, just be there."

"Call if you need anything."

"I will."

"I'll see you Saturday if not before."

"Bye."

Susannah hung up.

She had to pick out something to wear to her mother's.

Taking care of her new clothes, she left out the lilac sheath she'd bought.

When she had her clothes lain over a chair in front of her vanity, she stripped down to her undergarments.

Putting on a long t-shirt she went to take a nap.

Waking up, Susannah felt refreshed and well rested.

She'd taken a shower that morning, so didn't need one. She could try hairstyles to see which she liked best.

By the time she was through testing hairdos it was time to get ready. Alexander would be there soon to pick her up.

Susannah dressed, looking in the full-length mirror to see how the dress hung on her frame.

She wanted to braid her hair but she also wanted to leave it down. Thinking for a moment, she came up with a way to have both. She'd braid part of her hair and leave the rest to hang down around her shoulders.

When she was ready, Susannah lightly applied her make-up.

Promptly at five thirty her doorbell rang. She went to open the door. Alexander stood in the hallway dressed in a black suit that set off his dark hair and skin.

Susannah's eyes began to water. Times like this made her want to cry.

"Are you all right, darling?" Alexander asked.

"Yes, fine. You surprised me." Susannah answered.

"Surprised you how?" He inquired.

"The way you're dressed. You look so handsome." She answered honestly.

"They're just clothes, Susannah. They don't make me who I am. This is what makes me who I am." He said, pointing to his heart.

"I'm well aware of that Alexander. Let's go I don't want to be late." She answered.

"You're not getting off the hook that easily, my dear. You are lovely in that lilac frock. Are you aware your figure shows very nicely?"

"I wore this dress because it's feminine, not because it's alluring."

"I'm not trying to start an argument, love. I want you to have a realistic view of who I am."

"I am realistic, Alexander. Images hit me sometimes and I can't help finding them appealing."

"I agree images are appealing. Just be realistic in the future."

"I've been living in reality for a long time, Alexander. After Wayne's betrayal I had to come to grips with the fact that people aren't always as they appear. We

~ 180 ~

should be going now or mother will think we aren't coming."

Susannah went to get her wrap out of the closet. After putting it on, she closed the door and headed toward her apartment door.

Alexander followed not happy she was brushing aside his concerns.

When they reached the elevator, Susannah pushed the down button to go to the lobby.

Alexander caught up with her.

Neither said a word as they waited for the elevator, when they walked into the compartment, or on the ride down to the lobby.

As they walked to the car, Alexander put his hand on the small of Susannah's back to guide her to the car.

She tried to move away, but his hold on her was strong and she couldn't break free.

Before opening the door he turned her to him. She looked up at him puzzled.

"This is reality." He put his hands on either side of her face and kissed her.

Susannah was stunned.

Alexander kissed her until she couldn't think. When he raised his head, hers was spinning.

After a few moments she came back to her senses.

"You call that reality? You make me senseless with a kiss and you call it reality." She said.

Opening her door, she stepped into the car then shut it, effectively cutting off any remark he would have made.

Alexander walked around to the driver's side, getting into the car.

"Do you always close yourself off when someone gets close?" He asked.

"I'm not closing myself off. I'm showing displeasure at your action." She stated.

"I want to continue this conversation, but I think now is not a suitable time. Will you talk to me later?"

"Alexander you can't solve all of my problems. I will talk to you later, but don't expect things to change."

"One day at a time." He reminded her.

Susannah nodded.

Alexander started the car and pulled into the street.

Susannah directed him to her mother's

Arriving at Laura's, Susannah pulled herself together.

Alexander stepped out of the car, going to her side to help her out.

Going to the door, Susannah opened it. "Mom." She called.

"We're in the kitchen, darling." Laura answered.

Alexander and Susannah went in. She put her wrap in the closet.

Going through the house they could hear Laura talking.

"Hello, Mom." Susannah said kissing her cheek.

"Hello, Susannah, Alexander." Laura greeted.

She made the introductions between them and Blaine.

"It's a pleasure to meet you both. Laura has told me so much about you." Blaine said.

"The pleasure is mine. Mom has hardly told me anything about you." Susannah replied.

"We can talk over dinner." Alexander said.

When the table was set everyone sat down around it.

"Help yourselves, there's plenty." Laura said.

"The food looks wonderful, sweetheart." Blaine said.

"Thank you." Laura said.

During the first few moments of dinner food was dished up and passed.

"Mom said you two met while volunteering." Susannah said to Blaine.

"Yes, to keep active after I retired I chose to do volunteer work. We found we have a lot in common." Blaine answered.

"You're retired from Western Chemical." She stated.

"Yes, I went to work there after graduating high school." He said.

"Western Chemical was in the infant stage about that time wasn't it?" Alexander asked.

"Yes, I began working there in its second year. I saw a lot of changes during the time I was employed there." Blaine said.

A variety of topics were discussed over dinner.

"While Susannah and I clear up from dinner you men make yourselves comfortable in the living room." Laura suggested.

Alexander and Blaine took the suggestion, going into the living room.

When they were out of earshot Susannah said, "Blaine seems quite nice, Mom. How is the relationship progressing?"

"Well, we have a lot in common and get along well." Laura answered.

"Why has it taken this long for you to get involved in another relationship?" Susannah asked.

"I wasn't looking for a relationship. Most of the men I've come into contact with over the years were either married or not someone I wanted to get involved with." Laura answered.

"How did you know you wanted to get involved with Blaine?"

"I didn't, it just happened. You don't always know you have to take a chance."

"Like with mine and Alexander's relationship."

"Yes."

Susannah hugged her mother tightly. "Thanks, Mom."

"For what?"

"Just being you."

The kitchen was clean and the dishes were loaded into the dishwasher.

Laura made a fresh pot of coffee to take into the living room. While it brewed Susannah put cream, sugar and mugs on a tray. Laura put slices of cake on saucers to go on the tray.

When the coffee was ready Susannah and Laura took the tray and coffee into the living room.

"Does anyone want coffee and cake?" Laura asked.

"Just right after that wonderful dinner you made." Blaine said.

Laura passed out the cake while Susannah poured coffee.

Alexander took a bite of his cake. After tasting it he said, "This tastes like the cake my mother makes. Is it from scratch?"

"Yes, I prefer making things from scratch." Laura admitted.

"You're a rare woman, my dear. These days most people want things pre-made, packaged, or otherwise prepared ahead so they have to do little or no work." Blaine stated.

"I'd like to cook from scratch, but don't always have time." Susannah voiced.

"No one is criticizing you, darling." Alexander told her.

"I wasn't implying they were, dear. I was expressing my opinion." Susannah said.

"Your mother told me you and Alexander recently became engaged." Blaine said.

"Yes, we first saw one another at Tilly's, then met again at Matilda's." Susannah answered.

"Have you set a wedding date?" Blaine asked.

"No, both Alexander and me are too busy with work." Susannah told him.

"You've been made an associate at the law firm where you work."

"Yes, I've had the job since graduating from the university."

"How is construction on the mall coming along, Alexander?" Laura asked.

"Well, we're ahead of schedule." Alexander answered.

"Alexander is building a house for himself." Susannah said.

"Are you going to live there when you marry?" Blaine asked.

"We have a choice between my house and Hawthorne Manor." Alexander said.

"Hawthorne Manor?" Blaine questioned.

"Yes, I have to decide if I'm going to accept the inheritance my late stepmother left me." Susannah told him.

"Your stepmother was Glenda Hawthorne?" Blaine asked.

"Yes, did you know her?" Susannah asked.

"I only saw her a few times. We never met, but I heard rumors that she stole a woman's husband and took him away from his family." Blaine said.

"The man is Susannah's father and my former husband." Laura said.

"We don't have to talk about it, darling. I understand." Blaine told her.

"It's all in the past. We should let the past stay in the past." Laura said.

"And live in the present, eh Mom." Susannah answered.

"We'll get you into the twenty-first century yet." Laura teased.

"I am in the twenty-first century. I'm just not sure it's where I belong." Susannah declared.

"On that note, it's time we leave, darling. You have a long week ahead of you." Alexander stated.

"I suppose we should go. I do have to work tomorrow." Susannah agreed.

Alexander stood. Extending his hand to Blaine he said, "It was nice to meet you. Next time we get together we can play cards or take the ladies dancing."

"I'm glad to have met you and your lovely fiancée, Alexander. Next time we'll go out to dinner so the ladies don't have to cook and clean up." Blaine said.

Susannah had come to stand by Alexander. Remembering her wrap, she went to get it then returned to his side.

"It was an honor to meet you, Blaine. I hope we can get together another time when we aren't so busy."

Turning to her mother and kissing her on the cheek, she said, "Thanks for dinner, Mom. I'll talk to you sometime this week."

"Thanks for coming. It's been a lovely evening." Laura told them.

Alexander escorted Susannah to the door, and out to the car.

When they were in the car Alexander asked, "Did you enjoy the evening, love?"

"Yes, Blaine seems very nice." Susannah answered.

"Does it bother you that your mother is dating him?" Alexander asked.

"No, why should it? She's an adult capable of deciding who she does or doesn't want to date." Susannah told him.

Alexander started the car and pulled into the street.

"So, you trust your mother's judgment."

"It's not a question of whether or not I trust mother's judgment."

"You think she's capable of deciding what's best for her."

"Yes, Alexander, what are you getting at?"

"You trust your mother to judge for herself who or what is best for her, yet you don't trust yourself."

"I don't trust my own judgment simply because of Wayne's deception and my father's abandonment."

"You had no control over either one. Why do you blame yourself for their mistakes?"

"I think if I were a better person I could have made others better."

"You weren't born when your father made his decision to leave. Loomis is a pathetic, excuse for a man."

~ 187 ~

"I've told myself that innumerable times, but it doesn't make a difference. I take the problems of the world on my shoulders."

Alexander pulled up in front of Susannah's building. He shut off the car.

Turning in his seat he said, "I'd like to come in and continue this discussion if you don't mind."

"I don't mind but things won't change because you want them to."

"I'm not trying to change things. I want to make love to you, Susannah."

Susannah's face went pale. She stared at Alexander as though he were someone she didn't know. "What?" She asked dumbly.

"Would you like me to repeat the statement?"

Susannah fumbled for the door handle wanting to escape.

"Is the thought of me wanting to make love to you so repulsive?" He asked.

Susannah opened her mouth to speak; not a sound came out.

Alexander leaned over and kissed her. Susannah responded with a hunger she didn't know she had.

After several moments of kissing and petting Alexander pulled away then he kissed her again.

His kisses were gentle, yet demanding, passionate, yet soothing. She didn't feel pressured or threatened. Susannah felt loved and cherished.

He felt her tense when he touched her between the thighs.

Alexander stopped. She was awed by his self-control. It took her a moment to control her body's reaction to his lovemaking.

Alexander held her to him as her heated body cooled.

When she stilled, he asked, "Are you all right?"

"Yes, why did you stop?" She questioned.

"You may be willing, but your mind isn't. I won't make love to a woman who resists in any way." He told her.

"You're quite chivalrous, Alexander, that's sweet." She answered.

"Not at all. I'd rather a woman be completely receptive to my lovemaking and not have any regrets."

"I still think it's sweet."

He gave her a disgruntled look.

"We can't continue to do this, Susannah."

"Why not?" She stuttered embarrassed.

"We're in a car, making out like teenagers with raging hormones." He answered.

All Susannah could manage was "Oh." After several tense minutes she said, "We should go inside."

"We can't go inside." Alexander stated.

"Why not?" Susannah asked.

"If I go into your apartment it won't be to talk, Susannah. I want to make love to you so bad it hurts." He said.

"Alexander, you're confusing me."

"You're not confused, love, you're afraid."

"What am I afraid of?"

"Afraid that if you give yourself to me I'll leave."

"Alexander that's absurd. I know you won't leave."

"In your heart yes, but your mind tells you something entirely different."

"Why are we even discussing this? You said you want to make love to me, I've agreed."

"If we make love now we'll both regret it and grow to resent each other."

"Okay, Alexander, you win. I'm going to my apartment. When you get this whole, whatever it is, figured out call me."

Susannah opened her door, stepped out of the car, shut it and walked into her building going to her apartment.

She didn't look back. If she had she would have seen Alexander wrestling with his conscience.

Alexander opened the door to get out and follow her then closed it. He waited a few seconds, opened it again, and closed it again.

"Brilliant, Arthur. You tell the woman you love you want to make love to her, she agrees and you turn her away."

Alexander clicked his seatbelt into place. Until he convinced Susannah to marry him without the pretense of engagement he had no right pursuing his wanton desires.

He knew several women who'd welcome him into their warm beds; he couldn't do that to Susannah. He'd made a commitment to her when he'd told her he loved her. He'd honor that commitment no matter what temptations he had.

Susannah shakily leaned against the door to her apartment. Why hadn't Alexander followed her? He'd said he wanted to make love to her, so where was he? She wasn't bold enough to go looking for him and invite him to her bed. She was faint with longing.

Forcing herself to move away from the door, Susannah went about her nightly routine of getting ready for bed.

When she wearily climbed into bed she fell into a fitful sleep. She lapsed into a dream state.

Alexander was kissing her, his hands wandering to her breasts, gently caressing. She made herself more accessible to him. His hands wandered to the heat between her thighs. Susannah cried out as he brought her to fulfillment.

Alexander brought her to release over and over. She couldn't break hold of the dream. Her response to him was amazing. She hadn't known she was so sexually hungry.

Her energy spent, she slept through until her alarms awoke her.

CHAPTER TEN

Alexander had awakened a hunger in her she didn't know she possessed. She wanted him and needed him like she needed air to breathe, food to sustain her.

Susannah wanted Alexander to make love to her with such intensity she didn't know herself.

Climbing out of bed she got ready for work and hoped Alexander would fulfill her soon.

When Susannah arrived at work she saw Nathan's car parked out front. She knew he was determined to get the office in order so he could help her with her inheritance and hire her assistant.

Going inside, she went about her morning routine then busily worked on her latest projects.

An hour later Nathan came out of his office.

"I thought you had an appointment with Linda this morning." He said.

"I completely forgot. I'll have to call and reschedule." Susannah answered.

"You must have had a hectic weekend, you don't usually forget your appointments with Linda or any appointment for that matter." Nathan said.

"I spent time with my father and siblings. Father and I talked about the past. I understand why he did what he did. His abandonment still hurts, but I understand." Susannah replied.

"Anything I should know about before I check into your inheritance?" Nathan asked.

"No, it has nothing to do with that. It was about my feelings for my father and what happened before and after he left." Susannah answered.

"All right. If you need to talk, I'm here."

"Thank you, I appreciate it Nathan."

"You're like a daughter to me and I take care of family."

Tears formed in Susannah's eyes, she was speechless. Both she and Nathan went back to work with a new understanding of their relationship.

At lunchtime Susannah checked her hair and make-up, let Nathan know she was leaving, then left.

Walking into Tilly's she saw Alexander. She turned to leave but was stopped by Olivia.

"Hi, Susannah. What can I get you?" She asked.

"I... I seem to have lost my appetite." Susannah said.

"Is something wrong?" Olivia inquired.

"No, suddenly I'm not hungry." Susannah responded.

Alexander walked up to Susannah.

"Hello, darling, I've missed you." He said.

"Alexander..." Susannah paused to form her thoughts.

"I know you're reluctant to talk to me, but our quarrel is over. We have to talk." Alexander told her while he guided her toward a table.

"We didn't have a quarrel, Alexander." She quietly reminded him.

"I know, love. I'm not going to let you avoid me because of last night." Alexander stated.

"I wasn't going to avoid you. I don't know what I'm supposed to do now when we're together." Susannah answered.

"You could greet me with a kiss to begin with."

"That's what got us into this uncomfortable situation, Alexander."

"No, my stating I want to make love to you got us into this situation. The kiss just heightened what we were feeling."

"I waited for you to come to my apartment."

"I couldn't and we both know why."

"Alexander, I can't do this right now. I have to eat and get back to the office."

"I'll come by your apartment after work tonight so we can discuss this. I'll be there after six."

"Alexander, you can't..."

"I promise we'll just talk unless you decide you want more, love."

"But..."

"Get lunch, I'll see you tonight."

Alexander kissed Susannah, gave her a gentle squeeze, then walked out.

Shaking, Susannah walked back to the counter.

"I've decided I'm hungry after all. I'll have number eighty-two, iced tea and traditional cheesecake." She told Olivia.

Olivia nodded her head, a twinkle in her eye and went to give the cook Susannah's order.

Susannah stood uncomfortably waiting for her lunch.

Olivia came back to the counter.

"I reccived my letter of interview, thanks for putting in a good word for me." She said.

"I didn't have to. Nathan chose you on your qualifications." Susannah said.

"Well I appreciate it. I came back here to work so I could stay in town." Olivia told her.

"You didn't want to go home?" Susannah questioned.

"No, I like Camille. It's small and homey. The residents help one another." Olivia answered.

"I take it you come from a large city." Susannah replied.

"Yes and everyone acts like they're always in a hurry and can't stop just to talk."

Susannah and Olivia talked for a few minutes more then Susannah's order was ready.

Olivia handed it to her.

"I forgot to order Nathan's lunch." Susannah said.

"No wonder. If Alexander only had eyes for me I'd forget everything except him." Olivia stated.

Susannah blushed. "He does have a way of making me forget things even when I don't want to." Susannah said.

"No need to feel embarrassed. Many women in love let their minds wander to their fiancées." Olivia told her.

In love, was she in love? Susannah wondered.

"I suppose you're right. I'd like to order number twenty-two, no onions or lettuce, strawberry cheesecake and iced tea to go." Susannah said, changing the subject.

"I'll put that right in. I didn't mean to make you uncomfortable. You just look so... lost."

"I'm sorry, Olivia. I'm not ready to discuss this yet."

"Don't be sorry. Sometimes I don't know when to mind my own business. I'll go put your order in now."

Olivia went to give the order to the cook.

Susannah was miserable. Twice in one day she was close to tears. What was wrong with her?

She didn't have to wait long for Nathan's lunch. Olivia brought it to her as soon as it was ready.

Susannah handed her the money and received the change back.

"Have a good day." Olivia said.

"Thanks, you too." Susannah said.

She left, carrying hers and Nathan's lunch back to the office.

"Here's your lunch, Nathan." Susannah said a tremor in her voice.

She turned to go, Nathan stopped her.

"Are you going to tell me what's wrong or do I have to drag it out of you?" Nathan asked.

Susannah turned back to him, her eyes filled with tears.

"I don't know what's wrong with me today. I just seem to be on the verge of tears." Susannah answered honestly.

"Is it Alexander?" Nathan said.

"No, Alexander hasn't done anything." Susannah said.

"That's not what I asked. I asked if it had anything to do with Alexander." Nathan told her.

"If I had the answer to the question I wouldn't feel like crying." Susannah told him.

"Emotions are funny things. We have them but don't always know why. Take love for example, we fall in love and feel miserable, but don't know why. We feel sad, but don't know why."

"I'm not sad, I feel lost. I'm pretending to be engaged to a man I hardly know. My father and siblings walked into my life after twenty-six years and I just finally got Wayne out of my life."

"That leaves love. Before you deny it, think about it. I mentioned love and sadness. You chose to speak of sadness. That leaves love."

"How could I be in love? I don't know Alexander well enough to be in love with him."

"Sit down, Susannah."

Susannah sat down across from Nathan.

"My dear child, you don't always know the one you fall in love with. Love knows what it wants even if we don't. Don't dismiss it out of hand."

"I'm supposed to believe I'm in love with Alexander and there's nothing I can do about it?"

"I'm not telling you what to believe or not believe. I'm advising you to keep an open mind."

Susannah stood, walked to Nathan and hugged him.

"Thank you, Nathan. I'll think about what we've discussed."

She took her lunch and went out to her office to eat.

After lunch Susannah called Linda's office to reschedule her missed appointment.

For the rest of the day she tried to avoid thinking about the conversations she'd had with Alexander and Nathan.

She was unsuccessful, so thought about what might happen when Alexander came over that evening. They could talk about 'the situation,' Allie's upcoming wedding...

She'd forgotten to invite Alexander to the wedding.

Susannah wrote down several topics of conversation they could discuss that evening. As the afternoon wore on she added to the list.

Nathan left his desk a few times to check on her. He noticed the list on her desk and smiled. She'd begun making lists again, that was a good sign.

When the alarm on her watch chimed at five o'clock Susannah hurriedly went through her closing up routine for the day.

When she was satisfied Susannah grabbed her purse and the list then walked out the door determined to put the past behind her.

On the way home Susannah stopped to pick up a few things she was getting low on. Passing by the pharmacy she noticed the contraceptives and debated whether or not she should buy them.

After considerable thought she picked out a box to purchase.

Going through the checkout she was anxious and embarrassed. Telling herself that people bought contraceptives everyday and that she was doing nothing wrong, she relaxed.

Making it through the checkout, she went to her car, packed her purchases in the backseat, stepped into the car and drove home.

After checking her mailbox, she went up to her apartment. Putting away her packages she tinkered around in her apartment until it was time for Alexander to arrive.

When he hadn't arrived by six forty five Susannah thought she had gotten a reprieve from having to deal with Alexander and 'the situation.'

Suddenly there was a knock on the door.

"Damn." She sputtered.

Calmly walking to the door, she opened it to an exhausted and irritated Alexander.

He walked passed her without so much as a kiss or hello.

"Please come in, Alexander. Make yourself at home." She said sarcastically.

"Don't start with me, Susannah. I've had a bad day and 'our situation' hasn't exactly made my day bearable." Alexander snapped.

"If you've had a bad day why bother coming over at all? You could have called and canceled." She said.

"I promised I'd be here. Let's get this over with." Alexander said.

"Go home, Alexander. I'm not going to discuss anything with you while you're in a bad mood."

Alexander walked over to her, took her by the arms and shook her.

"I'm not going home until we get 'the situation' cleared up. You know how I feel and what I want, don't play games with me, Susannah."

"Let go of me. I will not be threatened. We have nothing to discuss."

Susannah took Alexander's ring off holding it out to him.

Looking at the ring, then back at Susannah, he let go of her.

"I'm sorry, love, after we met at lunch my day started going bad. To top it all off Miss Langley showed up at the construction site. She made it very clear that her father's mall and she were a package deal."

Susannah's face went white. "She tried to seduce you?"

"That's putting it mildly, but yes. Put the ring back on Susannah. We both know you aren't going to give it back."

Susannah stubbornly refused to put the ring back on.

Alexander took it from her and put it back on her finger.

"Never, ever take this off again. We both know you're going to be my wife, sleep in my bed and bear my children."

Susannah tried to pull her hand away but Alexander held onto it and pulled her to him. Before Susannah could utter a sound Alexander's mouth captured hers and he kissed her.

The kiss was undemanding. Susannah fought the urge to push herself against Alexander. He put his hand on the small of her back and held her to him.

The kiss seemed to go on forever. She thought Alexander was going to make love to her. She didn't think she could hold back any longer. Alexander drew away from her.

After she came back to her senses Susannah looked at him quizzically.

"I promised we wouldn't go any further than you wanted to." He told her.

"But..." She stuttered.

"No, love, you're not ready. When we make love it will happen naturally." He said.

Susannah burst into tears. Alexander held her as the tears flowed down her cheeks.

She didn't know how long they stood like that, but when the tears finally stopped Susannah felt better than she had in years.

At that moment she knew Alexander was right, she would be his wife and bear his children.

Realizing Alexander was still holding her, Susannah went to pull away from him. He held her to him.

While they stood there Susannah came to the realization that she was in love with Alexander. She began to cry again.

Feeling her body shudder from the tears Alexander asked, "What's wrong, love?"

"I love you, Alexander." She stated clearly.

"I know my love." He said.

"You know? How could you know? I just realized it myself." She said.

"A man knows when a woman is in love with him."

"How?"

"Instinct."

"Alexander..."

"It's all right, love. Remember we're supposed to be taking one day at a time."

Susannah nodded and held onto Alexander as if she'd never let go.

Her mind whirled, she loved Alexander, he loved her. Everything she had to do came to the forefront of her mind.

"Alexander." She said.

"Yes, love." He answered.

"Allie is getting married this Saturday." Susannah said.

"Yes?" He asked.

"If you're not busy I'd like you to go with me."

Alexander held her away from him, but still held onto her.

"Susannah, you do that a lot you know." He told her.

"Do what?" She asked.

"Expect me to be available to escort you at the last minute." He said irritably.

"I said if you're not busy." Susannah reminded him.

"The point isn't whether I'm busy or not. I don't like being thought of at the last minute." He said.

"Alexander I don't think of you at the last minute. Allie just told me this last weekend. She and John we're going to get married within the month but recently changed their plans."

"How long have you known about Allie's wedding?"

"A while now but as I said they recently changed their plans."

"You're just now asking me to be your guest. Susannah you have to break this habit of asking me to escort you at the last minute."

This time when Susannah pulled away from him, Alexander let her go.

She wasn't sure what to say or do now that she knew she was in love with Alexander.

Susannah wordlessly paced back and forth across her living room.

Knowing she was warring with her emotions, Alexander didn't try to stop her pacing. Instead, he watched as she mentally worked things out.

"Should I tell Alexander I bought contraceptives today? Do I let things progress naturally as Alexander said?" Susannah silently asked.

After several moments of silent contemplation Susannah decided to let nature take its course. She'd wait for the time to be right to make love with Alexander.

"One day at a time." She said aloud.

Turning to Alexander she said, "I apologize if I've made you feel as if you're unimportant to me. It's just that..." She stopped to gather her thoughts.

"You have a lot on your mind and haven't had to consider anyone else in your plans for years." Alexander finished for her.

Susannah looked at him stunned. "How did you know what I was thinking?" She asked.

"I've been able to read you since we met. I couldn't tell you until now for fear of scaring you." He told her.

"All this time you've known what I've been thinking and haven't said anything." She stated irritably.

"Yes, and as I said I was afraid of scaring you." Alexander repeated.

"You know everything I'm thinking?"

"Not everything. There are still parts of yourself you keep hidden from me."

"I'm not hiding. I'm cautious."

"You don't want to take the chance of letting me get too close for fear of being hurt."

Susannah opened her mouth to deny what Alexander had said then closed it when she realized he was right.

Alexander walked to her, pulled her to him and kissed her.

Susannah gave herself to him the only way she could. She kissed him back like she never wanted the moment to end.

Breaking the kiss, Alexander put her from him. Looking into her eyes he could see the little devil she wasn't very good at hiding.

"You're very tempting, my love but as I said when we make love it will happen naturally." He said.

With a sparkle in her eye Susannah innocently said, "Alexander whatever are you talking about?"

"You know very well what I'm talking about. Don't be coy with me or I'll throw my good intentions out the window and take you up on your offer."

Susannah looked at him trying to tame the amusement in her eyes.

"You little flirt. I'm tempted to throw you over my shoulder, march into your bedroom and have my way with you." He said stepping toward her.

"All right, Alexander I'll behave myself but I can't promise for how long."

"I'm going home and take a cold shower. I'll see you tomorrow." He said.

Alexander walked out without so much as a kiss or backward glance.

When she heard the door close with a thud, Susannah burst out laughing. She laughed so hard her sides ached and tears streamed down her face.

What she was laughing about she had no clue, but it was going to be interesting finding out.

Going to her room, Susannah readied herself for bed. When she climbed into bed she was happily exhausted if not a little frustrated.

She had many sensuous dreams. One lead into another and each was increasingly more provocative.

When she awoke Susannah was flustered. Getting out of bed she went through her morning routine of getting ready for work.

She couldn't help but think of the look on Alexander's face the night before when the little devil inside her decided to appear and play games with his libido.

~ 205 ~

Giggling, Susannah went out to her car unmindful of anything except the fact that she was playing with fire and just might get burned.

Walking into her office she was still smiling. Nathan was just coming out of his office.

"What has you in a good mood this morning?" He asked amused.

"Alexander." Susannah said happily.

"Remind me to thank him when he comes in." Nathan said.

"I'm sure I won't have to. He's a smart man, he'll be able to figure it out for himself." Susannah said.

"I'd like to know what he's done to make you so happy."

Susannah's face turned bright red.

After several minutes of trying to make the color leave her face, she simply said, "He loves me."

"By the way you're smiling I'd say the feeling is mutual."

Again Susannah's face suffused with color. She couldn't deny Nathan's observation, so simply nodded her head and went to work.

Nathan went back to his office.

Susannah was in a good mood all week. Alexander stopped by each evening after work and left the same way he had Monday evening, frustrated to the point of needing a cold shower.

He left Susannah each night with a sensual kiss that promised more, all she had to do was ask.

She couldn't bring herself to ask. She couldn't ask Alexander to make love to her, she didn't know how.

When Friday arrived Susannah was up early excited that Nathan and she would be hiring her part-time assistant today.

She pulled out her most professional business like suit. After tinkering around her apartment for several minutes she left early for work.

Susannah couldn't stay at her apartment to wait until it was time to leave. She wanted to get the interviews started and over with so she could begin training her assistant.

When she arrived at work Nathan was waiting for her.

"I've called the answering service to let them know we won't be open today due to interviewing for your assistant." He told her.

"Are you sure we'll need to close the office for the whole day? We may be done interviewing by afternoon." Susannah said.

"I decided to close early today after the interviews. We've both been working hard and need time away from the office." Nathan said.

"Is there something you're not telling me?" Susannah asked.

"No, we're both tired of the long days and closing the office for the day won't hurt business."

"Okay, you would tell me if something was wrong wouldn't you?"

"Yes, child. Don't worry, nothing is wrong. I've decided we both need a break from this place."

"Okay."

The bell above the door tinkled.

Susannah turned around to greet the visitor. It was Alexander.

"Hello, love, how are you today?" He asked.

"I'm fine, Alexander. What are you doing here?" Susannah asked.

"I'm afraid I may have to miss Allie's wedding." Alexander told her.

"Why? What's wrong?" Susannah questioned.

"I have to go out of town and don't know if I'll be back in time for the wedding."

Susannah's face showed her disappointment. After all the loving Alexander and she had shared this week she may have lost her opportunity to let herself get close to him.

Alexander smiled inwardly at the look of disappointment on her face. "I'm sorry, love, if it weren't important I'd wait until after the weekend." He told her.

"I can't expect you to neglect your business." She answered.

"Well... it isn't my business." He said.

"Alexander, what's going on?" Susannah asked.

"Nothing, I have to go out of town."

"What are you two doing?" Susannah demanded.

"Nothing, we do have lives away from work." Nathan answered.

"You're closing the office for the day. Alexander has to go out of town but it's not business related. What's going on?" Susannah demanded again.

"Susannah, you're being paranoid." Alexander said.

"No, I'm suspicious. What aren't you telling me?" She asked.

"Nothing that you need to worry about... yet." Nathan said.

"You are doing something that I don't know about. Tell me what it is." Susannah said.

Alexander took Susannah by the arms, pulled her to him and kissed her. The kiss seemed to last longer than the mere moment it happened.

"Stop asking questions and trust us, please." Alexander asked.

Susannah's mind still on the kiss just nodded her head, putting her trust in Alexander and Nathan.

"Now that's settled, we have interviews to get ready for." Nathan said.

Embarrassed, Susannah said, "I'd forgotten."

"Don't think another thing of it. You have more important things on your mind right now." Nathan told her.

Alexander looked at his watch. "I have to go, love. I have an appointment. I'll call you when I get back." He said.

"All right, I'll see you when you get back." Susannah said.

Alexander bent his head and kissed her. The kiss was like all the ones he'd given her during the week.

"I love you." Alexander said.

"I love you." Susannah responded.

Shaking Nathan's hand, he wished him good luck on the interviews and left.

"Now, young lady, do we have everything ready for the interviews?" Nathan asked.

"Yes, would you like to go over the list of questions before we start?" Susannah answered.

"Yes." He said.

Susannah went to her desk, opened the top drawer, withdrawing the list of questions.

"Would you like to read the list or would you like me to read it to you?" She asked.

"Read a few of the questions so I have a general idea what we'll be asking." Nathan told her.

Holding the list, Susannah read the first few questions. She continued down the list until she'd read all of the questions.

"We have everything covered. Make coffee and set up for the day as you usually do except call the answering service." Nathan told her.

Susannah nodded and went about her morning routine. When she finished she joined Nathan in his office.

"We're ready." She told him.

Nathan looked at his watch. As he did the bell above the door in Susannah's office tinkled.

"Right on time." He said.

CHAPTER ELEVEN

Susannah went to meet the applicant. All morning Susannah and Nathan greeted and interviewed applicants for Susannah's assistant.

The interviews were concluded by two o'clock.

Unable to sit in Nathan's office and wait for his decision, Susannah went to her desk to work.

At two thirty Nathan had one applicant who met all the requirements to do the job.

"Susannah, I've made my decision." Nathan said.

Susannah put aside the paperwork she was working on and went into Nathan's office.

"I'm anxious to know who you chose." She said.

He handed her the paperwork he had.

Susannah smiled. "You're sure this is the applicant you want?" She asked.

"Yes, she's the best qualified applicant." Nathan answered.

"I'll call her now. When do you want her to start?" Susannah said.

"She'll have to give her current employer notice. Tell her she can begin two weeks from Monday." Nathan said.

Susannah nodded and went to her desk. Picking up her phone she dialed the number on the application.

She didn't get an answer. Susannah hung up. Putting the paperwork aside, she went into Nathan's office.

"I didn't get an answer. I'll go to Tilly's." She said.

Nathan smiled and said, "All right."

Susannah left Nathan's office and walked to Tilly's.

Walking in Susannah smiled. She looked for Olivia, finding her at the counter.

Olivia saw her and smiled. "Hi, Susannah." She said.

"I tried calling the number you left with us, not getting an answer I thought you might be working." Susannah told her.

Tilly walked up to the counter. "I take it you have good news for Olivia." She said.

"Yes, Olivia I'm honored to extend an offer of employment with the firm." Susannah said.

Olivia's smile lit up her face. She was so full of emotion she was speechless.

Susannah waited for Olivia to take in the news before she continued.

"Nathan wants you to start two weeks from Monday. That will enable you to give two weeks' notice to Tilly." Susannah said.

"She doesn't need to give notice. She'll start Monday." Tilly said.

Olivia looked at Tilly, tears in her eyes.

"Don't get all teary-eyed with me, child. You can make more money working for Nathan the next two weeks than you can here. That will enable you to pay off your student loans that much sooner." Tilly said.

Hugging her, Olivia said, "Thanks, Tilly. I appreciate your thoughtfulness, won't you be shorthanded?"

"I'm not going to make you give notice because I'll be shorthanded. Accept the job and agree to start work on Monday." Tilly commanded.

"Thanks, Tilly. Yes, Susannah I accept the job offer and if Nathan's agreeable I'll start Monday." Olivia said.

Susannah smiled and held her hand out to Olivia.

"Congratulations." She said.

Olivia shook Susannah's hand. "I'll see you Monday morning. What time should I be there?" Olivia said.

"The office opens at eight o'clock. I get there at seven thirty to get ready for the day." Susannah said.

"I'll see you Monday at seven thirty." Olivia agreed.

"Have a nice weekend and congratulations again." Susannah said.

She left Tilly's in a joyful mood believing everything could only get better.

When she walked into Nathan's office she found him hard at work.

"I thought we were closing the office today." Susannah said.

"We are. This work is for your inheritance. I have a confession to make." Nathan said.

"I'm listening." Susannah said.

"Alexander and I have been working on the details of your inheritance for the last few weeks." Nathan told her.

"Why didn't you tell me?" Susannah asked.

"We didn't want to overwhelm you with everything else you've been going through." Nathan said.

"What have you come up with?" Susannah questioned.

"Sit down, Susannah."

"What's going on, Nathan?"

"Alexander and I have checked into your inheritance and rechecked the stock prices. As Alexander told you he didn't go out of town on his business."

"Nathan..."

"Susannah there's no easy way to tell you this."

"Just say it, Nathan."

"We can't be sure until we've seen a copy of your late stepmother's will, but according to what we've learned you're a wealthy young woman."

"I'm sorry, Nathan. I'm a little confused. How can that be with a small inheritance and stock in Western Chemical?"

"As I said we rechecked the stock prices..." Nathan began.

He pulled a sheet of paper from the pile in front of him, showing it to Susannah.

She gasped aloud at the figures on the paper. After several moments she was finally able to speak.

"How can you be sure how much my inheritance is worth without knowing how much stock I own and how much money I've inherited?" She asked.

"I've based the amount of stock you own by the average holdings of a stockholder." Nathan told her.

"You guessed." Susannah said.

"Yes, before we get off track Alexander asked me to tell you where he went and what he's doing." Nathan said.

Becoming suspicious and dreading what Nathan might tell her Susannah said, "What is it, Nathan? What is Alexander hiding from me?"

"He's not hiding anything from you. There hasn't been a good time to tell you."

"Out with it, Nathan. What hasn't Alexander told me that I should know?"

"Alexander is able to help determine the worth of your inheritance and get the information we need because he has a law degree."

"I'm sorry, what?"

"I know what you're thinking. Alexander hasn't been upfront with you about everything."

"Why would Alexander not tell me he has a law degree?"

"He hasn't practiced regularly and has decided he wants to be active in the firm."

"He's decided he wants to practice law?"

"Yes."

"Why?"

"You know how busy it's gotten around here."

Susannah nodded.

"His father was my partner before he decided to work in construction."

"Is Alexander going to be your partner?" Susannah asked.

"Not going to be... is." Nathan said.

"What do you mean is?" Susannah questioned.

"Alexander's father, Alexander senior, didn't sell his half of the partnership. When he passed on Alexander, his son naturally took over the partnership." Nathan said.

"All this time Alexander, my Alexander, has been able to practice law." Susannah verified.

"Yes."

"He didn't go out of town on business. Where is he, Nathan?"

"Rose Lake."

"I've had all the surprises I want for one day. I'm going home. If I hear from either one of you I just might throttle you."

Before Nathan could utter a sound, Susannah walked out of his office, grabbed her purse and left.

"Nathan can close the office, serves him right." Susannah sputtered as she walked to her car.

For the rest of the day Susannah stewed over Alexander's secret while she put together an outfit for Allie's wedding.

"Alexander should know that I don't like surprises, especially surprises that catch me off guard. Why didn't he tell me he has a law degree? Is he trying to hide something from me? What else don't I know about him?" Susannah asked herself.

She kept busy so the questions she had wouldn't put her into a panic attack.

Later that evening the phone rang. Susannah went to answer it.

"Hello." She said.

"Hi, love." Alexander said.

"Alexander." Susannah stated.

"Yes, were you expecting someone else?" He asked gruffly.

"No I didn't expect to hear from you." She told him.

"Why?"

"Have you talked to Nathan?"

"No, why?

"We had a conversation this afternoon. He told me what the two of you have been up to."

"You sound angry, love. What's wrong?"

"I don't like to be kept in the dark, Alexander. You know I don't like surprises. Why would you keep it a secret you have a law degree?"

"If I had known you'd be this upset I'd have told you sooner. I'm not hiding anything, Susannah."

"Why did you call, Alexander?"

"I miss you and wanted to hear your voice."

"You've heard it, good-bye Alexander."

Susannah hung up the phone as gently as she could considering the mood she was in.

Waiting for Alexander to call back, she became anxious when he didn't

Getting ready for bed, Susannah worried about her relationship with Alexander.

Falling into a fitful sleep, she pushed away the nightmare when it tried to invade her sleep.

She tossed and turned anxiously when Wayne appeared in her sleep.

"Susannah you might as well give Alexander his ring back. You can't marry him, he lied to you." Wayne said in the dream.

"No, he didn't lie, he didn't tell me he could practice law." Susannah cried.

"He lied by not telling you. A lie is a lie." Wayne said.

"No, Alexander isn't like you. He loves me and I can trust him." She stated.

Susannah struggled in the dream. Wayne tried convincing her that Alexander wasn't trustworthy and she shouldn't marry him.

Finally she did something she hadn't been able to do in the four years since the nightmares began... she broke free coming fully awake.

Surprised, Susannah looked around her. She was in her room, in bed completely awake.

She'd done it, she'd broken the hold Wayne had on her and she loved Alexander.

Climbing out of bed, Susannah couldn't wait until morning to talk to him, she had to talk to him now.

Going to the phone, she dialed Nathan's number; he'd know how to contact Alexander.

"Hello." Nathan said sleepily.

"How do I contact Alexander?" Susannah demanded.

"Susannah, do you know what time it is?" Nathan asked.

"Yes, how do I contact Alexander?"

"Hold on, let me get the number."

There were several minutes of silence. It took so long for Nathan to come back on the line Susannah thought he'd fallen back to sleep.

"Are you still there, Susannah?"

"Yes."

Nathan read off the number to her.

Susannah wrote the number down, thanked him and hung up.

Nervously Susannah put in the number Nathan had given her.

"Hotel Haven, how may I help you?" The desk clerk answered.

"Alexander Arthur's room please." Susannah said.

"I'm sorry miss, but I can't wake up a guest." The clerk said.

"This is his fiancée, I have to talk to him." Susannah demanded.

"I'm sorry, miss, we're not allowed to ring through to a guest's room until nine o'clock."

"I'd like to speak to a manager."

"I'd be happy to take your name and number and have the manager return your call."

"I don't have time to wait."

Susannah hung up the phone in frustration.

She picked up the phone and put in her mother's number.

Laura's answering machine picked up.

"Hi, Mom, it's Susannah. I need to talk to you, call me when you get this." She said.

After hanging up Susannah paced her living room, wringing her hands repeatedly.

Her phone rang. She practically jumped on it.

"Alexander?" She asked picking up the phone.

"No, Susannah it' s your mother." Laura said.

"Oh, hi Mom." Susannah said disappointment in her voice.

"Are you expecting a call from Alexander?" Laura asked.

"No I was hoping he'd call. I got angry with him." Susannah told her.

"That's why you called me at the crack of dawn." Laura stated.

"Yes, I tried reaching him at his hotel, the desk clerk wouldn't ring through to his room."

"What's going on, Susannah?"

"I had a nightmare. Wayne was telling me Alexander lied to me and I can't trust him."

"I get the feeling I'm missing part of the story."

Susannah related to her mother what had happened with Nathan the day before and how she'd hung up on Alexander when he'd called.

When she was through telling her mother that part of the situation she told her about how she'd broken free of the nightmare.

"I love Alexander and I can trust him, Mom." Susannah told her.

Letting out a deep breath, Laura said, "Does Alexander know you love and trust him?"

"Yes, but I'm afraid he won't want to talk to me after last night." Susannah said.

"Alexander is an intelligent man, he'll realize you were trying to protect yourself and call you." Laura stated.

"I'm afraid he won't talk to me."

"Don't lose hope. I'm sure Alexander won't give up on you, he loves you."

"Thanks Mom. I have to go."

"Remember, Alexander loves you."

The line was disconnected.

Susannah felt better than she had before talking to her mother.

Knowing she had to get ready for Allie's wedding, she went to draw a bath.

While soaking in the bubbles Susannah thought about how to convince Alexander that she loved and trusted him.

After bathing, Susannah wrapped her hair in a towel turban style and put her bathrobe on.

While waiting to dry and for the next few hours Susannah concentrated on her duties as Allie's maid of honor.

Ignoring her anxiety, she concentrated on making Allie's wedding day the best she could.

Susannah's phone rang. She didn't get her hopes up that it was Alexander.

"Hello." She said.

"Hi, Susannah, it's Allie." Allie announced.

"Hi, how are you?" Susannah asked.

"A nervous wreck. Can you come to my parents' house early?" Allie asked.

"Of course. I just have to dress and I'll be on my way."

"Good, I'll see you soon."

"All right, hang in there. Your day is going to be perfect and beautiful."

"I keep telling myself that but I'm not very convincing."

"I'll be there soon."

"Thanks."

Susannah hung up the phone.

No matter how anxious she was to talk to Alexander she had to pull herself together for Allie's sake.

Only one of them could be nervous today and since it was Allie's wedding day Susannah had to let her worries take a backseat to Allie's.

Going to her room, she dressed quickly, threw together a small bag of items she thought Allie would need and was out the door.

Arriving at Allie's parents' house, Susannah was greeted by an agitated Allie.

"I'm so glad you're here. Mother is complicating things." Allie told her.

"What's going on?" Susannah asked.

"Mother doesn't like the flower arrangements or the menu, she's ruining everything." Allie said.

"Calm down, Allie. Go to your room and relax, I'll talk to your mother." Susannah said.

"Thanks."

Allie walked into the house.

Susannah found Emma Cole in the backyard arranging the guests' chairs.

"Hello, Emma." She said.

Looking up from her work Emma said, "Hello, Susannah how are you?"

"Fine, can I help with anything?" Susannah said.

"You can tell me if these chairs line up with one another." Emma told her.

"The chairs are perfect. Let's take a break, have a cup or two of chamomile tea and relax." Susannah said.

"I don't have time to take a break or relax. Allie is getting married today."

"Emma, you aren't going to help Allie by upsetting yourself. Allie needs you today. Come in the house."

Susannah led Emma into the house, straight into the kitchen. Filling the tea kettle with water, she sat it on the stove and turned the burner beneath on.

"While we wait for the water to boil what can I do for you?" She asked.

"Nothing, Allison is getting married today. I have to put things in order." Emma told her.

"Allie's wedding day is going to be perfect. The only thing that matters is that at the end of the day your daughter will be married." Susannah stated.

Emma looked at Susannah, stunned that she was so calm and logical about the situation.

Tears began to roll down Emma's cheeks. "It never ceases to amaze me that the little girl I knew has become such a caring, unselfish young woman." She said.

"I'm not unselfish. I just know when it's time for someone else to be the center of attention." Susannah answered.

"I thank God Allie has a friend such as you. You've both been through so much." Emma told her.

"I've been blessed to have Allie as my friend all these years." Susannah said.

The teakettle began to whistle.

Susannah went over shut off the burner and made a cup of tea for Emma and herself.

"Drink this, it'll make you feel better." Susannah said.

Emma took a drink of the hot liquid.

The two women sat in quiet companionship as they drank their tea.

After the tea was drunk Susannah took their cups and made another cup for Emma and herself.

When they had finished their second cup of tea Emma was visibly calmer than when Susannah had arrived.

"I'm ready to marry off my daughter." Emma said, a trace of humor in her voice.

"Let's see how the bride is holding up." Susannah said.

Susannah and Emma walked through the house to the stairs leading to the upper floor of the house.

They found Allie pacing in her room, wringing her hands in agitation.

Seeing her mother and Susannah Allie announced, "I can't get married."

Emma looked ready to faint.

"What?" Susannah asked.

"John deserves better than me. I can't tie him down." Allie said.

"Of course John deserves better, but you're all he has. He has to make the best of what life has given him." Susannah told her.

Allie visibly grew stronger, drawing herself up.

"John could do worse. I'm caring, loving, hell, I'm the best damn thing that ever happened to him."

"I don't know. There's the blonde at his office who'd jump through hoops for him if he asked her to." Susannah said.

"That little hussy can find her own man. John is mine and I'm not giving him up." Allie said coldly.

"Okay, if you're sure. I still have time to tell John you don't want to marry him."

"You so much as breathe a word to him and you'll be looking for a new best friend."

Susannah smiled mischievously.

"Susannah Kay Roberts, you just wait until it's your turn to get married." Allie threatened.

Even though she felt like crying, Susannah didn't let the smile fall from her lips.

"What are best friends for?" She asked.

Allie walked over and hugged her with a force so strong Susannah thought she'd break a rib.

"Okay, are we ready to get this show going?" Susannah said.

"Ready." Allie announced firmly.

Emma stepped toward her only daughter. "We have time yet. I am so proud of you Allison. I've dreamed of this day for so long, I can't believe it's here." She stated.

"I know, Mom. I don't believe it myself. You're not disappointed about my not having a big, formal ceremony?" Allie said.

"That was my dream. Every bride has her own dream ceremony, this is yours. A friend recently told me 'the only thing that matters is that at the end of the day you'll be married'." Emma answered.

Susannah smiled, the tears she was holding back threatened to spill over onto her cheeks.

A knock came at the door. "Allison, there's a young man who is anxious to make you his wife. He says if we don't begin soon he's leaving." Roger Cole announced.

"You tell him we'll start when I'm darn good and ready and if he takes one step to leave I'll have his hide." Allie said.

Roger chuckled.

"That's my cue to go down and let the minister know we're ready to begin." Emma said.

She hugged Allie tightly, kissed her on the cheek and said, "I love you."

Allie hugged her mother back responding with "I love you, too."

Emma walked to the door, opened it, gave her husband a quick kiss and was off to wait for her daughter to get married.

Roger stepped into the room. "You're beautiful, Princess. I couldn't be prouder of you." He said.

"Thank you, Daddy. Now let's go get married." Allie said.

Susannah took that as her cue to start the procession. She took up her bouquet off of Allie's vanity and began the walk to take her best friend to the man she loved.

During the ceremony Susannah had difficulty keeping her mind on her duties as maid of honor.

When the minister pronounced John and Allie husband and wife Susannah couldn't have been more relieved.

Waiting in the receiving line for the guests to congratulate John and Allie, Susannah wondered if she'd ever have what they shared.

Susannah and Allie joined the guests in the lively celebration.

Although she felt like crying, Susannah forced back the tears of a broken heart

Later, in the early evening, Susannah was dancing with John; he'd noticed how quiet she had become during the celebration of his marriage to Allie.

"Allie is worried about you." He said.

"Why? She shouldn't be worrying about me. Her attention should be focused on her new life with you." Susannah said.

"Allie is funny that way. You're like sisters, she can't help but feel your pain." John told her.

"But..."

John interrupted, "You've been best friends since you were five. She understands you're anxious about Alexander. Why do you think it took her so long to set a wedding date after I proposed?"

"I guess because she was afraid of getting married."

"No, she wanted to be sure it was right. You know Allie, she doesn't jump into anything without analyzing it to death first."

Susannah felt a sudden change in John's feelings. Her heart began to beat wildly.

"Not unlike you, Susannah." Alexander said.

Susannah turned around to find Alexander standing behind her with a solemn look on his face.

"Alexander how long have you been here?" She asked.

"Not long." He said.

Seeing that Alexander had the situation under control, John placed Susannah's hand into Alexander's and left to find his wife.

"How did you know where to find me?" Susannah questioned.

"I called Nathan, he gave me directions." Alexander answered.

"I tried reaching you at your hotel this morning."

"After you hung up on me last night I checked out and drove home."

"Why didn't you let me know you were home or come to my apartment?"

"You needed time to think about the situation and come to your own conclusions."

"But we could have..."

"No, Susannah making love wouldn't have solved our problem."

Susannah's face was awash with color.

"How did you..."

"You've been anxious to make love since I first told you I wanted to make love to you."

"Alexander, we need to talk."

"Yes, love, we do but now is not the time."

"Now is the perfect time. I hate seeing Susannah so miserable when I'm so happy." Allie said.

"Have you been eavesdropping, Mrs. Sanders?" Susannah asked.

Smiling at Susannah's use of her new name, Allie said, "Of course, how else am I supposed to know what's going on with you when you don't talk to me?"

"Allison Emma Sanders you ought to be ashamed of yourself." Susannah reprimanded.

"Just returning the favor." Allie said.

"Allison, so help me..."

"I'm going."

Allison walked away smiling, content to know that her friend would soon have the kind of happiness she'd found.

The music started to play again. Alexander held his hand out to Susannah.

She graciously accepted his offer to dance.

Alexander took Susannah in his arms and they danced to 'Slow Dancing (Swaying to the Music)'.

As if they had a mind of their own, Alexander's hands gently caressed Susannah's back.

When she melted against him he massaged her arms down to her fingertips.

Susannah felt the desire for Alexander begin to build.

They didn't notice when the songs changed. Next they danced to 'Nights Are Forever Without You'.

After that was "I'd Really Love To See You Tonight'.

Alexander sang the songs to Susannah as they played.

With their foreheads touching Alexander brushed his nose back and forth against Susannah's.

Although the movement was meant to be soothing, Susannah's body reacted as though he were caressing her naked body.

"Relax, love, we have as much time as we need." Alexander told her.

"Alexander, I said we have to talk." Susannah reminded him.

"All right start with why you tried to reach me at my hotel this morning." He suggested.

"I had another nightmare last night." She began.

Alexander bristled at her statement.

"No, Alexander, not about you. Wayne was telling me I couldn't marry you because I couldn't trust you." She continued.

Alexander's stance remained the same and he seemed to withdraw from her.

"Alexander, please listen to me." She begged.

"I'm listening." He said stiffly.

"The more Wayne tried to convince me I couldn't trust you the more convinced I became that I can trust you." Alexander relaxed a little. "The nightmare continued until I did something I haven't been able to do in the four years since they began. I broke free, I woke up. No more nightmares. I broke the hold Wayne had on me. I'm completely free. When I broke free of the nightmare and woke up I knew that I could trust you with my life and that I love you." She said.

Alexander took a step back from Susannah.

"You're sure."

"I've never been more sure of anything in my life."

Alexander wanted to let out a whoop of delight. Instead he pulled Susannah to him and kissed her hungrily.

Susannah responded to his kiss with a hunger of her own.

When the kiss ended Susannah tried to urge Alexander to kiss her again.

"I'm afraid if I kiss you anymore my love, I won't stop there." He told her.

Susannah blushed a becoming shade of red.

"Let's get out of here." She whispered.

"You still have duties to attend to, love." He said.

"I'd forgotten." She said.

"That is obvious, love."

Susannah threw her head back, stuck her chin in the air and walked as regally as she could away from Alexander.

He chuckled and followed behind her.

When Susannah reached Allie's side, she hooked her arm through hers.

"Are you ready for the traditional reception events?" Susannah asked.

"Let's skip all of that. I'm tired and want to get out of here." Allie said.

"Are you sure?" Susannah questioned.

"I'll just throw the bouquet, John can toss the garter and then we'll leave." Allie told her.

Susannah clapped her hands together.

"If I can have everyone's attention, please." She said.

When the guests quieted down enough so Susannah could be heard she said, "Mr. & Mrs. Sanders are anxious to start their new life together. The bride is going to throw the bouquet and the groom is going to toss the garter."

Everyone applauded.

"All single ladies stand in the center of the yard." Susannah instructed.

All of the single women gathered at the spot Susannah had indicated.

She found herself in the front of the group.

Before she could wonder how she had gotten there, Allie threw the bouquet.

Seconds later Susannah was holding the bouquet in her outstretched hands.

Alexander walked up to her and whispered, "Looks like you're the next bride, darling."

"Shut up, Alexander." She said.

"I'll do my best to catch the garter love then ours will be the next wedding." Alexander said chuckling.

Knowing the tradition of the maiden who caught the bouquet and the man who caught the garter, Susannah said, "Alexander don't you dare."

"I'm not letting another man put that garter on your leg. I plan to do that myself and slowly take it off later." He told her.

Susannah's face turned red.

The best man announced that John would be tossing the garter.

All of the single men stood in the center of the yard, all vying to catch the garter.

With very little effort, Alexander snatched the garter out of the air when John tossed it over his shoulder.

Knowing the odds of getting away before anyone saw her were slim, Susannah slowly began to back away from the rowdy crowd.

"Going somewhere, love?" Alexander asked.

Everyone turned toward Susannah.

She stopped mid-step and threw Alexander a 'I'll make you pay for this look.'

Allie brought a chair to the center of the yard.

"All right, Alexander and Susannah your turn." She said.

Reluctantly Susannah walked to the chair and sat down.

Alexander walked to her telling her, "Relax, love it's only in fun."

"I'm not used to being the center of attention." She whispered.

"For this brief moment pretend we're the only two people in the world." He said.

Susannah smiled and nodded.

Putting her leg out for Alexander to place the garter on, Susannah thought only of the two of them.

Alexander took off her shoe and using his teeth pulled the garter up her leg to an embarrassingly high position.

As he did, the crowd urged Alexander to go higher as he slid the lacy garment up her leg.

After Alexander took the garter up her leg as far as he dared he put his hands on either side of Susannah's face and drew towards her to kiss her.

The rowdy crowd whooped and hollered as Alexander kissed Susannah long and seductively.

Drawing away from her, Alexander whispered, "We need to get out of here."

Susannah still in a seduced haze was slow to respond. "A little anxious are we, Mr. Arthur." She said seductively.

The crowd dispersed from around Alexander and Susannah.

"You're fortunate I don't want to embarrass you anymore than I have." He growled.

There was a commotion near the entrance to the yard.

Alexander and Susannah looked up to see John and Allie being pelted by birdseed and shouts of well wishes.

Content where they were Alexander and Susannah stayed back from the crowd and watched as John and Allie made their escape from all of the well-wishers.

Alexander turned to Susannah.

"All right my future wife it's our turn to escape." He said.

Alexander took Susannah's hand, leading her to Allie's parents

When they came to them Alexander asked, "Would you like us to help clean up?"

"No, we have hired help to clean up. You two go on." Emma said.

"Thanks for everything." Roger said.

He pulled Susannah close to hug her. Turning to Alexander he shook his hand.

Alexander and Susannah made their way through the throng of people, into the house, to gather the few things she had brought.

Afterward he walked her to her car, kissed her and promised to meet her at her apartment.

Susannah nodded, climbed into her car and drove the few miles to her apartment.

CHAPTER TWELVE

When Susannah reached home Alexander hadn't yet arrived.

She guessed he stopped to buy contraceptives. Logically he hadn't thought she might have already done so.

She went into her apartment and put away the things she'd taken for Allie's wedding.

Changing her clothes, she became nervous as the night ahead crept into her mind. She finally felt like she was ready to commit to Alexander in every way.

Would Alexander be disappointed in her? Would he leave because she wasn't as experienced as the other women he'd dated?

After half an hour of waiting, Susannah became panicked. It shouldn't take this long for Alexander to get here; even stopping to buy contraceptives wouldn't take him this long.

Susannah had a sick knot in the pit of her stomach. Something was wrong, she could feel it.

If something had happened to Alexander she wouldn't be able to bear it. They were so close to committing to each other it couldn't be taken away now.

Another quarter of an hour ticked away on the clock.

Susannah could feel the contents of her stomach start to rise and almost begin choking off her breath.

She fought the urge to run to the bathroom and empty the contents of her stomach.

Suddenly there was a knock on the door. Susannah panicked. It was bad news she could feel it.

"Who is it?" She asked.

"Your future husband, open the door woman." Alexander demanded.

Susannah quickly went to the door, threw it open and fell into Alexander's arms.

"What's wrong, love? Has something happened?" He asked.

"I was so frightened. You weren't here within half an hour; then another fifteen minutes went by and you weren't here." She sobbed.

Alexander held her to him, rubbing her back comfortingly.

"I stopped to pick up a package then was on my way here and got stuck behind an accident." Alexander explained.

"I thought something awful had happened to you." Susannah whimpered.

"As you can see I'm all in one piece. I'm all right, safe and sound." Alexander assured her.

Susannah pulled Alexander into the apartment.

"Who's anxious now, love?" He chuckled.

"Alexander, don't laugh, I was really frightened." She told him.

"I know, I'm sorry, love. Let's snuggle on the couch until you calm down." He said.

Alexander noticed she was a little jittery.

"Relax, love, we'll only go as far as you're comfortable with." He told her.

"Alexander, I can't wait any longer." She told him.

Alexander led Susannah to the couch where they lay together comfortably content to be in each other's arms.

When Alexander knew Susannah was once again calm he tilted her head up. Looking into her calm face he lowered his head to kiss her.

The hunger that had begun to build earlier in the day returned slowly at first, then started a fire Susannah couldn't control.

She squirmed to get better contact with Alexander's body. He refused to let her rush.

"Slow, love. We have all the time we need." He told her.

He had to slow her wandering hands and curious mouth.

Deliberately, Alexander took her slowly toward the edge and brought her back.

After several attempts at pushing him to go faster Susannah fell into the rhythm he set.

Alexander kissed her slowly, letting his tongue entice her. When she licked her dry lips, he captured her tongue with his lips and gently sucked to bring her to arousal.

Susannah caught her breath.

Moving from beside her, Alexander's hands made lazy circles down her leg as they wandered down to her ankles. Coming back up her leg, he caressed her shin making his way up to the hollow behind her knee. Slowly he made circles up her thigh.

Susannah wanted his hands to go higher to her most intimate part.

"Alexander, please." She begged.

"Not yet, love. I want to enjoy every inch of you before I make you mine." He said.

Alexander's hands continued to arouse her as they climbed higher and he began to undress her.

When he came to her bra, his head dropped into the valley between her breasts. He kissed her breasts before releasing the catch.

"Alexander..."

He laughed, knowing he was driving her mad with his slow seduction of her body.

Susannah lay helpless as he pursued his seduction of her body; she couldn't lift her arms to touch him the way she wanted.

He had her begging for release and she couldn't do anything except wait for him to satisfy her growing, painful hunger.

At last he stopped. Susannah cried out. Alexander picked her up going to the bedroom.

Their nude bodies lying together on the bed clung together as Susannah pulled her body against him for closer contact.

Alexander pulled away to get the protection he'd brought.

"Alexander no..." Susannah cried.

"Protection, love." He said.

"Top drawer, night stand." She managed.

Alexander left her briefly to find that she had also thought of contraceptives.

Knowing the teasing was over Alexander quickly opened the box, took out a packet covered himself and went back to Susannah.

He captured her warm, moist mouth with his whispering loving words to her.

When Susannah indicated she was ready he slowly entered her.

Feeling her tense at the welcome invasion, Alexander slowed until she relaxed while accepting him inside her.

Alexander knew he couldn't stop the pain that was to come, he quickly thrust inside making their union complete.

He captured her cry and whispered words of love to her. When he felt her accept him, he started a steady rhythm to bring her to climax.

She forgot the instant of pain as Alexander made love to her.

Finally Susannah was able to touch him as she wanted to. Her hands caressed him, making him more passionate in his pursuit to give her the ultimate conclusion to their lovemaking.

When it came, Susannah's climax brought Alexander's name to her lips and she cried out as the waves of pleasure coursed through her.

Feeling his climax begin, Susannah began moving her hips in a seductive way to give him more pleasure.

Alexander called her name as the waves of pleasure overwhelmed him and he couldn't hold back any longer.

Making love to each other they didn't know how much time passed and they didn't care.

When the waves began to subside Alexander felt Susannah relax beneath him. Sated, he rolled to his side bringing Susannah next to him with an arm wrapped around her.

Alexander listened to her breathing; it went from climactic release to sounds of sleeping.

She'd fallen asleep. How had she fallen asleep? He was disappointed that he'd put her to sleep instead of readying her for more lovemaking.

He cautioned himself not to let Susannah know he hadn't made love to her the way he'd wanted to.

Several minutes went by and he felt her begin to stir beside him.

She hadn't fallen asleep, she'd passed out. Alexander smiled.

"Alexander." She said.

"Yes, love." He said.

"Did I fall asleep?" She asked.

"No, love, you passed out." He told her proudly.

"Was I supposed to?" She questioned.

"It does happen, darling. Your body gets so overwhelmed by feelings of lovemaking that you lose consciousness for a moment."

Susannah smiled. "That's a good thing, right."

"That's a very good thing."

"Alexander." She said, letting her hands slide down his chest to his still aroused manhood.

Alexander jumped. "Woman don't start something you can't finish."

Susannah looked up at Alexander. " I wanted to ask if we could make love again." She said.

"We can make love as long as we want." He told her.

"Good, because I've decided I like lovemaking." She told him.

In answer Alexander kissed her and began the cycle of slowly arousing her again.

This time when they made love Alexander let Susannah set the rhythm.

Alexander and Susannah made love into the night and early morning hours.

Finally exhausted they lay spoon fashion. Susannah put her leg between Alexander's.

Their quiet slumber was disturbed by a knock on Susannah's apartment door.

Slowly waking, Susannah wondered who could be at the door.

"Ignore it and go back to sleep." Alexander said gruffly.

"I can't it may be important." Susannah said.

Alexander looked at the clock on Susannah's bedside stand.

"It's ten o'clock on a Sunday morning, who visits at this time of morning?" He grumbled.

"Go back to sleep. I'll get rid of whoever it is and come back to bed." Susannah promised.

"I'm not letting you out of this bed alone. I'm coming with you." He told her.

Susannah gave Alexander a quick kiss then swung her legs over the side of the bed.

Seeing Alexander's shirt from the day before she picked it up off the floor and put it on. By the time she had it buttoned Alexander had slipped on his briefs and pants.

Together they made their way to the door.

Opening it, Susannah was ready to tell whoever was on the other side they had a nerve knocking on her door at this time of morning.

Any thoughts that had formed in her head instantly left her when she saw a police officer standing at the door.

"May I help you officer?" Susannah asked.

"Susannah Roberts?" She asked.

Susannah nodded.

"I've come to let you know Wayne Loomis has been in an accident. He's in the hospital and requests that you come right away." The officer told her.

Susannah stood staring at the officer feeling numb.

"What about his family? Have they been contacted?" Susannah questioned.

"No ma'am. He requested we contact only you." The officer said.

"I'm sorry you wasted your time officer but I won't be going with you."

"Ma'am?"

"Susannah he's asking for you, you should go. Loomis will just have another officer come back." Alexander told her.

"Alexander I'm not responsible for Wayne." Susannah told him.

"I'm not suggesting you go alone, love. I'll go with you. We'll be along shortly, officer. Thank you." Alexander said.

"Yes sir."

The officer turned and walked away.

Alexander shut the door.

"Alexander why did you say we'd go? You know I don't want anything to do with Wayne." Susannah said.

"I know, love, but the sooner we get this over with the better. Now before we leave I have something I want to ask you." Alexander told her.

Taking her hands in his and going down on one knee, Alexander looked lovingly at Susannah.

"Miss Susannah Roberts will you marry me?" Alexander asked.

Tears forming in her eyes, the only response Susannah could manage was a nod of her head.

"I intend to stay down here until I get a proper response to my proposal my love." He told her.

"Yes." She squeaked out.

"I'm sorry, what?" He asked.

"Yes." She said firmly.

Alexander stood, pulled Susannah to him and kissed her.

Susannah got lost in the kiss, completely forgetting the officer who'd just been there and her request.

Alexander broke the kiss with disappointment.

"We have to go, love." He said.

"Wayne isn't going anywhere. Let him wait." Susannah said.

"Sorry, love, but they'll be expecting you at the hospital." Alexander reminded her.

Susannah swore under her breath and walked toward her room to change out of Alexander's shirt and into her own clothes.

Alexander put on the shirt Susannah just took off.

Running a brush through her hair, Susannah let Alexander know she was ready to go.

Walking hand in hand, Alexander and Susannah went to the lobby and out the door to his car.

Susannah dreaded what she'd have to deal with when they arrived at the hospital.

Alexander pulled into a parking spot. He and Susannah walked to the reception area of the hospital.

"May I help you?" Ada, the volunteer asked.

"Wayne Loomis' room please." Susannah said.

"Your name." Ada asked.

"Susannah Roberts." She answered.

Ada looked up Wayne's information and gave it to Susannah.

Alexander and Susannah started to walk away.

"I'm sorry, Miss Roberts you'll have to go up alone." Ada told her.

"I'm not going up without my fiancée." Susannah said firmly.

"I'm sorry, the rules." Ada said.

"You'll have to call the nurses' station on Mr. Loomis' floor to tell them I'm not coming up." Susannah said.

Ada picked up the phone and dialed the nurses' station on Wayne's floor.

When the line was picked up she said, "This is Ada in reception. Miss Roberts is here to see Mr. Loomis. She refuses to come up unless her fiancée can accompany her."

Ada was silent as she waited for the nurse to get instructions. She hung up the phone.

"Please go up Miss Roberts, your fiancée is welcome to accompany you." Ada told her.

"Thank you." Susannah said.

Alexander took Susannah by the hand, leading her to the elevator.

Susannah shuddered as they waited for the elevator door to open.

"What's wrong, Susannah?" Alexander asked.

"I have a bad feeling about this. I wonder what Wayne is up to." Susannah said.

"What kind of bad feeling?" Alexander asked.

"Something about this isn't right." She told him.

The elevator door swished open. Alexander and Susannah stepped into the elevator car.

On the ride up to Wayne's floor Susannah felt a knot form in her stomach.

When the elevator door opened on Wayne's floor Gina Langley descended on them.

"He's dying and all the can think about is you." Gina said accusingly.

Caught off guard, Susannah took a step back.

Alexander held the elevator door so it wouldn't close.

"Who the hell are you?" Susannah asked sharply.

"Gina Langley, Wayne's fiancée." Gina said.

"My condolences." Susannah said.

"He was drinking and talking about how he'd lost you. He couldn't give you up. He had to have you." Gina whined.

"I'm sorry, Miss Langley, I haven't seen Wayne in weeks. Since he gave up on winning me back." Susannah told her.

"He didn't give up. He was waiting for you to come running back to him when Alexander learned how you'd duped him and he dumped you."

"What are you talking about?"

"Wayne told me how the two of you planned to fool Alexander into signing over Arthur and Sons Construction to you."

Susannah felt Alexander tense beside her.

Turning to him she said, "It's a lie, Alexander. I haven't seen or talked to Wayne since the night he came to my apartment and told me good-bye."

Alexander looked at Susannah.

"Oh, God he doesn't believe me." She thought.

"Alexander say something." Susannah demanded.

Alexander turned and walked away.

Susannah watched him walk away not able to do anything. She couldn't force him to trust and believe in her. He had to trust her of his own free will.

She wanted to shout at him, to say he couldn't believe the lies Gina was telling, not after last night.

Hopelessly she stood watching as the man she loved walked away from her. Again Wayne had lied and ruined her life.

Dejected, Susannah turned back to Gina.

"Now that you've ruined my life tell me why Wayne asked that only I be contacted." Susannah hissed.

Gina smiled. "Wayne said you'd come back to him when Alexander dumped you and I'd have my chance to take Alexander from you." She said.

"That's what this is about. Wayne couldn't have me so he wants to ruin my life and you're so desperate to have a man that you concocted a story so Alexander would come to you for comfort." Susannah stated.

"I am not desperate. Alexander should be with me not some prude virgin." Gina said.

"You're pathetic. Alexander may leave me, but when he realizes what you've done he'll cast you off like an old shoe." Susannah told her.

Gina's face turned red. "You bitch, you'll pay for that." She said bringing her arm up and swinging at Susannah.

Realizing Gina had been drinking, Susannah easily moved out of her way.

Making a complete circle when she swung at Susannah, Gina fell into a heap on the floor.

Laughing, Susannah walked around her to the nurses' station.

"I'm here at the request of Wayne Loomis." She said.

The nurse gave Susannah directions to Wayne's room.

Susannah thanked her and headed in the direction she'd indicated.

When she turned the corner to go to Wayne's room Susannah saw two police officers standing at the door.

Approaching them Susannah smiled.

"May I help you, miss?" One of the officers asked.

"I'm Susannah Roberts. I believe you're expecting me." She said.

"Yes, Miss Roberts please come with me." Officer Thompson said.

Susannah followed Officer Thompson into Wayne's room.

When she saw Wayne, Susannah nearly passed out.

"Why is he hooked up to these machines?" She asked.

"The accident Mr. Loomis caused was fatal. The machines are helping to sustain his life." Officer Thompson told her.

"Miss Langley said he's dying." Susannah said.

"That's right, Miss Roberts. He instructed the doctors to prolong his life long enough to marry you." He said.

"We're not getting married." Susannah stated.

"You'd deny a dying man his last wish?" Wayne asked.

"Under ordinary circumstances I'd grant the wish, this isn't an ordinary circumstance." Susannah told him.

"Let me die happy, Susannah. Marry me." Wayne begged.

"I'm sorry, Wayne but I can't marry you. I'm going to marry Alexander." She said.

Wayne snorted. "Not after what Gina told him you're not." He said.

"Regardless of whatever story you and your girlfriend have come up with to push Alexander away from me, you will not convince me that marrying you is the right thing to do." Susannah jeered.

"I'm a dying man, you have to honor my wish."

"No, Wayne, I don't. You're selfish and controlling to the end. You're only thinking about yourself. Besides you don't want to marry a woman who's pregnant with another man's child."

Wayne winced. "You're not pregnant. You're just saying that."

"Actually there is a possibility that I am pregnant. Alexander and I are lovers."

"You're lying. The Susannah I know is a prude."

"Why would I lie?"

"You want to hurt me."

"I can't hurt you anymore than you've already hurt yourself."

Susannah turned and walked out of the room, running into Alexander.

"How long have you been standing here?" She asked sharply.

"The entire time you've been in there." Alexander responded.

"Why did you come back? Did you think I'd confirm what Gina said?" She questioned.

"I came back because I realized I know you better than that. You'd never hurt me that way, not after what Loomis put you through." He told her.

"How could you even doubt my feelings for you Alexander?"

"Male pride, it does a lot to batter a man's ego."

"You should have trusted me."

"I'm sorry, love. I'll never doubt you again."

Alexander took Susannah's hand and together they left the hospital and Wayne behind.

On the way to Alexander's car and on the ride to Susannah's apartment there was a tangible silence.

Alexander held onto Susannah's hand even though it was obvious she wanted to be as far away from him as she could get.

When Alexander pulled up in front of Susannah's apartment building she quickly undid her seatbelt, withdrew her hand from Alexander's and went to her apartment.

Knowing he'd hurt her, Alexander followed Susannah to her apartment.

When they were inside and he'd shut the door, Alexander said, "How long are we going to play this game of I can't trust Alexander, Susannah?"

"I'm not playing a game, Alexander. You believed every word that drunken woman said. You didn't trust me and that hurt. You walked away so easily… just like my father." Susannah told him.

"I'm not your father. I've already apologized, what more can I do to tell you how sorry I am?" He questioned.

"I don't know that there is a way for you to do that. It felt like you were throwing me away."

"Susannah…"

Alexander took Susannah by the arms and pulled her to him.

Susannah tried to pull away but it was only a half-hearted attempt.

Hugging her, Alexander rubbed his hand over Susannah's back determined to make her understand how much he loved her.

She knew his intent wasn't meant to get her to make love with him.

He was genuinely sorry he'd doubted her feelings for him, but could she marry a man who ran at the first sign of conflict?

Just like before, Susannah had to make the choice of whether to trust and believe in Alexander.

She pulled away from him, turning away.

"I'm not dumping you or throwing you away, Susannah." He said.

"If you ever make me feel this way again I will walk away from you Alexander." She told him.

Simply he said, "Understood."

"There will not be another chance. I've been hurt too much." She said.

"I promise I'll never doubt your feelings for me again."

Susannah turned back to Alexander her eyes shining with the love she couldn't hold back.

He looked into her eyes and saw a genuine need for love and understanding.

Taking her hand, Alexander led her to the couch.

They cuddled together on the couch.

"Susannah." Alexander said.

"Yes." She answered.

"Why did you tell Loomis we're lovers?" He asked.

"To let him know I'm completely free of him and that I belong to you." She told him.

"You weren't trying to hurt him?" He questioned.

"Maybe a little." She said yawning.

Alexander kissed the top of her head.

"I love you." He said.

"I love you, too." She responded sleepily.

"Are you going to sleep?" He asked.

"Maybe." She said teasingly.

"Go to sleep, my love. I'm not going anywhere." He told her.

"Okay." She agreed

She let herself fall asleep in Alexander's arms. She was safe and protected.

Alexander knew when she fell asleep. Her breathing became deep and even.

Suddenly Susannah was awake.

"He's gone." She said.

"Who's gone, love?" Alexander asked.

"Wayne." She told him.

"Sweetheart, Loomis is in the hospital." He told her.

"No, I mean he's passed on." Susannah stated.

"What are you talking about?" Alexander questioned.

"Officer Thompson said Wayne had caused a fatal crash. Now he's dead."

"How do you know?"

"I feel it. Don't ask how, I just feel it."

"How do you feel about it?"

"I'm sorry he passed on, but I'm also relieved."

"Relieved how?"

"I know for certain he won't be pestering me anymore."

"Would you like me to take you to the hospital?"

"No, there's nothing I can do."

Alexander pulled Susannah closer to him inhaling her sweet scent.

Lying next to Alexander, Susannah thought about Wayne's death. She was genuinely sorry he'd passed on but the relief she felt was overpowering.

She could relax knowing that he wasn't lurking around a corner waiting to jump out at her.

For four years she'd waited for him to come back to threaten her calm, predictable life. The wait was over and she could move on with Alexander.

"I'm hungry." Susannah said.

"Would you like to make something here or go out?" Alexander asked.

"Go out." She told him.

"First I have a question."

"Okay."

"When we first met you said you didn't intend to make love until you were married, what changed your mind?"

"After all that's happened today that's what's on your mind?"

"It's been in the back of my mind for a few days; since last week actually when we were getting closer emotionally."

"You changed my mind."

"How?"

"Your loving made me curious. I wanted to know what it was like to be intimate and how making love would make me feel."

"How does it make you feel?"

"Closer to you than I thought it was possible to be. I also realized waiting for marriage is almost impossible."

"No regrets?"

"None, can we eat now?"

Alexander kissed Susannah; she responded to his kiss with a hunger she was getting used to.

When Alexander tried to pull away Susannah darted her tongue into his mouth.

Groaning, Alexander held her to him wanting the feel of her naked body beneath him.

Helping her up off the couch, and without losing contact with her mouth he led Susannah into the bedroom.

Once there, Susannah forgot how she wanted to tease Alexander.

He held her to him sensuously kissing her jaw, leading down to her neck where he sucked at her throat evoking soft gasps of pleasure from her.

"Alexander..."

Alexander fondled her breasts, gently kneading them until her nipples became hard nubs aching for his mouth to possess them.

Stripping her of her shirt and bra, Alexander drew one hardened nipple into his mouth, suckling like a nursing baby.

Susannah held his head to her breast while he sucked and teased her nipple to the point of pleasurable agony.

When he was satisfied he had the breast sufficiently excited he moved his mouth to the other hardened nub repeating the process with the second hardened nipple.

"Oh, God... Alexander I want..."

She couldn't finish her thought. Alexander's hand was working it's way up her leg to the warmth between her legs.

Susannah held him to her as he suckled her breast, getting pleasure from his warm mouth surrounding her aching nipple.

Several minutes ticked by on the clock while Alexander excited her with his mouth at her breast.

Finally he pulled his head up and captured her warm, moist mouth with his.

Undressing, they touched, stroked and otherwise gave pleasure to one another with their hands until they couldn't stand the heat their lovemaking was creating.

Alexander took a contraceptive from the box in Susannah's top drawer and enclosed his hardened manhood.

Holding Susannah's waist, he plunged inside her warm, moist center of desire, eliciting short, pleasurable gasps from her.

Susannah closed around him, making him gasp in response.

He made love to her while they stood against the side of the bed; Susannah's climax made her hold onto Alexander while the waves of pleasure coursed through her soft, sensitized body.

When she thought she couldn't stand, Alexander brought her legs to wrap around his waist.

He thrust deeper inside her, making her climax again.

When he felt her loosen her grip with her legs he said, "Not yet, my love, I'm not through loving you."

Alexander gently laid her on the bed and began a slow, steady rhythm.

Susannah's climax was stronger than the first two had been.

"Alexander I can't..."

Alexander let himself go then and she felt him pulse inside her.

"Oh, God Alexander..."

With his release, Susannah lost consciousness.

Moments later Susannah awoke to find Alexander still inside her."

"Alexander?"

When he'd known she was coming back to consciousness he felt himself harden again.

"Eating is going to have to wait, love. I need to make love to you again." He told her.

Susannah's only response was to clamp her legs at his waist.

He pulled himself away long enough to remove the contraceptive, replacing it with another.

Going inside her again, Alexander touched every part of her.

When he made love to her again it was with such intensity Susannah couldn't catch her breath.

He drew out their lovemaking until Susannah cried out for completion.

"Alexander please."

He brought her to completion over and over taking her to new heights of ecstasy.

When Susannah began to drift off Alexander had completed his climax.

After she drifted off, Alexander smiled to himself. He'd been as randy as a teenager having his first sexual experience.

It had been some time since he'd felt that with a woman. He was glad Susannah was the woman who'd made him feel like it again.

Alexander had a sobering thought. If Susannah made him feel like a teenager how would he continue to remember to use contraceptives when they made love?

As he began to drift off he thought about asking Susannah to get the pill.

CHAPTER THIRTEEN

Susannah dreamed that Alexander was making love to her again. She was pregnant... again.

How many children would this make, three no four. Four years of marriage and she was pregnant with their fourth child.

She had to do something. They were multiplying like rabbits.

Contraceptives were useless if you didn't use them. Alexander didn't remember to use them most of the time because he always wanted to make love and his brain hadn't caught up with his libido.

Susannah was suddenly awake. She sat up, swung her legs over the side of the bed and went to her desk.

Pulling a pad to her, she wrote a note to remind herself to call Dr. Hanson, her gynecologist, to discuss getting a prescription for the pill.

Going back to her room, she pulled her robe off the hook on the back of the door and went into the bathroom.

She closed the door and started a bubble bath.

Alexander's lovemaking had made her tender in a few areas.

She smiled. Alexander had been like a teenager making love. He'd wanted to make her his and he had.

While taking her bath, Susannah heard Alexander get up and start moving around.

He came to the door and knocked.

Knowing the bubbles covered her she said, "Come in."

Alexander opened the door and stuck his head in.

"Need someone to wash your back." He asked hopefully.

"Alexander we both know if you climb into this tub neither one of us would do any washing." Susannah told him.

"You can't blame a guy for trying." He said.

"You have a one track mind, Mr. Arthur."

"Are you complaining, love?"

"No."

Susannah winced and brought her hand up to her side.

"Are you all right?" He asked.

"Yes, mother nature decided to visit." Susannah said panting.

"You're not all right. I have two sisters remember. From experience I know you have cramps and along with them you're in a bad mood."

"Alexander I don't want to talk about this."

Alexander walked over and kneeled beside the tub.

Stroking the hair back from her forehead he said, "Love, don't be embarrassed to talk to me."

"I'm not embarrassed. Speaking of which there is something we need to discuss."

"Contraception."

"Yes, I don't think the method we've chosen is going to work for us."

"I agree. Would you be offended if I asked you to see your doctor?"

"No, I actually thought about that after I woke up from a troubling dream." She said opening her eyes.

Alexander looked at her quizzically.

"I dreamed that we were making love and I was pregnant."

"Why would being pregnant be troubling?"

"It wasn't being pregnant that was troubling. We'd been married four years and I was pregnant with our fourth child."

"And that's a problem why?"

"Alexander four pregnancies in four years? It's not exactly how I picture our future."

"You don't want children?"

"I'll have as many children as you'd like. I'd just rather not have them one after another."

"We'll have to practice just to make sure we get it right."

"First we have to get married."

"What date have you picked? I don't want to be engaged long."

"Alexander you only proposed this morning. I haven't had time to think about a wedding date."

"When your mother discovers we're lovers she's going to want to know when I intend to make you my wife."

"I know. We're both so busy with work. There isn't going to be a good time in the foreseeable future."

"Our lives do not revolve around work, love. We pick a date and make our wedding plans."

"Right now I'd like to finish my bath and then get something to eat."

Alexander leaned over to kiss Susannah. Being aware of her condition made it difficult to give her a chaste kiss. He wanted more but knew they'd have to wait.

He left to get his bag.

Susannah finished bathing, climbed out of the tub, wrapped her hair in a towel and put on her robe.

When Alexander came back into her apartment Susannah was in the kitchen making coffee.

While she waited for it to brew and Alexander took a shower, Susannah puttered around her apartment eventually settling at her desk.

She remembered her conversation with Nathan on Friday. He'd said if he and Alexander had all the facts in order she was a wealthy young woman.

Would she be able to move into Hawthorne Manor and be happy there? She'd have plenty of room to roam around.

What about Alexander's house? She couldn't expect him to give it up. What were they going to do?

Alexander came out of the bathroom freshly shaven and showered. He saw Susannah sitting at her desk.

"Is something on your mind, love?" He asked.

"I was thinking about a conversation I had with Nathan on Friday." She told him.

"Something I can help with?" He queried.

"What information did you get when you went to Rose Lake?"

"I read your late stepmother's will. According to her attorney you not only inherited Hawthorne Manor you have been bequeathed the same amount of stock and money as your brothers and sister."

"Why would Glenda leave me a small fortune?"

"Her attorneys' records show that she intended you to have everything you would have received had you been born to her."

"Alexander, that doesn't make any sense Father must be keeping something from me."

"Susannah, it isn't uncommon for someone like Glenda to give her children everything."

"Alexander, I'm not her daughter. Why would she force my father to leave us and then on her death will me a fifth of her estate?"

"I don't know, love. Why are you so agitated?"

"Something isn't right, Alexander. Glenda must not have told me everything."

"It isn't likely you'll get any answers; she can't be brought back to answer your questions."

"Alexander you're not helping."

"Susannah quit thinking about it. You're already in a bad mood."

Susannah threw her hands up. "You don't understand."

"Love, you're over-analyzing the situation. Let's get out of here."

Susannah stood up and walked into the bedroom to gather her clothes to get dressed.

Going into the bathroom, she closed the door with a thud.

She hated it when Alexander was right. No she didn't. Her monthly was making her quarrelsome and irrational.

When she finished dressing Susannah went out to Alexander. Putting her arms around him she hugged him tightly.

Alexander wrapped his arms around her, kissed the top of her head, holding her.

Standing together locked in a comfortable embrace neither wanted to move.

Alexander moved first.

Susannah rebelled. "Alexander no..."

"Come on, let's get you out of here."

Susannah went to get her purse. Checking that she had her keys, she followed Alexander out the door after securing the lock.

The ride to Matilda's was quiet. Alexander parked the car and they went inside.

The hostess seated them. "Your server will be right with you." She said.

"Thank you." Alexander said.

Michael, their server appeared. "What can I get you to drink?"

"Coffee." Alexander told him.

Michael walked away.

"Oh." Susannah gasped.

"What's wrong, love?" Alexander asked.

"I left my coffeemaker on." She told him.

"Don't worry it'll shut itself off." He said.

"What if something happens?" She asked.

"Nothing will happen. Susannah you worry too much."

"I'm beginning to think you don't worry enough."

"I have enough to worry about without creating things to worry about."

Michael came back with their coffee. "What can I get for you folks?" He asked.

"We'll have the buffet." Alexander said.

"I do not create things to worry about." Susannah said after Michael left.

"That's enough, Susannah. You're trying to start a fight."

Susannah, on the verge of tears, stood up. Without looking at Alexander she fled to the ladies' room.

She knew Alexander couldn't follow her but she wished he'd have tried.

Knowing she was being irrational, Susannah let the tears come.

Crying, she wanted to throw something, break something or hit something. She didn't care what, she just wanted the physical pain to stop.

Thankfully no one came in as she cried. When the tears subsided Susannah splashed cold water on her face, patted it dry and started back to Alexander.

When she stepped into the hallway Alexander asked, "Feeling better?"

"I don't know. The pain is awful and my emotions are messed up." She said.

"I can't help with the pain, but I can get you a nutritious meal." He told her.

"I'm sorry I'm so irrational." She apologized.

"You have nothing to be sorry for. I'll just have to remember on days like this, not to take things personally."

Susannah kissed Alexander.

"You're too good to be true."

"I have my faults too. I can't think of any right off, but I'm sure I have them."

Susannah laughed they walked to the buffet, filled plates with food then went to their table.

"After we finish eating I'd like to stop at the Chocolate Hut." Susannah stated.

"The Chocolate Hut?" He asked.

"Yes, I have a friend who makes a special box of chocolates for me when I need them." She told him.

"Would this friend happen to be a man?" Alexander questioned.

"Yes, you have nothing to worry about. He's married and has nine children."

"Married men have been known to have mistresses."

"Are you jealous, Alexander?"

"If I am what would you do?"

"I can't stop your being jealous. I can only assure you that Garth is just a friend."

"Garth, he's your friend."

"Yes."

"I want to meet the man who's been flirting with you."

"He does not flirt with me, Alexander. I promised I'd bring you in so he could meet you."

"Why does he want to meet me?"

"He wants to know the man who is to take me away from him."

"He is more than just a friend. Susannah..."

"Now who's being irrational?"

Susannah smiled at the look of consternation on Alexander's face.

"I am not being irrational. I'm protecting what's mine."

"I am not an object Alexander and I can protect myself."

While they finished eating Susannah could see that Alexander was warring between being furious with himself for being jealous and believing she and Garth were no more than friends.

After they finished eating Alexander possessively took Susannah by the hand, went to the cashier and paid their bill.

"Be grateful I can't make love to you right now because if I could I'd take you back to your apartment and make love to you so thoroughly that you wouldn't remember your own name let alone that of another man." Alexander told her when they were in the car.

Susannah knew there wasn't any sense answering him. He was jealous of Garth and there wasn't anything she could do about it.

Driving out of the parking lot, Alexander reluctantly turned in the direction of the Chocolate Hut.

After he parked the car he turned in his seat saying, "I'll warn you before we go in that if this Garth so much as winks at you I won't be responsible for my actions."

"Alexander you have nothing to be jealous of." Susannah told him.

"Let's go in and found out." He said.

Susannah opened her door and stepped out of the car. Alexander joined her on the passenger side of the car.

Together they walked hand in hand into the Chocolate Hut.

Seeing them come in, Garth smiled.

Going to Susannah, he kissed her on both cheeks. "You've brought your young man to meet Garth." He said.

Susannah could feel the tight control Alexander had on his temper.

"Yes, Garth, this is Alexander." She said.

Garth extended a hand to Alexander.

Reluctantly Alexander shook hands with him.

"He's a jealous one, eh?" Garth stated.

"I am not jealous." Alexander stated firmly.

Alexander and Garth looked at each other determining whether they could be friends or if they were destined to be enemies.

After several tense minutes Susannah said, "Garth I'd like a medium box of Susannah's Buttons."

Deciding Alexander was worthy of Susannah's affection Garth said, "This month I think you need a large box."

"Why?" Susannah asked.

"Your Alexander, he's a big one. You need the energy to keep him in the bedroom, no." Garth said.

Flushing and in a warning tone Susannah said, "Garth."

Susannah felt Alexander relax. "Yes, Garth she does." He said.

"Alexander!" Susannah reprimanded.

"Susannah, people aren't blind. They can see the change in you." Alexander teased.

Susannah sputtered about men being horses behinds and walked to another part of the store followed by Alexander and Garth's laughter.

Several minutes later Alexander caught up with her.

"He loves you very much." He said.

"Garth? I don't think so." Susannah answered.

"He loves you like a daughter. Do you know he has nine sons?" He asked.

"Yes, Alexander. I told you we're friends. How do you know he loves me like a daughter?" She asked.

"The way he protects you. How long have you known him?"

"Since I was a little girl. Mom used to bring me in every so often and let me stay with Garth while he worked."

"I'm sorry I didn't believe you're just friends. Are you going to ask him to give you away when we marry?"

"I haven't thought about it. Alexander why are you in a hurry to get married?"

"Honestly?"

"No, I want you to lie to me. Of course honestly."

Alexander took Susannah's hands in his and looked into her eyes. He saw love shining in them.

"I hate the thought of having to leave you to a cold, empty bed every night. I want yours to be the first face I see in the morning and the last face I see at night. I love you and can't imagine my life without you." He told her honestly.

"Are you afraid I'll change my mind?" She asked.

"Yes." He stated.

"You have nothing to worry about, Alexander. I'm not planning on running away." She told him.

"I'd like to get married as soon as possible."

"Alexander we're not going to discuss this in public. Let me get my chocolate then we can go back to my apartment."

"Don't expect me to change my mind."

Susannah shook her head. He was going to be difficult about their marriage. She wasn't going to rush the wedding because Alexander was afraid she'd run away.

Alexander took Susannah by the hand and led her to where Garth waited with her box of chocolates.

Taking the box from him Susannah said, "Thank you, Garth."

"It is my pleasure, cherie. You let me know when you get married." Garth said.

Alexander stuck his hand out to shake hands with Garth.

"Thank you." He said.

"You mustn't keep Alexander waiting Susannah. You must have babies." Garth told her.

Susannah blushed. "Let's not rush things. The babies will come when it's time." She said.

"It's always time for babies. The mama must be ready." Garth told her.

"All right, Garth we'll let you know when the wedding is." Susannah said.

She wanted to get out of there and stop this conversation.

Alexander took Susannah to the checkout, paid for the box of chocolates and led her out to his car.

"Garth is right you know." He said.

"Right about what?" Susannah asked.

"Having babies. I'm in my thirties. I'd like to have children while I'm able to get out and play catch with them." Alexander told her.

"Alexander we may just have girls you know." She said.

"Then we'll have tea parties." Alexander said.

Susannah pictured Alexander sitting at a table with his daughters playing the gentleman at a tea party for stuffed animals and dolls. She giggled.

"What's funny?" Alexander asked.

"A picture of you sitting at a small table with little girls, stuffed animals and dolls having a tea party." She told him.

Alexander chuckled.

They were in the car and he was driving towards Susannah's apartment.

Pulling up in front of the building, Alexander put the car in park, shut off the engine and turned towards Susannah.

"Your new assistant starts tomorrow doesn't she?" He asked.

"Yes, I told her to be there at seven thirty but forgot I have an appointment with Linda in the morning." Susannah said.

"I'll be at the office in the morning. What can I get her started on?" Alexander said.

"You're going to be at the office?" Susannah questioned.

"I am an active partner. I'm going to start practicing law." He told her.

"Why now? What about your construction company?" She asked.

"There's no sense in letting my law degree sit on a shelf collecting dust. Charles is capable of running the construction company."

"Why did you study for a law degree when you wanted to work in construction?"

"Father knew I'd need it to negotiate contracts and thought I might possibly need it if construction work slowed."

"Latham, Arthur and Associate is the name of the firm."

"Arthur, Latham and Associate."

"Why didn't Nathan tell me this before?"

"We didn't think I'd pursue law. The construction industry has been doing well."

"You're getting married and need a steady, uninterrupted source of income to take care of your family."

"Yes."

"Speaking of family, father and my siblings have gone home."

"I saw them when I went down. They're anxious for you to visit."

"I don't have time for a vacation, Alexander. I have to train Olivia and get my work caught up."

"It's not going to take as long as you think to get Olivia acclimated to running the office."

Together they went into Susannah's apartment.

When they walked in Susannah saw the steady light on her answering machine, no messages.

She took the box of chocolates to the kitchen, putting them in the refrigerator.

Alexander made himself comfortable on the couch.

When Susannah went back into the living room she sighed.

"That bad, huh?" Alexander asked.

"Not bad, just tiring." Susannah said.

"What do you want me to get Olivia started on in the morning?" Alexander asked again.

"I hate this. It's like giving instructions to someone over the phone when they have absolutely no idea what they're doing." Susannah told him.

"Start with the least tiresome project and work from there." Alexander suggested.

Susannah walked him step-by-step through her daily routine, missing nothing.

"Obviously we'll need your login name and password, which of course you'll change when you get in tomorrow." Alexander said.

Susannah tore a sheet of paper from the pad on her desk and wrote down her login name and password. She handed the paper to Alexander.

He folded it and put it in his pocket.

Susannah lay next to him on the couch.

They lay like that for some time.

There was a knock on the door.

"Who could that be?" Susannah asked.

She started to get up to answer the door.

"You lay still, I'll answer it." Alexander told her.

Susannah nodded in agreement. She sank into the cushions when Alexander went to open the door.

"Where the hell is she?" Gina demanded.

"What are you doing here, Gina?" Alexander asked.

"I came to tell your girlfriend my husband's obsession with her killed him." Gina said.

"From what the police say Loomis killed himself. He caused a fatal car crash." Alexander told her.

"If he hadn't been so obsessed with having that bitch this never would have happened." Gina told him.

"Watch how you talk about my fiancée, Gina." Alexander warned.

"Are you threatening me, Alexander?"

"If you choose to take it as a threat be my guest. I'm warning you to be respectful of my future wife."

Gina walked past him into the living room where Susannah stood in the center of the room.

"What is it you want Miss Langley?" Susannah asked deliberately using her maiden name.

"Mrs. Loomis. After you left I convinced Wayne I loved him and he married me." Gina snapped.

"Again my condolences." Susannah said.

"You killed my husband the same as if you'd put a bullet in his head. We'd been drinking and were arguing when the accident happened. He couldn't stop talking about how if you had trusted him and had more faith in him you'd have been married years ago. If you had married him I could have had my chance with Alexander." Gina stated.

"Your husband's obsession with me is not my fault. I broke things off just before he left town. I'd rather not speak ill of the dead. I think you better leave." Susannah told her.

"I just came to tell you my husband is dead and you're not welcome at his funeral."

"My condolences on the loss of your husband. I had no intention of attending his funeral."

A shocked looked came over Gina's face. She'd come to warn Susannah and it had backfired. With her head held high she walked to the door and left.

Alexander closed the door and walked to Susannah.

She was shaking.

"What's wrong, love? Did Gina's visit upset you that much?" He asked.

"No, Gina's visit didn't upset me at all. It's her remark about Wayne being obsessed with me." Susannah told him.

"You didn't know." Alexander said.

"No, I'm wondering if I somehow encouraged him." She said.

"Susannah, don't start blaming yourself. Loomis' obsession with you was his own creation. No one would have had to encourage him." Alexander said.

"I know you're right." She told him.

"You have more important things to think about. Like a wedding date."

"Three months from now."

Alexander gave a delighted whoop, picked Susannah up and whirled her around.

"All right, Alexander you're going to make me sick." Susannah told him.

Putting her down Alexander kissed her; his kiss was pure joy.

"In three months' time we'll be husband and wife." Alexander said excitedly.

"Alexander, people get married every day we're no different." Susannah told him.

"The Arthur family tradition is intact." He told her.

Growing suspicious, Susannah asked, "Alexander what family tradition?"

"For several generations Arthur men have fallen in love with and married their soul mate within six months of seeing her for the first time."

"Alexander Arthur is that why you wanted me to set a wedding date so quickly?"

"Partly, I'm also anxious to make you my wife"

Discussing wedding plans they decided on a small, simple ceremony with close family and friends.

"Mother will want to have an engagement party for us." Alexander stated.

"You said 'small, simple ceremony,' Alexander." She reminded him.

"As simple as we can with mother."

"Call her so we can get started making plans."

"Susannah, I can't tell my mother we've set a wedding date over the phone. We'll have to go to her house."

"We'll have to go to my mother's as well. Hopefully we can talk them into planning one engagement party."

"Yes, get your things so we can go to mother's."

Susannah went to get her purse and a sweater.

They left to tell Alexander's mother they'd set a wedding date.

CHAPTER FOURTEEN

Susannah realized she'd actually made a commitment to marry him when Alexander pulled up in front of his mother's. She was excited as well as nervous.

Alexander opened his door and stepped out of the car.

He composed his face into a smug mask when he walked to Susannah's side.

When he reached Susannah he held out his hand to help her out.

Susannah saw the smugness on his face and ignored his hand, becoming angry.

"I still have time to change my mind." She threatened.

"You won't." He said too confidently.

"What makes you so sure?" She asked.

"Because you love me too much." He crowed.

He took her hand in his and squeezed it reassuringly.

Opening the door to his mother's house he called, "Mother."

Tina Arthur came out of the sitting room.

"Alexander, Susannah is something wrong?" She asked.

"No, Mother. We came to tell you we've set a wedding date." Alexander said.

"How wonderful, when are you getting married?" Tina asked.

"In three months and before you start making plans we've decided on a small, simple ceremony with only close family and friends." Alexander stated.

Tina's face showed her disappointment. "You don't want me to give you a nice wedding like Patricia's?" She said.

"That's exactly why I've chosen a small, simple ceremony." Alexander told her.

"You've chosen? Doesn't Susannah have a say in her own wedding?" Tina asked.

"I'm fine with the small, simple ceremony, Mrs. Arthur." Susannah assured her.

"Mrs. Arthur? You must start calling me mother, child." Tina admonished with a smile.

"Okay, Mother." Susannah obeyed.

"Is the dress going to be casual or formal?" Tina asked.

"Semi-formal. I believe Susannah would like to wear a traditional wedding gown." Alexander stated.

"Traditional wedding gown?" Susannah asked.

"Yes, you know the lace and fluff." Alexander said.

Susannah snorted. I... do... not... want... lace... and... fluff." Susannah stated sarcastically. "I'll wear a simple, tasteful dress."

Alexander knew Susannah was already in a bad mood because of her condition.

"Love, don't get upset. I thought you might like to have a wedding gown you can cherish." He said.

"I do not need a wedding gown to remember the most important day in my life." Susannah said an edge in her voice.

Tina decided to take over the conversation before Alexander made things worse.

"I'd be happy to go shopping with you, Susannah. Of course you'll want your mother there." She said.

"We haven't told Mom we've set a wedding date." Susannah said.

"You'll want to tell her about the wedding before you make any decisions." She stated.

Susannah looked at Alexander.

"Just a wedding or are we planning a reception as well?" Tina asked.

"A small reception is allowable, nothing elaborate, Mother." Alexander warned.

"You're determined to make this as unromantic as possible, Alexander." Tina stated.

"I am not being unromantic, Mother. I don't want to put undue stress on Susannah." Alexander answered.

Tina turned to Susannah. "How do you see your wedding day Susannah?" She asked.

Susannah's mind was blank. She struggled to think.

After several minutes she was able to speak.

"I haven't thought about it." She confessed.

"You are agreeable to a small, simple ceremony?" Tina questioned.

"Yes, I'm sure of that." Susannah told her.

"Mother, what are you plotting?" Alexander asked.

Tina smiled innocently. "I'm not plotting anything, Alexander. I think the bride should at least have a say in her own wedding."

Susannah could feel herself getting angry.

"I am not invisible, stop talking as if I'm not standing here." Susannah spat.

Alexander looked at her, she was glaring at him.

"Calm down, love, we know you're not invisible..." Alexander began.

"Yet you talk as though I'm not here. You can't have a wedding without a bride." Susannah sputtered.

She turned and walked out the door, slamming it behind her.

Alexander was rooted in the spot he was standing.

Tina laughed. "She's not submissive. Susannah will keep you on your toes, Alexander. I suggest you and your bride-to-be discuss wedding plans before making any decisions." Tina said.

Still stunned by Susannah's reaction, Alexander slowly got over the shock that his soon-to-be wife was a forceful woman.

"I'll keep that in mind, Mother." He said.

He kissed his mother's cheek and went to find Susannah.

He found her pacing back and forth in front of the house.

She looked up when she heard the door close. Susannah looked at him coldly.

Alexander put his hands up in surrender.

"I'm sorry, love. I was so pleased you'd set a wedding date I didn't think we needed to discuss the decisions that need to be made." He apologized.

Alexander hadn't thought it was possible for her to look any less approachable.

Susannah's look was incredulous.

"You didn't think? What were you going to do Alexander, plan the wedding and have me just be there like a prop?" She asked angrily.

Alexander was speechless.

"By your response I'd say I'm right." Susannah said dumbly.

Pulling his thoughts together, Alexander said, "You're right. I expected to put the wedding together without your input. I'm sorry, Susannah that is inexcusable."

Susannah softened slightly.

"I am not one of your employees, Alexander. I expect you not to treat me like one." She snapped.

Alexander smiled. "I'll keep that in mind in the future." He promised.

Susannah's posture softened to the point that Alexander knew he could go to her then.

Taking her in his arms when he reached her, Alexander hugged her tightly to him.

"What would you like to do?" He asked.

"You mean besides hit you over the head with a frying pan?" Susannah said.

Alexander chuckled. "Yes." He said.

"Go back to my apartment. We can discuss wedding plans." She told him.

Alexander let go of her then. Taking her hand, he led her to his car and helped her in.

He walked around to the driver's side.

After settling into the seat, he picked up Susannah's left hand and kissed it.

"Alexander!" Susannah said sharply.

Surprised he innocently asked "What?"

"Behave yourself." She reprimanded.

"I'm sorry, love, I missed something?" He asked.

Susannah leveled a look at him.

"I'm sorry, love, I don't understand." He confessed.

Susannah rolled her eyes at him. "Alexander, my condition doesn't stop the urges my body feels, it enhances them." She explained.

Alexander smiled. "So we could..." He said.

"No! We will not. Please behave yourself." She said through clenched teeth.

Laughing, Alexander started the car and began the drive to Susannah's apartment.

Once they arrived Susannah headed for the refrigerator where she'd stored the chocolate Alexander had bought at Garth's.

Alexander's smile needed no interpretation.

"You say one word and I'll find that frying pan." She threatened.

"I find this very interesting." He admitted.

"Interesting? Having your head bitten off without warning and your fiancée in a bad mood is interesting?" She asked.

"Yes, I've never experienced anything like this before." He said.

"You're crazy, you know. Most men would be running as far away as they could get." She told him.

"I'm not most men, Susannah." He said.

"Didn't your mother or sisters ever..." She trailed off.

"If they did none of them ever showed it. The men in our family were blissfully unaware."

Susannah snorted. "I would not call this bliss. Having this condition is hard on most relationships."

"I can handle anything that comes along, Susannah. Don't keep things from me. Be yourself, bad mood or not."

"Have you been hit in the head recently? You're being very reasonable."

"Would you rather I left?"

"No, I've never met a man like you before. You should be ready to run at the first sign of temper. Women can be irrational with this."

"I don't run away from problems, love. Your condition and mood are not permanent, they'll pass; until then I'll have to think before I act."

Alexander walked to her, took the box of chocolates and sat it on the table.

Pulling her into his arms he kissed her.

Susannah put her arms around his neck, pulling him closer. She wanted him to make love to her, but knew they'd have to wait.

She contented herself with the kiss.

Pulling himself free, Alexander chuckled.

"You forgot to mention how persuasive you could be." He said.

Susannah smiled "I'm new at this too, Alexander. We'll have to work through it by trial and error." She told him.

Taking her hand, Alexander led Susannah into the living room. Sitting on the couch, he pulled her to him.

"Relax, love. We'll discuss wedding plans later. Right now I just want to hold you in my arms."

Susannah snuggled contentedly into his arms and let her eyes close.

Alexander held her close as he closed his eyes.

Startled awake by another dream that she was pregnant, Susannah pulled free of Alexander's arms.

She went to the bathroom.

Several minutes later she was eating the chocolate Alexander had left sitting on the table.

Looking at the wall opposite from her, she wondered why she was dreaming of being pregnant. In the latest dream Laura and Glenda had fought over who was better suited to give her maternal advice; seeing her mother and stepmother together brought back the oddly familiar feeling she'd had when she'd watched the DVD Glenda had left her.

Not noticing Alexander come into the room, she was startled when he spoke.

"Are you all right, love?" He asked.

"I had another dream that I was pregnant." She told him.

"Is being pregnant a problem?" He questioned.

"No, I'm wondering why I'm having these dreams now." She said.

"You've never had them before."

"No, not until we became..."

"Until we became lovers."

"Yes."

"Does it bother you?"

"No."

"Would calling your mother help?"

"She hasn't been receptive to talking about sex in the past."

"Call her, you may feel better."

Knowing it was late and unable to wait, Susannah stood then walked toward the living room.

Alexander put his arm around her waist as she passed.

He pulled her to him so he could kiss her.

She responded hungrily.

"Interesting." He said laughing.

Susannah scowled at him and went to the phone to call her mother.

Putting in her mother's number, she waited impatiently while it rang.

Laura answered on the third ring.

"Hello." She said.

"Hi Mom." Susannah said.

"Hi, what's going on?" Laura asked.

"Actually, I have something I'd like to talk to you about." Susannah said.

"You sound serious." Laura said.

"It's not so much serious as confusing." Susannah said.

"Would you like to come over."

"Yes, are you busy now?"

"Er, um... now isn't a good time."

"Why?"

Laura hesitated. "Blaine is here."

Susannah wondered at the tone in her mother's voice.

Beginning to understand, she quickly stuttered. "Call me later."

Laura giggled. "I'll do that."

Perplexed, Susannah hung up the phone.

"Susannah?" Alexander questioned.

Susannah looked at him with wonderment in her eyes.

"Blaine is at my mother's. She'll call me later." Susannah said.

"Why do you look confused?" He asked.

"Alexander, Mom and Blaine they're..." She said and shuddered.

Laughing, Alexander said, "Did you not know? Or were you pretending it didn't happen."

"How would I know? This is my mother we're talking about; the same woman who advised me to abstain so I wouldn't get hurt." She said.

"People change love. You did say your mother hadn't dated since her divorce."

"Dating and this are two different things, Alexander."

"This, you can't say it can you?"

"No and if you value your health you won't either."

Becoming serious, Alexander put his hands on her waist, pulling her close.

Pressing his forehead to hers he kissed her.

Pulling away from him, she sighed.

"Why is life so complicated?" She asked.

"It's only complicated if you let it be." He said.

Susannah wanted to ask Alexander to make love to her but knew he'd refuse.

"I'm hungry." She said.

"What would you like to eat?" He asked.

"Something oozing with chocolate." She answered.

"Not a chance. You're going to eat something filling and nutritious." He told her.

Susannah stuck her tongue out at him. "Killjoy." She muttered.

"You'll thank me later." He told her.

Susannah gave him a disgusted look.

Amused, he kissed her again.

This time Susannah put more force into the kiss, holding him to her when he would have pulled away.

Several minutes later she let him up for air.

"You are dangerous, my love." He said raggedly.

Alexander took Susannah out for a filling and nutritious meal, dropped her off at her apartment, then went home.

The next morning Susannah woke before her alarms went off.

She headed to the bathroom, to shower. Leisurely taking her shower, Susannah thought about her wedding. She'd wear an elegant white dress and shoes, rubies at her throat and on her ears to match her engagement ring.

Alexander would wear a white suit and shoes...

Why was it hard to imagine her wedding day? It wasn't like she hadn't thought about it as a teenager.

Of course at the time her thoughts had been childish and wistful.

It was all romantic and outrageous. Her wedding was going to be something to behold.

This wedding wouldn't be without romance she was sure, but there wouldn't be lace and fluff.

Turning off the water and stepping out of the shower Susannah took her robe off the back of the bathroom door.

Putting it on she tied the belt at the waist afterwards wrapping her hair in a towel and went to the kitchen to make coffee.

While she waited for it to brew she looked out the window of her apartment.

It was going to be a warm, sunny day. The kind of day you wished only came on weekends so you didn't have to sit in an office all day.

Susannah brought her thoughts back to the wedding. She was clueless as far as what she wanted.

Should she let Alexander and Tina plan the wedding? Would Alexander think her indifferent?

She couldn't muster up the energy it took to plan the wedding. Something was nagging at her.

It wasn't doubt or cold feet. Was she afraid? No, that wasn't it. Suddenly it was there, springing from the back of her mind.

Glenda bequeathing a fifth of her estate, plus Hawthorne Manor, to her brought on the nagging feeling. The story her father had told her about her conception and birth; the dreams of her being pregnant, they only began appearing after she and Alexander began making love.

She still had to make an appointment with Dr. Hanson. After she saw Linda she'd stop in and make the appointment.

Deciding she wasn't going to work today, she headed to the phone.

While dialing Alexander's number her hand shook.

"Hello." Alexander said.

Susannah didn't answer.

"Hello." He repeated.

Still she didn't respond.

"Susannah what's wrong?" He asked.

Susannah snapped out of her reverie.

"I don't know, Alexander but I'm going to talk to my mother today." She said.

"I take it you won't be going to work today." He said.

"No, I won't. Things aren't making sense. Glenda left me a sizable inheritance, my father told me my conception and birth were difficult situations and the

~ 286 ~

dreams I've been having about being pregnant." She told him.

"Would you like me to go to your mother's with you?" He questioned.

"No, but plan on going to Rose Lake. I'm sure I'll get my answers there." She said.

"You don't think your mother will be much help."

"I'm sure she'll want to be but won't be able to."

"You'll call me after you've talked to your mother."

"Yes."

"Okay, I love you."

"I love you, Alexander."

Susannah hung up the phone, then went to pour herself a cup of coffee.

Leisurely drinking it, she avoided thinking about the conversation she'd have with her mother. She was sure it would lead her to visit her father and siblings in Rose Lake.

Impatiently she waited for the time to pass so she could get ready for her session with Linda, make an appointment with Dr. Hanson then visit her mother.

Susannah anxiously waited for Linda to come out of her office to call her back.

She was relieved when she saw Linda coming to the door.

"Susannah." Linda said.

She nearly jumped out of her seat she was so anxious.

After she settled in a chair in Linda's office she bounced her leg in agitation.

"Is everything all right, Susannah?" Linda asked.

"No!" Susannah said.

Linda waited for Susannah to say more. Several minutes passed before Susannah continued.

"My late stepmother left me a sizable inheritance; my father said my conception and birth were complicated situations and I've been dreaming that I'm pregnant." Susannah finally said.

"What bothers you most?" Linda asked.

"All of it. Why would Glenda leave her stepdaughter, whose father she tore away, a sizable inheritance? I'm not blood related." Susannah said.

"I can't tell you, Susannah. She obviously had her reasons. Have you talked to your father about your concern?" Linda answered.

"No, I'm going to talk to my mother later today after I stop to do an errand." Susannah told her.

"You said your father told you your conception and birth are complicated situations, do you plan to speak to him?" Linda said.

"Yes, after I talk to my mother. There's something else I need to say... I'm not sure how to tell you."

Linda waited while Susannah gained the courage to tell her.

"Alexander and I have become lovers."

"Are you upset about it?"

"No, it's wonderful." Susannah hesitated. "I've begun having dreams that I'm pregnant; they started after we began making love."

"You think the two are connected?"

"I don't know. I have to talk to my mother about it. Alexander and I have set a wedding date."

"Congratulations, when is the big day?"

"In three months. The errand I have to do after I leave here is to make an appointment with my gynecologist to get a prescription for birth control."

"Are you okay with that?"

"That's the only other thing I am sure about."

"The only other thing?"

"I'm sure about marrying Alexander."

Susannah made her next appointment with Linda, left the clinic and headed to Dr. Hanson's office.

The receptionist greeted her.

"Hi, Susannah, what can I do for you?" Mary asked.

"I'd like to make an appointment with Dr. Hanson to discuss birth control." Susannah told her.

Mary looked at her appointment book. After a moment she gave Susannah a date and time.

Susannah agreed. That would give her plenty of time to start the medication before the wedding.

She thanked Mary and left, driving to her mother's.

Arriving Susannah began to feel ill.

Why do I have this feeling of dread? What am I afraid of? She questioned herself.

Walking to the door, Susannah composed herself and walked in.

"Mom?" She said.

Laura came out of the kitchen. "Susannah, why aren't you at work?" Laura asked.

"I have to talk to you." Susannah told her.

"Come into the kitchen." Laura said.

Susannah followed her into the kitchen, sitting in a chair at the table.

Looking at her hands, Susannah said, "Mom if I ask you a question will you tell me the truth?"

"Of course, you know I will." Laura assured her.

"Why did Glenda leave me a sizable inheritance?"

"Susannah, there is something that you should know, but right now is not the proper time to tell you. I can't discuss that without your father present."

Susannah looked up then. Her mother suddenly looked her age. She knew that there was no use in trying to convince her mother to tell her because she knew her mother too well.

Susannah decided she was going to get nowhere and decided to call Alexander to go with her to visit her father in Rose Lake. She walked to the phone dialing the number to her office.

Susannah told Alexander her mother couldn't be of any help and that they'd have to go to Rose Lake.

Alexander promised to tell Nathan about the situation and that she wouldn't be in the office all week; he also told her he'd meet her at her apartment and that he loved her.

Susannah hung up. Turning to Laura she said, "Alexander and I are going to Rose Lake tomorrow morning, will you be joining us?"

Laura resigned herself to the fact she wouldn't be able to change Susannah's mind.

"I'll ask Blaine to drive me down." She said.

"Why? Is there some reason you won't ride with Alexander and me?" Susannah asked.

"There's no sense in having your father drive me home." Laura said.

Susannah grew angrier. Her mother wouldn't discuss the situation with her, she refused to go to Rose Lake with her and Alexander, she believed they wouldn't drive her home.

"I'm guessing I have to wait until tomorrow to learn why you're covering your bases." Susannah stated.

Laura's only acknowledgement was a slight nod of her head.

"I'll see you tomorrow." Susannah said.

She left her mother's more anxious than when she'd arrived.

Driving home, Susannah concentrated hard on not having an anxiety attack.

Her breathing became shallow and labored, her ears were ringing, her heart pounded wildly and she had tunnel vision.

She let herself into her apartment. She had just finished starting a pot of coffee brewing when there was a knock on her door.

Going to answer it she hoped Alexander was there.

Opening the door she was relieved to see Alexander standing in the hall.

Letting go of the doorknob Susannah went to take a step toward Alexander and felt herself falling.

"Susannah!" Alexander said.

He caught her before she hit the floor. Carrying her into the apartment, Alexander closed the door with a thud.

Alexander was patting her cheeks to wake her up. She felt disconnected from her body.

Susannah tried to turn away from Alexander.

He refused to let her.

"Susannah, love wake up." He said.

She shook her head.

Alexander laughed. "Sweetheart open your eyes." He said.

She wrinkled her nose at him, but obeyed his command.

"What happened?" She asked.

"I'm not sure. One minute you were greeting me at the door, the next you were falling." Alexander told her.

"I passed out?" Susannah asked incredulously.

"I'm afraid so, love." He confirmed.

She covered her face with her hands. "Oh." She sighed.

Alexander pulled her to him, soothing her.

"It's all right, Susannah. You're exhausted. Do you want to talk about it?" He said.

"There's not much to talk about. You know the problems I'm having. Mom said she couldn't discuss anything with me without father present which means they are both hiding something from me. I have a feeling that it has something to do with my birth and inheritance."

Susannah pulled away from Alexander, standing she walked to the kitchen poured herself a cup of coffee going to the table to drink it.

"We're going to Rose Lake tomorrow." Susannah reminded him.

"I remember, love." Alexander said.

"Mother refuses to ride down with us because she believes we won't bring her home and she doesn't want to put father out." She said.

"This is getting more and more mysterious." Alexander mused.

Susannah sank back in her chair watching while Alexander made toast for her and an omelet for himself.

"You've never cooked for me before." Susannah blurted.

Amused, Alexander responded with, "It doesn't mean I can't cook."

"I wasn't implying it did. I was making an observation." She told him.

"As you've recently learned I have many hidden talents. Take the bedroom..." He began.

"Shut up, Alexander." She said her face turning red.

"Don't you want to hear about my extraordinary talents?"

"No, I've experienced them first hand. Talking about that will just make me more agitated than I already am."

"If you're sure..."

"Alexander... don't push your luck."

He put a plate in front of her then sat down next to her.

They ate silently. Alexander thought about their upcoming trip to Rose Lake.

Susannah contemplated what she'd have to do when they arrived.

Alexander gathered their dishes from the table, rinsed them in the sink and put them in the dishwasher.

Susannah stood up, walked to Alexander and put her arms around him.

"The situation will get better." He promised.

"How can you promise that, Alexander? We haven't a clue what's going to happen tomorrow." Susannah said sarcastically.

"Faith." Alexander stated.

Susannah eyed him skeptically.

He leaned down to kiss her. Kissing him back, Susannah clung to his body like she'd never let go.

Disengaging her from his body, Alexander put Susannah away from him.

At the hurt look in her eyes he said, "Making love is not an option, Susannah."

"It'll make me feel better." She pleaded.

"You're forgetting one important factor." He reminded her.

Susannah blushed. "Being a woman sucks sometimes." She said.

Alexander laughed. Taking her hand he led her into the living room.

Cuddling with her on the couch, he rubbed her back in a slow, circular motion.

While Alexander made the circular motions on her back Susannah could feel herself nodding off.

She tried in vain to stay awake, finally drifting off to sleep.

CHAPTER FIFTEEN

While she slept she had a dream that she and Alexander eloped to Las Vegas.

Susannah knew in her dream that wasn't what Alexander wanted he only did it to please her.

Pleasing her seemed to be his main goal in life, in and out of bed.

She shifted uncomfortably as she slept.

Alexander patted her soothingly.

Was she awake or dreaming?

"Susannah love wake up." Alexander said.

Definitely awake.

Alexander gently shook her.

Susannah pushed at his hand.

He chuckled.

"Wake up, my love." He told her.

She burrowed into the couch.

Alexander pulled her away from the back of the couch.

She struggled to get back.

"Susannah, wake up." He said sternly.

"Don't want to." She said childishly.

"Susannah!"

Her eyes flew open at the command in his voice.

"What? Is there an emergency?"

"I've been trying to wake you up for half an hour."

"Why?"

"It's seven o'clock."

"In the morning!"

"Yes, you slept all night. I was beginning to worry."

"Why didn't you wake me sooner. You couldn't have been comfortable sleeping on the couch."

"Who slept. When you went to sleep I watched TV for a while expecting you to wake up. When you didn't I guessed you needed the rest."

"You didn't sleep... at all?"

"On and off. You kept mumbling about eloping to Vegas and other things that weren't coherent."

"I dreamt we eloped to Vegas to get married and your main goal in life was to please me."

Susannah read the unasked question in his eyes and blushed.

"Yes, both in and out."

Alexander laughed.

"We'll have to try that."

Susannah rolled to her side letting her legs dangle on the edge of the couch.

"I'm going to take a shower."

She stood up and walked to her bedroom to get her robe.

"Want me to help?"

Susannah grunted.

She let the hot water run over her for several minutes to loosen the knots in her body.

While showering she thought about the idea of getting married in Las Vegas. If they decided to elope that would be one less thing to worry about.

She realized today she'd learn the mystery of her conception and birth.

The thought made her tense again. She quickly finished her shower.

After putting her robe on and wrapping her hair in a towel, she went to find Alexander.

"Are you okay to drive to Rose Lake this morning?" Susannah asked when she found him.

"Of course, why wouldn't I be?" He said.

"You didn't get much sleep." She reminded him.

"I'll be fine. I've gone with less sleep." He told her.

Susannah wondered, not for the first time, how she'd gotten so fortunate.

Alexander interrupted her thoughts. "Would you like breakfast?" He asked.

"I don't think I can handle breakfast this morning." She admitted.

Alexander nodded. "After we visit your family." He said.

"I can't promise anything, Alexander. My mother has me worried. She has rarely been unable to talk to me." Susannah said.

"Is there a chance you're making this worse than it is?" He questioned.

"I don't think so. I'm receiving a sizable inheritance from my stepmother, my mother can't talk to me about my conception and birth without my father present; something's definitely wrong."

Alexander walked to Susannah, put his hands on her waist and drew her to him.

Susannah clung to him like she would a life preserver.

They stood that way for several minutes.

"I have to get dressed." Susannah said.

"We'll stop in town to get coffee." He told her.

Susannah nodded then headed to her bedroom to gather her clothes and toiletries to get dressed.

She took one last look in the mirror before joining Alexander in the kitchen.

"Ready?" He questioned.

"There's no reason to put this off any longer." She said.

Alexander took her hand, leading her out the door.

For a change, Susannah didn't check that her apartment was in order before she left.

The trip to Rose Lake was quiet and tense.

Alexander knew trying to make Susannah relax would be useless.

He listened to the radio while he drove. Susannah picked up the mood of the music.

When they finally arrived at her father's house Susannah felt sick to her stomach.

"This was a bad idea." She said tensely.

Alexander looked at her. She was pale.

"Do you want to postpone?" He asked.

"No, let's get this over with." She said.

While Alexander stepped out of the car and walked around to her side Susannah took several deep, calming breaths.

The breathing didn't help, she still felt sick to her stomach.

When Alexander opened her door she forced herself to step out.

As they walked to the door Susannah gathered her strength.

Knocking on the door, Susannah refused to let the bile rise in her throat.

Thomas answered the door looking like he hadn't slept in a week.

"Hello Susannah, Alexander." He said, gesturing for them to enter.

Stepping into her father's house, Susannah could feel his tension.

As they walked into the sitting room, Susannah said, "I'm sure mother has told you why I'm here."

"Yes." Laura said.

Susannah hadn't noticed Blaine's car out front but she wasn't surprised to see her mother.

Phillip, Martin and Jennifer all sat nervously on the sectional sofa that occupied the room.

"Please sit down, Susannah." Thomas advised indicating an empty chair.

Susannah nervously sat in the chair indicated.

Alexander stood next to her holding her hand in support.

"Laura told me you've questioned her about the inheritance Glenda left you." Thomas said.

"Yes. I want to know why she would leave me a fifth of her estate." Susannah confirmed.

"You're her daughter." Thomas stated.

"Stepdaughter." Susannah corrected.

"No, you are Glenda's biological daughter." Thomas said.

The shock didn't register immediately.

"I'm sorry, what?" Susannah asked dumbly.

"You are Glenda Hawthorne's biological daughter. She conceived you, carried you and gave birth to you." Thomas said.

"No, Laura Roberts is my mother." Susannah denied.

"Laura is Glenda's half sister; biologically she's your aunt."

The shock broke through Susannah's numb brain.

"Is this some kind of joke?"

"I'm afraid not." Laura said.

Susannah sat in silence for several minutes.

"Glenda's my mother, you're my aunt, what about you father, who are you, my uncle." Susannah said.

"I am your biological father." Thomas said.

"How did all of this work?" Susannah questioned.

Thomas drew in a ragged breath.

"I met Glenda at Western Chemical when her father came to the plant. I was smitten from the moment we met. Shortly after meeting we began an affair." He said.

Susannah drew in a calming breath that didn't calm her at all.

"Glenda became pregnant in the beginning. I couldn't keep the news from your mother, Laura Everyone at the plant knew of the affair. Laura was furious when I told her Glenda was pregnant and I wanted a divorce." Thomas continued.

"I couldn't believe your father would betray me that way." Laura said.

"You said Glenda and mother are half sisters." Susannah said.

Thomas replied, "Yes, Glenda's father, Adam, was engaged to Glenda's mother when he met Constance, Laura's mother. He convinced Glenda's mother, Susannah to postpone the wedding indefinitely hoping she'd call off the engagement so that he could be with Constance."

"Susannah, I was named after Glenda's mother?"

"When Susannah, your grandmother learned that your mother, Glenda was pregnant she insisted you be put up for adoption. To spite your grandmother, Adam named you before you were given up for adoption."

Susannah put her hand to her throat trying to push back the bile that was rising there.

"My mother Constance wouldn't let her pregnancy interfere in my father's life. Before giving birth to me she met Grandpa Nelson, they married and he raised me as his own." Laura said.

"I don't understand, Glenda is my mother, you're my aunt; how is it that you raised me?"

Thomas held up a hand to Laura.

Dragging in a breath he continued. "As I told you your biological maternal grandmother insisted you be put up for adoption. Laura couldn't conceive. We didn't know, not that we tried often. We assumed our timing was bad."

Thomas stopped to take a another breath to calm himself.

"When Glenda told me she was pregnant I didn't believe her. Your mother and I had been married for five years and didn't have a child."

Laura choked back a sob. "I went to my doctor and had some tests. He told me I could never conceive; I'd never have a child of my own. Glenda was eighteen, she wasn't ready for a child, being a child herself."

Susannah put her hand to her mouth letting her family see how their revelation was affecting her.

"I agreed to the divorce on the condition that Glenda allow me to adopt and raise you." Laura said.

Susannah flinched at her mother's words. "I was the consolation, the trade-off for father's freedom?" She asked standing.

"No! You were not a consolation. Glenda wasn't prepared to be a mother. As I said she was still a child herself when you were born. I was willing to adopt you and raise you as my own daughter." Laura said.

Sickened by the news she'd just received, Susannah couldn't hold back the contents of her stomach.

Quickly putting her hand to her mouth, she looked helplessly at Jennifer.

Jennifer quickly led her to the bathroom with Alexander following close behind.

Forcing the door shut, Susannah let go of the bile that rose in her throat, crying softly as she did.

Her stomach was nearly empty so she had nothing to bring up.

Susannah lay against the commode with her head hanging over the bowl.

When she finally felt able to stand, Susannah put the lid down, stood up and went to the sink to put a cool cloth to her face.

"Susannah, are you all right?" Alexander asked through the door.

"I'll be out in a minute." She choked out.

Putting the cloth under cold water again Susannah rinsed it twice then washed her face and neck.

After cooling herself down, she rinsed her mouth as best she could with cool water.

Knowing she couldn't hide what had just happened Susannah calmly opened the door stepping into Alexander's waiting arms.

"Is she all right?" Laura asked anxiously.

"She's just learned that the woman she thought is her mother is her aunt and the woman who took her father away is her mother; I'd say no she's not all right." Alexander snapped.

"How could they do this to me? Hide the truth for twenty-six years?" Susannah sobbed into Alexander's shoulder.

"Shh. Don't think about it now. Let's get you home." Alexander said soothingly.

"No, I want to know why no one told me, why they let me live a lie." Susannah demanded.

"You were never supposed to know the truth. We agreed on that when Laura adopted you." Thomas said.

Susannah lifted her head from Alexander's shoulder. "Why?" She questioned.

"We thought it would be better that way. Glenda got what she wanted, Laura got a child and I left you alone never knowing how much I was hurting you by not revealing the truth." Thomas told her.

"Alexander get me out of here." Susannah demanded.

Alexander put his arm around Susannah's waist and led her out the door without a backward glance.

Once in the car Alexander asked, "Do you want to go home?"

"No, they'll look for me there.. I don't want any contact right now. Is there somewhere we can go they won't know where to find us?" Susannah questioned.

"Yes, my house. No one except my brother Charles knows where it is. He'd never tell if we went there." Alexander said.

"That's where we'll go." Susannah decided.

"We'll stop by your apartment to pack a bag for you." Alexander said.

"I don't want to be there long. That's the first place mother will look for me."

Alexander started the car and began the drive back to Camille.

While driving, Alexander watched Susannah. Occasionally she put her hand to her mouth like she was going to empty the contents of her stomach again. The feeling quickly passed each time.

Alexander worried that the news Susannah received today would alter their future.

Pulling herself up, Susannah said, "After I pack a bag I'm calling Allie. Would you mind very much if we eloped to Las Vegas?"

"Are you sure? I don't want you to act in haste." Alexander said.

"Marrying you is one thing I'm absolutely sure about." She stated.

Alexander smiled at her. "Your dream about us eloping will become a reality after all." He said.

Susannah smiled back. "Yes, I can't wait to become Mrs. Alexander Arthur." She stated.

When they walked into Susannah's apartment she quickly threw together a few changes of clothes, her toiletries and anything else she thought she might need for the trip to Vegas.

When she had everything she needed she called Allie.

Allie answered on the third ring. "Hello." She said.

"I'm eloping to Vegas and want you to be my matron of honor." Susannah quickly told her.

"What?" Allie asked.

"I'm eloping to Vegas..." Susannah said.

"I heard you. Is this a joke?" Allie said.

"No, I'll explain on the trip." Susannah told her.

"When are we leaving?"

"As soon as we can get a flight."

"Call me when you have flight arrangements."

"I will."

Susannah hung up.

"Remember that phrase." Alexander said wrapping his arms around her.

"We won't have much of a honeymoon." Susannah reminded him.

"We have the rest of our lives together, I can wait a few days for our honeymoon." He told her.

Susannah turned in his arms and kissed him.

Pulling away from her ardent kiss Alexander chuckled.

"I'd better call Charles. He'll be happy to stand up with me." He said.

"I'm sorry we're not having the small, simple ceremony with family and friends." Susannah told him.

"Don't be, we'll have another wedding in a few years." Alexander told her.

"Your mother will be disappointed." Susannah said.

"As long as I'm happy she won't mind." He said.

Susannah hugged Alexander with all the love she had in her.

"How'd I get so lucky?" She asked.

"Luck has nothing to do with it." Alexander stated.

He gave her a quick kiss then went to call Charles and the airline.

Several minutes later Alexander was back at Susannah's side.

"Our flight is in a few hours. I'll go to my apartment and pack a bag then come back to pick you up." He said.

"Not a chance, I'm coming with you. I told you my apartment will be the first place my family will look for me." Susannah said.

Alexander saw the stubborn set to her jaw and knew he wouldn't be able to budge her on this.

"Okay, wife-to-be get your bags and let's go." He said.

Susannah gathered her bags and together they walked out the door.

On the way to Alexander's apartment Susannah used his cell phone to call Allie to arrange meeting her and John at the airport.

Alexander called Charles to tell him when to meet them at the airport.

As Alexander packed his bags Susannah paced back and forth across his living room.

"Nervous, love?" He questioned.

"Not so much nervous as anxious. I've never been a patient person." She responded.

"In a few hours we'll be on a flight to Vegas and then shortly after we'll be married." Alexander said.

"I can hardly wait." Susannah said enthusiastically.

"I have one question." He said.

"Yes?"

"Why are we eloping? Are you running away from your family?"

"No, you are the one person in my life I am sure of, I see no reason to postpone getting married."

Alexander pulled Susannah to him, kissing her.

"I love you, Susannah."

"I love you, Alexander."

Susannah pulled out of his embrace and began pacing again. The few hours they'd have to wait was going to be difficult.

"I have an idea." Alexander said.

"I'm listening." Susannah said.

"Let's get something to eat. The time will pass quicker and you'll have something in your stomach before we leave." He said.

"Alexander I wasn't able to eat this morning, what makes you think I'll be able to eat now?" Susannah asked.

"You were nervous this morning. Now you're anxious, you should be able to eat something." He said.

Susannah thought for a moment.

"I'd like to try to eat before we leave." She agreed.

Alexander picked up his bags and they walked out the door to get something to eat.

"You were right, I do feel much better after eating." Susannah admitted.

Alexander kissed her in response.

Holding Susannah's hand on the way to the airport, Alexander intertwined their fingers.

Meeting John and Allie at the airport, Susannah hugged them.

"Are you going to tell me what's going on?" Allie asked.

"When we're on the plane, settled in our seats." Susannah said nervously.

"Alexander, what's going on?" Allie questioned.

"Susannah must be the one to tell you." He answered.

Charles arrived to their party.

"When's the party start?" He asked.

Alexander made the introductions between Allie, John and Charles.

There wasn't time for celebration or congratulations. A short time later their flight was announced.

After everyone was on the plane Alexander asked for their attention.

"As you know this trip was not planned. Susannah asked that we elope after being told of her parentage." He said.

Everyone looked to Susannah for explanation.

She obligingly told the gathered group what her mother and father had revealed to her that morning.

When the shock settled in Allie asked, "Are you going to accept your stepmother's... mother's inheritance to you?"

"Yes, by birth it's mine. I see no reason not to accept it." Susannah said.

"All these years you didn't have a clue?" Allie questioned.

"No, I wouldn't have been told if Glenda hadn't left me a sizable inheritance. I didn't understand why she would do it so I questioned my mother." Susannah answered.

"Wow, talk about family secrets, this one's a whopper." Allie said impressed.

"Allie, this is not something to be impressed about. My parents lied to me for twenty-six years. If Glenda hadn't left me the inheritance I wouldn't have known."

"Would you rather not have been told?"

"No, I would rather my parents hadn't kept it from me. I'll wonder what else they're keeping from me."

"Don't stress yourself over it, love. No matter how you found out, you know now." Alexander said.

Susannah was going to argue, the look on Alexander's face stopped her.

"I know now." She repeated.

Alexander smiled.

The remainder of the flight Susannah and Allie discussed the type of dress Susannah would wear for her wedding and the wedding details.

After the plane landed and they had their luggage Alexander asked the porter to get them a shuttle to their hotel.

Once at the hotel Alexander checked everyone in. Everyone went to their respective rooms and unpacked meeting back in the lobby when they finished.

"I'll take Susannah to buy a dress for the wedding. We'll meet you back here in two hours." Allie said.

"Two hours." Alexander agreed.

Allie dragged Susannah out of the hotel onto the strip in search of a dress shop.

"Slow down, Allie we have two hours." Susannah said.

"We have to get your dress, get you in the shower and do your hair and make-up." Allie said.

"Two hours?" Susannah asked.

"Two hours just to find the dress." Allie said.

Susannah let Allie drag her through the shops to find the perfect dress.

Finally they were back in Susannah's room opening the packages they'd purchased.

"Get in the shower. I'll lay everything out." Allie said.

"If Alexander comes back don't let him in. Send him to Charles' room." Susannah said.

"I will, I will get going." Allie said.

Susannah obediently went into the bathroom to shower. When she emerged twenty minutes later she had a healthy pink glow.

"Finally, some color in your cheeks." Allie said.

She pulled the towel from Susannah's head and dragged her to where the blow dryer was to blow dry her hair.

When she finished Susannah gathered her dress and ensemble to dress in the bathroom.

Coming out she had tears in her eyes.

She wore a long, white strapless A-line dress which showed far too much cleavage and matching jacket.

Underneath the dress she wore silky nylons, matching lacy bra and panties, on her feet were satiny white pumps.

Allie clapped in delight.

"You're beautiful, now your hair and make-up." She said.

"I'm wearing my hair down and using very little make-up. We're keeping this simple, Allie." Susannah told her.

Allie pouted. "Can't I have any fun?" She teased.

"Simple, Allison." Susannah said.

"Oh, all right. I have a gift for you."

"What?"

Allie handed Susannah a small, black box.

Susannah slowly opened the box and gasped.

"Allie, they're beautiful."

"They're my contribution to make your wedding day more special." Allie said.

Susannah examined the ruby necklace and earrings Allie had given her.

They were beautiful and something she had wanted to wear on her wedding day.

"I knew my best friend since kindergarten would want something to complement her engagement ring." Allie told her.

"Thank you." Susannah said hugging her.

"Let's see how they look." Allie said.

She took the box from Susannah and released the necklace and earrings from the plastic twist tie wrapped around them.

When she'd helped Susannah put them on Allie stepped back.

Tears formed in her eyes. "Beautiful. You won't need make-up the way you're glowing." She stated.

Susannah blushed.

There was a knock at the door.

"Susannah, are you ready?" Alexander asked.

"Give me a minute." She answered.

Looking at Allie she said, "The groom isn't supposed to see the bride until they meet at the altar, it's bad luck."

"I think fate will make an exception in this case. I've never seen two people more suited to each other; well except John and me of course." Allie told her.

"Open the door." Susannah said.

Allie walked to the door to let Alexander in.

When Alexander saw Susannah he mouthed the word "wow."

Susannah blushed.

Charles and John were close behind Alexander. They were dumbstruck when they saw Susannah.

Alexander was the first to recover. "Shall we go?" He asked.

Susannah nodded.

Half an hour later Alexander and Susannah sat with their guests in a cozy little restaurant celebrating their marriage.

"I love you, Mrs. Arthur." Alexander said.

"I love you my dear husband." Susannah told him.

EPILOGUE
Five Years Later

Susannah paced the living room in Alexander's house. He'd finished building it after they'd gotten married.

They lived in the house she'd inherited from Glenda and came here to relax when things became too stressful at the big house.

Susannah forgave her parents for keeping her parentage from her.

A year after their marriage they'd renewed their wedding vows with family and friends in attendance.

Fifteen months later Aurora Louise had come along. Now Susannah awaited the birth of their second child.

"Mama, are you going to wake up daddy." Aurora asked.

Aurora had acted like a mother hen since Alexander and Susannah had told her she had a sibling coming to join her.

"Yes, darling, give me a few more minutes." Susannah said.

"Little Alexander isn't going to wait much longer." Aurora said exasperated.

"How do you know it's little Alexander?" Susannah asked.

"He told me." Aurora said.

"He who?" Susannah questioned.

"The baby silly." Aurora told her.

"The baby talks to you." Susannah said.

"He comes in my dreams."

"You see the baby in your dreams?"

"Yes and he told me he was coming today. We need to wake up daddy."

Susannah and Aurora walked into the bedroom together to wake Alexander.

Aurora patted her father's cheek.

Alexander was instantly awake.

"Is it time?" He asked.

"Almost, I told Mama little Alexander talks to me in my dreams." Aurora told him.

"Apparently I'm the only one who doesn't know our three year old daughter can communicate with our unborn son." Susannah admonished.

"You said you didn't want to know, love." Alexander reminded her.

"Since when did the two of you start listening to me?" Susannah asked.

Aurora began giggling.

Susannah looked at her suspiciously.

"What are you two up to now?" She questioned.

"Nothing." Aurora said still giggling.

"Alexander Arthur I suggest you tell me what's going on or you'll be spending the next six weeks in this house... alone." Susannah threatened.

Alexander looked at his daughter who was unrepentant.

Exasperated, he said. "I allowed Aurora to call your mother."

"You what!" Susannah demanded.

"Now, love, calm down. She feels bad that she wasn't here for Aurora's birth." Alexander said.

"Alexander, she broke her hip while learning to water ski on her honeymoon. There was no way she could have been here. Last I heard she and Blaine were on a cruise." Susannah said.

"They planned their vacation around our son's birth."

"I suppose our daughter told them when he was going to be born."

"She had to otherwise your mother would have postponed her vacation."

A sharp pain shot through Susannah's swollen abdomen. She put her hand up to the spot where the pain was.

"Time to go to the hospital." Alexander said.

After the pain passed Susannah said, "No more secrets, promise me."

"We promise." Alexander and Aurora said in unison.

They left for the hospital.

Three hours later family and friends surrounded Susannah and her newborn son.

"Very well done, Mrs. Arthur." Alexander whispered.

"No swearing this time?" Susannah asked.

Alexander chuckled. "You didn't have time, love." He answered.

"I have time now." Susannah threatened.

"I'll pass, my love." Alexander told her.

"I love you, Alexander."

"I love you, Susannah. I'll love you beyond the end of time." Alexander promised.

"A Time to Heal" is the second full length novel written by Cassandra J. Sperry. She is also the author of *"Kyle's Passion* and is currently working on her third novel, *"Quinton's Desire"*. Each of these novels are linked and could be considered a trilogy, but each tells a unique stand-alone story of love, passion and romance.

These wonderful and powerfully emotional stories are available in all formats. Please visit our website for purchasing options.

www.BadgleyPublishingCompany.com